Christmas

CANCELLATION

EVIE JAMES

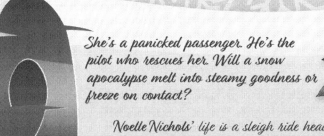

She's a panicked passenger. He's the pilot who rescues her. Will a snow apocalypse melt into steamy goodness or freeze on contact?

Noelle Nichols' life is a sleigh ride heading for a cliff. After her aunt's tragic accident and boyfriend's cruel betrayal, the twenty-six-year-old workaholic is now jobless, single, and desperate to make it back to her hometown. If she doesn't claim her inheritance by Christmas Eve, Eve—she'll lose it all. And it only gets worse when a snowstorm throws her plans into the kind of madness only New York winters and canceled flights can bring.

Captain Kol Vinter can't help but overhear the distraught blonde beauty's rage-filled rant and doesn't hesitate to defend his airline and shut her down. Yet when he catches her wishing she'd never been born, the valiant vet can't walk away and instead reluctantly makes her an offer that could change both their lives: a one-way trip to Saratoga Springs, the quintessential Christmas town that's lost all its magic for Noelle.

Annoyingly, Noelle realizes he's the only person who can help her get home. But Kol isn't your typical holiday hero—he's got scars of his own and walls he's not keen to let down. And as Kol struggles to navigate the growing winter storm, he finds ignoring his desire for the down-on-her-luck spitfire harder than keeping the car on the road.

He may be a grumpy "guardian angel," but what if he's exactly who Noelle's been waiting for? Will Kol's protective heart and smoldering presence be enough to remind her that life—even when it's messy and shadowed by loss—can still be wonderful?

Christmas Cancellation is a holiday romance set in Saratoga Springs, New York. The story includes elements such as perilous situations, death, graphic language, emotional trauma from the loss of parents, and sexual activities that are shown on the page. Readers who may be sensitive to these elements, please take note.

"What is it you want, Mary? What do you want? You want the moon?

Just say the word and I'll throw a lasso around it and pull it down."

~ George Bailey

It's a Wonderful Life

Noelle Nichols

Chapter One

12/23 late morning

"Life's a bitch, and then you die," I muttered, expelling an exasperated breath and dropping into one of the stiff, faux-leather seats by Gate 73. I shoved my coat through the handles of my suitcase and tossed my new Dior tote into the seat next to me. It hadn't just been one of those days; it had been a no-good, rotten week. Actually, my life had sucked in general since that night four years ago. Today was merely another example of the dark cloud that had moved in and taken up permanent residence over my head.

Since my plans for today had been screwed up big time, I scrolled through my phone, desperate for a miracle. Maybe I could rent a car? Nope. Nothing. Nada. The screen mocked me with a big, fat "No Availability." Every car in the city had been snatched up by other stranded passengers and holiday visitors.

Okay, maybe a hotel room? I tapped through a few options, only to find that the cheapest one was some no-name motel charging three times its regular rate, all because it was the holiday season. At the moment, my only option was my seat at Gate 73. Perfect. Just perfect. I was stuck, stranded, and hopeless.

I needed to vent. Needed Amanda. She was the only one I could count on to talk me off the ledge—my best friend, my ride-or-die, the one person who always had my back. Ever since I moved to Atlanta to start at the Martindale Agency as a social media coordinator, she'd been there for me, literally and figuratively. I'd met her the day I moved into my apartment, when her goldendoodle knocked me on my ass in the hallway and slobbered all over me. And instead of being pissed, I'd laughed, because who could stay mad with a face full of goldendoodle?

Right now, I'd have preferred to be in her apartment, a glass of wine in hand, with that goofy dog sprawled across my lap, than stuck here in this damn airport, waiting for a flight that wasn't going to happen.

I yanked my earbuds out of my tote and shoved them into my ears—hoping to muffle the annoyingly cheerful holiday music that was being piped through the airport speakers—then dialed Amanda's number, and waited. She picked up after the second ring.

"Hey, girl. What's up?" she asked. Fluffers barked in the background.

"Hey!" I replied.

The guy sitting across the aisle jerked back a little, startled, as his head snapped up from his phone. I'd shouted, forgetting how loud I could be with the earbuds in.

"You will not believe this," I said. "My flight's canceled. The leg to Albany. So, now I'm stuck in LaGuardia with no rental cars, no hotels, and a snowstorm that's apparently bad enough to ruin my life but not bad enough to be visible. Merry fucking Christmas to me."

Amanda laughed softly. "Well, shit. I'm sorry, babe. Did you talk to the gate agent? Can they rebook you?"

"Oh, sure, I talked to the gate agent. She smiled at me as if I was a toddler who lost her balloon. Then, in her oh-so-fake-nice voice, told me the weather was to blame—it was out of her control. An act of God. That's it. No options, no nothing for today. They're saying they can rebook me for tomorrow night at the earliest. Which is great and all, except I need to be at the attorney's office today to sign those papers." I let out an exasperated huff. "Just add it to the list of things that have gone wrong this week."

"God, Noelle. I'm not sure what to say," Amanda replied. "That...sucks."

"Tell me about it," I all but shrieked, my voice hitting an out-of-control pitch. "And don't even get me started on the airlines. They don't give a crap about passengers. You know, ' .' But there's no freakin' weather! I can see out the giant windows overlooking the tarmac, and my phone says it's thirty-four degrees and partly cloudy. Partly cloudy, Amanda! What storm?"

"Noelle, calm down and breathe before you pass out, okay?"

I inhaled, catching the smell of Cinnabon—sickly sweet—making my stomach churn. "I'm pretty sure the flight's half full, and am guessing the greedy airline doesn't want to waste money flying to Albany. Or it's some pilot who didn't want to work today. Most likely wanted to be home, drinking eggnog with his perfect little family."

Amanda snorted. "You think a pilot called in sick? *'Hey, boss, got holiday fatigue. Can't make it to Albany today.'*"

"Exactly!" I shouted, earning me a few irritated glances from people sitting nearby. The guy across the aisle scowled at me.

"Or perhaps the entire crew is sitting at Starbucks right now drinking hot cocoa, laughing their asses off, and contemplating ways they can ruin people's Christmas since *they* have to work."

"Do pilots even drink hot cocoa?"

"Shut up, Amanda. It's a metaphor."

"Pretty sure it's not," she said, laughing into the phone. "I don't think that's how metaphors work, Noelle. You're being paranoid. Maybe it's only bad luck. Or maybe—"

"No. No, this is a conspiracy. Who cancels a flight to Albany on Christmas Eve, Eve? It's practically un-American! I bet the crew is trying to avoid rowdy passengers excited for the holidays. God forbid anybody be happy on Christmas. Or maybe they're screwing with us for fun, always keeping us in suspense—guessing if our flight will, in reality, make it out, as though it were some twisted holiday thriller."

"Okay, now you're just making random stuff up."

"Am I?" I threw my hands up. "Who the hell cancels a flight for *partly cloudy*? I'm telling you, Amanda, it's the airline or some lazy pilot with a God complex."

Amanda chuckled again. "Calm down. You sound like a maniac. As if you actually believe the universe is out to get you."

"Yeah, well, the universe can bite me," I said, laughing. By now, several people were staring at me. I could tell I was annoying the hell out of them with my ridiculous ramblings. I didn't care. What did it matter? I was stuck here, my life falling apart around me, and now the universe had decided to pile on more nonsense. I was fully aware I was acting unhinged, but considering all the wine I'd had earlier and the deplorable circumstances I found myself in, unhinged was the best I could do. "Just so you know, if I ever meet the person who made the decision to cancel this flight, I'm going to give them a piece of my mind. And possibly a swift kick in the shin."

"Good luck with that, Noelle. And lower your voice a little. I'm sure everyone in the terminal can hear you, and the last thing you need is to be arrested."

I shrugged. "Oh, everyone's too busy plotting their own escape routes to care."

With a frown, I snatched up my phone and started furiously scrolling again, searching for a hotel or a rental car. At this point, I would take anything.

Digging my heels into the floor beneath me, I groused into the phone, "There are no rental cars anywhere in the city. Absolutely none. And the hotels? Not a single room in the entire area unless I want to shell out a couple of grand for some five-star suite with a chandelier in the bathroom or risk my life at a fleabag charging triple their normal rate."

Amanda sighed. "Of course they'd price gouge right before Christmas. It's all about the money."

"Yeah, and guess who doesn't have that kind of cash lying around? Me. The girl who lost her shot at a promotion and just quit her job because her snake of a boyfriend stabbed her in the back." I was sure Amanda was rolling her eyes at the mention of Blake.

"I always hated that guy," she said. "Remember, I warned you? I told you he was a fake, selfish jerk, only out for himself."

I sighed. "Yeah, you did. And you were right. He was a walking red flag. I just...I wanted to believe he was different. I mean, he was hot and charming when he wanted to be, and I thought...well, you know what I thought."

"You thought he was the one," Amanda finished for me. "But instead, he was a jackass who played you. He didn't deserve you, either. You're too good for him, Noelle. You always were."

I swallowed, and a lump formed in my throat. "I don't get it, Amanda. Why is it always me? Why is it always my life that's

5

a damn train wreck? It's like...it's like, ever since..." I glanced around the bustling gate area. The emotion started to push its way up, but I wasn't about to cry here, not in front of all these strangers. "It's as if I've been cursed or something. Nothing ever goes right." I lowered my voice. "You know, I shouldn't have quit. I should have just sucked it up at least until I could find another job. But my pride got the better of me, and here I am."

Amanda knew better than to push me. She remained quiet for a beat, waiting, and I pictured her biting her lip, trying to find the right words to say.

"Noelle, Blake did you dirty. You're human. You had every reason in the world to quit," she finally said. "And you're also strong. You've been through a lot and have handled it all better than most people—so much better than I ever could have."

"Yeah, well, I'm tired of handling it," I said softly, trying to blink away the prickle in my eyes. The bustle around me—the blaring announcements over the intercom, the rumble of suitcase wheels, the hurried conversations—blurred together into one chaotic buzz, and frustration frayed my last nerve. "I'd hoped to make it in the nick of time to the attorney's office to receive whatever it is my aunt left me. I'd hoped it was going to be some money or something I could sell to tide me over until I found another job. But now that's not happening. Looks like I'll be going on a starvation or dumpster-diving diet... I want something to go right for once. Just once. Is that too much to ask?"

"It's not. It's not at all," Amanda said in that reassuring, motherly voice that I both loved and hated. "But sitting in that airport isn't going to change anything. Maybe...maybe you need to get out of the terminal. Take a walk and—"

"Where the hell am I supposed to go, Amanda?" I snapped more loudly than I'd intended. "I'm trapped here."

She didn't say anything for a moment; she simply let me stew in my misery. "You're not trapped, Noelle. It's only a setback. You'll figure it out. You always do."

"Sure," I scoffed. "Like I figured out Blake? Like I figured out how to stop my life from going to hell after…" I shook my head, the words catching in my throat. "Never mind. I just wish things were different. I wish…I wish a lot of things. I'm sorry to unload on you. Thanks for letting me vent though. I'm so lucky to have a friend who listens when I'm going off the rails and isn't afraid to set me straight. God knows we've both been there for each other when life's thrown the worst at us."

Amanda snorted. "You're right about that. And don't think I've forgotten how much I owe you for dealing with my meltdown over that lying, cheating, wannabe country star, Jason Owens, who couldn't keep his pants zipped if his life depended on it. If you hadn't dragged my sorry ass out of that pity party, I'd still be hiding under my blankets, binge-watching rom-coms on Netflix and eating pint after pint of ice cream."

I chuckled and then let out a long sigh. "You've got that right. It was clear I had to intervene when I came over that day and pint containers were stacked in a pyramid like champagne glasses at a wedding."

She giggled even though, at the time, she'd been the most miserable I'd ever seen her. I crossed my legs and relaxed into my seat, catching sight of a pilot standing at the gate agent's station. He glanced over his shoulder, shooting me a side-eye that could have killed. His presence registered, but at the moment, I didn't care if he had heard my rant. I was past caring. Let him think what he wanted.

"Ugh, I've got to escape this airport, make my way to Saratoga, sign those papers, and wrap this part of my life up.

But, naturally, the universe has different plans." I took a deep breath, contemplating my lack of options. "Hmm, I know...I'll hitchhike," I joked.

"Yeah, and end up as the next victim of a serial killer. I don't think so," Amanda snapped. "It would be better to lose whatever your aunt is giving you in her will than end up dead trying to get home."

Out of nowhere, Mr. Captain strutted over with an air of authority, stopping right in front of me, his expression screaming, *I'm about to school you.* Damn, I loved a guy who thought he was capable of taking me on, a man who looked as though he was about to start a war. Oh, yeah...let's fight, hot stuff.

He was tall, and his broad shoulders filled out his uniform in a way that made me clench my thighs together. His dark, wavy hair was casually tousled, with that perfect balance of messy and stylish. And those brown eyes flecked with gold? Dangerous. Oh my God. He was a total daddy. So fucking hot. Seriously, how was this man so gorgeous? Any man in a uniform was sexy as hell, but this guy? Holy moly.

"Mind if I sit?" he asked, his tone brooking no argument. His voice was like gravel mixed with honey whiskey—a hint of rough around the edges but smooth enough to go down easy.

I blinked up at him, trying to play it cool. Oh, shit. He actually looked as if he wanted to murder me, and that wasn't some fantasy in my head. "Uh, Amanda, I gotta go," I mumbled. Not waiting for her reply, my thumb jabbed the "End Call" button.

I shrugged nonchalantly as I popped my earbuds out. This was a challenge I was more than up for. *Let's play.* "It's a public space," I said, crossing my arms. "You don't need my permission."

He didn't crack a smile, didn't even blink, just lowered himself into the chair next to me like he owned the place. The fabric of his jacket appeared ready to burst from the strain of his bulging muscles. His eyes flicked my way for a second before he turned to stare out the window. He leaned forward, resting his forearms on his thighs and clasping his hands together, ignoring me for a minute. Tension radiated from him.

"All your assumptions about the cancellation are total bullshit," he said calmly, but his words had a sharp edge to them.

I stiffened, not expecting the bluntness. Who did this guy think he was, anyway? But before I could snap back, he continued.

"First of all," he said, lifting his hands to make air quotes, "the *tarmac* isn't a place. It's a product used as a surface coating for roads and airfields. What you're looking at out there, where all the people and equipment are, is called the ramp. That's where planes are parked and serviced. The taxiways are the"—more air quotes—"*roads* planes use to move to and from the runways. And the runways? That's where airplanes take off and land."

He rattled this off as though he was a kindergarten teacher explaining the ABCs. My eyebrows shot up; I was taken aback by his unexpected aviation lesson.

"Okay," I said slowly, giving him my best *who the hell cares* look. "Thanks for the...clarification."

He didn't acknowledge my sarcasm. Instead, he reached into his pocket, pulled out his phone, tapped it a few times, and then shoved it in front of my face. "Second, the information on weather apps isn't always accurate. We pilots use a TAF—the official FAA forecast for aviation. It tells us if the weather is dropping below the minimums for ceilings or visibility at either the departure or *arrival* airports and whether we can be legally dispatched for a flight. We use a whole host of meteorological tools, dispatchers, and meteorologists to determine if the weather's good enough to fly. It's not as simple as looking out the window, sweetheart."

His words stung, not because he was wrong, but because he was being a dick about being right. I blinked, staring at the jumble of numbers and letters on his screen. "I—"

"Basically," he said, rudely cutting me off, "for this flight, the rules say we can take off but we can't land at Albany. We don't have a choice in the matter." He huffed.

"And thirdly, so that you're more grounded in reality, the number of passengers on a flight doesn't determine whether it goes or stays. We don't just cancel flights because there aren't enough people on board. Planes need to be positioned for their next scheduled leg, and there are strict FAA regulations. It's not about saving a few bucks or skipping a leg because we're feeling lazy. The airline would get fined up the ass if we pulled a stunt like that."

I glanced down at his chest, catching sight of the name badge below his wings. "Yes, sir, Captain Vinter." What kind of name was Vinter? Sounded like something out of a Norse myth. Made sense, I guess. Everything about him screamed Viking—he was all hard lines and had a gaze frigid enough to freeze hell over.

He leaned back, turning to rest his elbow on the back of the seat, his dark eyes locking onto me. His jaw was clenched with the kind of look that made it clear he wasn't here to play games. "I want to make this flight happen as much as you do because I don't want to be stuck here either. I didn't haul my ass into work just to sit around and listen to bratty girls complain. We aren't paid for delays or for listening to girls like you yap. I only get paid when the jet is moving."

His gruff words hit me square in the chest. I snapped my mouth shut, unsure whether to be pissed off or impressed by the way he'd put me in my place so easily.

I moved around in my seat, trying to get comfortable and failing as the armrest dug into my back, and sighed. Dropping my hands in my lap, I glanced down from his dark, steady glare, my cheeks burning from more than the heat of the conversation. My skin prickled with irritation at being called out by Mr. Captain here. I deserved it, though. It wasn't fair to rip into the airlines or make accusations about pilots, especially during this busy season when they were all working their asses off.

"Okay, fine, you're right," I muttered, glancing back up at him. "Sorry for being dramatic as fuck. I was just ranting to my friend. Taking my frustration out on the airline and the crew was a bit much, maybe. I know it's not your fault the flight got canceled... It's just...I'm having a really shitty day."

He stood and sneered as he pocketed his phone. Without a word, he turned and walked away.

Could my life be any more pathetic? The way he had scolded me had whisked me back to my elementary school classroom—standing red-faced in front of the class, murmuring an apology. My eyes dropped to the floor as I let out a frustrated sigh. "God, I wish I'd never been born."

His footsteps paused, his boots scuffing against the tile before he continued moving, leaving me alone with my thoughts.

I slumped down in my chair, biting my lip to keep it from trembling. Blake's face flashed in my mind—the smug grin he'd had on his face yesterday in the office, the way he'd paraded around as if he'd won some grand prize after screwing me over, the swagger he'd donned when he'd walked into my office acting like he'd done me a favor by ending our relationship before telling me he was now my boss.

His words replayed in my mind: "*No hard feelings, right?*" As though he was merely my buddy, parting ways with me after a casual lunch, not a man who had made me fall in love with him and then stolen my work.

Why was it so impossible to find anyone to love me? Was that really so difficult? Guys today sucked. Really, they did; it couldn't be me, right? That was what I kept trying to convince myself of. But deep down, I knew better. Of course it was me. Me. I was the problem.

I pressed my lips together, fighting the sting in my eyes. I wasn't a bad person. I didn't lie; I didn't cheat—I didn't hurt people on purpose. But I was...a lot. I was loud, emotional, and undoubtedly a bit of a drama queen when I'd had a glass or three of wine, like today. Mr. Captain over there probably thought I was a total bitch after that little display on the phone with Amanda. I didn't blame him. I wore my heart on my sleeve, especially when I was pissed off. It was beyond my control. I'd never learned to play it cool or keep my mouth shut.

I twisted in my seat again, trying to find some comfort that didn't exist. The gate area buzzed with activity, people moving to and fro, while I sat here dejected. I was frustrated about everything. I was upset about being stuck here and pissed about how my life was unraveling in a dozen different directions. My vision blurred as the emotions bubbled up, spilling over in hot, silent tears that rolled down my face. I wiped them away with the sleeve of my comfy gray sweater dress, hating that my world was crashing down around me.

Kol Vinter

Chapter Two

12/23 late morning

As I walked away from the cheeky blonde, her sass about the airlines and crew still irritated the hell out of me. She was a damn firecracker; that much was clear. Sure, she had the air of someone who'd never worked a hard day in her life—probably spoiled rotten by her parents—but there was something else about her, the way she challenged me, as though she were a wild mustang daring me to try and break her. Her fiery spirit and sharp tongue contrasted with her delicate features and petite frame, but it had stirred something reckless in me. I'd been compelled to confront her. People always have a way of chasing what's bad for them, and I wasn't immune. Maybe it was that instinct, that primeval pull to run straight at what could take you down, that appealed to me. Hell, that was how men like me ended up heading off to war.

Her half-hearted apology had come off as an invitation, as if she was letting me win this skirmish but wanted to take me on as a challenge she couldn't resist—like she was testing me, curious to see if I could handle her. The way she'd been mouthing off about the flight cancellation had indeed made me want to either shut her up with a hard kiss or throttle her—maybe both. As I headed back toward my bags, I thought about how good those pouty lips would look wrapped around my cock, her deep blue eyes gazing up at me as she kneeled in front of me. Too bad she was such a smartass and full of herself, but damn if she wasn't gorgeous.

I wondered how it would be to come home to a woman like her—feisty and hot-tempered, someone who would keep me on my toes. But, in reality, she was the kind of hassle I didn't need. Too much attitude, too much trouble. But she was something else; I'd give her that.

Although I'd thought about marriage, it hadn't been in the cards for me. I had always figured I would have plenty of time for that sort of thing once I was out of the Army, but here I was at thirty-four, still single, and the idea of settling down seemed like more of a joke with each passing year. Mom was always on me about finding a good Catholic wife, but I'd been able to dodge that bullet for years. I shook my head, dismissing the thought. Women were more trouble than they were worth.

I had a nice, quiet cabin up in Rotterdam, and right now, the only person I had to worry about was me. Honestly, I liked it that way. My old man always joked that a good woman was hard to find, and an even better one—like my mom—was damn near impossible. He wasn't wrong.

I walked past the gate agent's station to where my luggage sat by the window, then reached into my flight bag and pulled out my tablet, tapping it awake to check my schedule. Crew scheduling had already updated it. All my flights for the day had been canceled, and I was willing to bet the rest of my trip would be too, with this storm coming in. It meant my whole day was down the drain with my commute, but at least I'd get to head back home. Silver linings, I guess.

Before I could dive deeper into my schedule, someone shouted my call sign across the terminal.

"Icehawk!"

I looked up to see Ryan McAllister charging toward me—his face lit up like a damn Christmas tree. Ryan and I went way back to our first days in the Army. He grabbed my hand, pulling me into a one-arm hug.

"McAllister," I said, grinning. "Been a minute, huh?"

Ryan chuckled, still holding onto my hand. "Hell yeah. Good to see you, man. How you been?"

I clapped him on the shoulder. "Not bad. You?"

He released my hand, a proud grin spreading across his face. "Good, good. The baby girl's keeping us busy. She's getting bigger by the day and got me wrapped around her little finger already."

I smirked. "That's what they do, I hear. How's Scarlett holding up?"

Ryan's expression softened a bit. "She had a rough go at first, what with the C-section and me being gone so much, but she's tough. You know Scarlett."

"Sorry to hear that. But I'm glad she's doing better now," I said, nodding. "Give her my best."

Ryan took a step back, eyeing the new stripes on my uniform. "Look at you, Captain. Moving up in the world."

I snorted. "Yeah, first flight off IOE just got canceled. Then I checked, and my other two flights for today are canned too. So now, it's go-home day."

Ryan laughed, shaking his head. "Man, days like this, you gotta think the crew schedulers are about ready to shoot themselves."

"No kidding," I said, smirking. "Good for me though. I get to head back to the cabin."

Ryan's face lit up. "Speaking of which, we should get the guys together and come out to your place for a few days once the weather warms up. Do some fishing and kick back with a few beers. You know, live the good life. I'm damn envious of your setup."

I shrugged. "It has its perks."

Ryan gave me a sideways glance. "I still can't believe no pretty blonde has cuffed you yet. What are you now, thirty-four? Thirty-five?"

"Thirty-four. And no, no blondes or brunettes or redheads either." I cracked a smile. "I've seen too many times how this life plays out. Whether it's in the Army or the airlines, some women are only after the paycheck and benefits. They want a baby daddy, not a partner. No thanks. I've seen divorce tear through too many guys in this line of work."

Ryan grimaced, grabbing my shoulder. "I don't know, having the right woman snuggled up warm and tight all night might be worth the risk as long as you have a good prenup." He laughed at his own quip, but I shook my head.

"Yeah, well, if the right woman's out there, she's gotta be the exception, not the rule. Too many guys in this job end up in a nightmare, with half their paycheck gone. I'm not signing up for that."

Ryan patted me on the back. "Good seeing you, Vinter. I gotta run though. Flight to Nashville. Take care of yourself, all right?"

"Always do," I replied, giving him a nod. "Safe flight, McAllister!" I called after him, watching him jog off, then stuffed my tablet back into my flight bag, ready to get the hell out of this place. As I turned to leave, I caught sight of the blonde again. She was brushing tears from her cheeks with her sleeve. She was all alone, looking like a stray puppy that had been kicked one too many times. Damn, she looked pitiful. Her words, "*I wish I'd never been born,*" played back in my head. Shit. That hit harder than I'd expected.

I had two younger sisters and a little brother. Growing up, I'd been taught to look out for them and always to do the right thing. I recognized her tone, that kind of desperation. It was the kind of thing I couldn't just walk away from, not when I could do something about it. This girl needed help, and I was standing right here, more than able to provide it. Didn't matter if I wanted to help or not—it wasn't about me.

I was heading right through Albany on my way home to Rotterdam. I'd also overheard her complaining about needing to get to Saratoga Springs. Either way, I'd be passing close enough to make a quick detour. It wouldn't be much out of my way to give her a ride. I'd already driven down from Rotterdam to LaGuardia this morning instead of catching one of the two flights I could have commuted in on. I liked having my truck at base so that I didn't have to worry about missing the flight home and getting stuck needing a hotel.

That storm could be a problem, though, seeing as we'd be heading straight for it. And it looked like it was going to turn into a blizzard. But I was going regardless. Besides, if one of my sisters were stuck in a shitty situation and stranded in LaGuardia, I would hope someone decent stepped up to help.

Even though spending three hours locked in a car with a smart-mouthed princess who thought the world revolved around her was the last thing I needed today, what choice did I have? It was the right thing to do. After all, I'd handled worse in Afghanistan—the worst humanity had to offer, really. How bad could one elf of a girl be?

I tightened my grip on the flight bag and started toward her. She still had that lost look—all guarded and defensive, as if she was stuck in her own head. I planted myself right in front of her, casting a shadow over her small frame. She blinked up at me, her watery eyes going wide. She didn't say a word; she just sat there, waiting for me to speak first.

"You got anywhere else to go?" I asked.

A little wrinkle formed between her brows in a flash of defiance. "Why do you care?"

I shrugged, trying to keep my expression neutral. "Because I'm driving through Albany, and it looks as though you need a ride. I heard you mention Saratoga Springs. It's not that far outta my way. Figured I'd offer."

She sniffed, wiping her nose with her sleeve again. "And why would I get in a car with a strange man, some playboy pilot?" Clenching her jaw, she glared at me. Stubbornness was written all over her face, as though she hated the idea of needing anything from me.

"Because right now, I'm the best option you've got," I said. "And coming with me is a lot safer than sleeping in this terminal. Not to mention, I've been vetted and verified more times than you can imagine. Served as a Night Stalker in the Army, and pilots go through FBI background checks to get hired. You're looking at one of the most checked-out people you're likely to meet."

She narrowed her eyes, a hint of a smile teasing the corners of her mouth. "So, you're a stalker. That's supposed to make me feel better?"

I let out a low chuckle. "Night Stalker. It's an aviation unit, not the creepy kind of stalker."

"Not so sure about the *not being creepy* part." She eyed me warily. Her mouth opened, then closed, as if she was trying to come up with some smart remark while weighing her options.

I waited, crossing my arms, then added, "Trust me, sweetheart, in a hub like New York, cancellations for weather cause a domino effect. By now, all the hotels and rental cars are booked. I'm just giving you an option that doesn't involve sleeping on the airport floor for the next few days."

She rolled her eyes. "Oh, I already figured that much out, Mr. Captain," she quipped.

Damn, this girl had a mouth on her. "Well, enjoy the floor then," I said, turning to walk away. "Merry Christmas."

I made it a few steps before she let out an exasperated huff behind me. "Wait!" she shouted, and I stopped and turned back to her.

"You're serious?" she asked.

"Why else would I offer? Look, we're both going the same way. Saves you from spending a fortune on a last-minute rental or a fleabag hotel. Besides," I added, smirking, "you don't strike me as the type who enjoys being stranded for the holidays."

She let out a dry laugh and gave me a small smile, one that didn't reach her eyes. "Fine. I'll take the ride. But if you try anything—"

"Yeah, yeah," I said, cutting her off brusquely. "You'll scratch my eyes out or some shit. Got it. Just grab your stuff, Stinkerbelle. We're burning daylight, and I'd rather not have to drive in that snowstorm heading straight toward Albany any longer than I have to."

She scrunched up her face, and with that, I started walking away from her again.

She mumbled to herself as she scrambled to her feet and grabbed her things, her spiky boots tapping against the floor. "Why do I always end up in these situations? With my luck, he's probably a serial killer. But what choice do I have? Gotta get home...gotta sign those damn papers...can't sleep on the airport floor..."

I kept walking, a grin spreading across my face. As she moved to catch up to me, she kept up her half-muttered rant, her words tumbling out as though she were debating with herself more than with me. "All right, all right, stranger danger and all that aside, I have no other way to get there on time." When she stepped up beside me, she was fumbling with her bags, trying to get herself organized. "I guess I have no choice but to trust you. It's not as if there's another way to Saratoga, and I really have to get there today."

I couldn't believe how she kept going on and on about it— did the girl ever stop talking? When she stopped for a breath, I glanced her way. She scrutinized me for a moment.

"Okay, okay, I'll do it. But I warn you," she said, straightening up and trying to look tough, "I'm a green belt in American Mixed Martial Arts."

I chuckled. If she had any clue who I was, she probably wouldn't be bragging. Green belt? Cute. I'd spent years doing CQC training and grappling with guys twice her size. I'd been in more hand-to-hand combat situations than I could count, and none of them involved students from some half-assed martial arts studio at a strip mall.

"Yeah, well, that's all good and well," I said, not bothering to hide my amusement, "but I don't think you could fight your way out of a paper bag in those spiky boots. You got any reasonable shoes in that bag?"

She frowned. "What do you mean, reasonable shoes? I'm wearing boots. The perfect winter shoe. They can be used to dress up a nice outfit or worn casually with jeans."

I stared at her, stone-faced, not letting even a twitch of my amusement show. "Doesn't mean shit if we end up walking in two feet of snow."

She pressed her lips together, clearly not happy with the criticism.

"Did you check any bags?" I asked.

"No checked bags, just what I brought as carry-ons."

"Good," I said. "Let's get moving. From the forecast, we'll be cutting it close to get upstate before the worst of the weather hits."

I led her through the terminal at my usual pace, my long strides eating up the distance fast. Years of running to catch planes had me used to navigating crowded airports with the precision of a man on a mission. The holiday chaos swirled around us—families shouting at one another, people dragging oversized luggage around, kids crying about dropped candy canes or stuffed animals. The overhead announcements were barely able to cut through the noise. Christmas at LaGuardia was always a zoo, but today, it was as though the gates of hell had opened and unleashed every traveler in the world on the East Coast.

Behind me, the mouthy blonde tried hard to keep up, her boots clacking furiously against the tile floor. I glanced over my shoulder. She was struggling to weave through the crowd, her suitcase bouncing along behind her.

"Hey, Mr. Captain!" she called out, her breath coming in short bursts. "What's the rush? Are we late for a flight or something? Or do you just like running around as if your hair's on fire?"

Not breaking my stride, I chuckled and called back, "This is my normal pace. Trust me, if I were running, I'd have left you behind after two gates."

She muttered something under her breath and kept hustling to stay close, but just then, some guy in a Christmas sweater barreled into her. Her suitcase toppled over, and she stumbled forward. Overcompensating, she then pitched back, her arms flailing, a yelp escaping her lips. Her red coat and bag flew out of her hands. Yep, she was going down. Before she hit the floor, my instincts kicked in. I dropped my bag and reached out, grabbing her around the waist. When I yanked her up, her body collided with mine, her hands landing flat against my chest.

Soft curves pressed against me as I gripped her hips with both hands, holding her in place. Her scent wrapped around us, a warm blend of vanilla with a hint of cinnamon, rich and sweet, like a holiday treat. Her breath hitched, those ocean-like blue eyes widening as she gazed up at me, clouded with raw desire. The way she focused on me, as if she wasn't sure whether to thank me or slap me, made my pulse kick up a notch. Damn, there was a spark there—a heat I hadn't expected.

Moving her so that she could stand upright, I leaned in and asked, "Are you okay?" My mouth was so close to her ear that her hair was brushing against my cheek.

She pulled back slightly, her hands still on my chest. "Yeah... Thanks. Good save."

I let go, but the space between us seemed charged now, as if something electric had passed through.

After taking a deep breath, she brushed herself off, then straightened her ridiculous boots.

I snatched up her suitcase and hooked it to mine, my flight bag dangling from the top. She spun around and leaned over in front of me to gather up her fancy bag and coat. As I watched her, my mind jumped to thoughts of taking her from behind. I squeezed my eyes shut and shook off the mental snapshot. Fuck! What was this girl doing to me?

"Come on," I said, heading toward the exit. "We've got a shuttle to catch. Try not to get run over this time."

She shot me a glare, but there was a hint of a smile on her face too. "It wasn't my fault. You're the one flying through here like a bat out of hell."

I didn't bother to slow down; I just glanced over at her. "Are you always that clumsy? Because if you keep throwing yourself at strangers, I'm gonna have to charge a rescue fee." I raised an eyebrow, smirking. "You know, some people walk without making it an Olympic event."

She muttered something about me being a smartass, but she managed to keep up, practically trotting alongside as we made our way through the throng of holiday travelers. At one point, a kid nearly plowed into us with one of those rolling backpacks, and she jumped to the side, bumping into me again. I steadied her without saying a word, cutting through the crowd like a hot knife through butter, dragging our bags behind me.

We finally made it outside, the cold air smacking us in the face. She pulled on her coat and fastened it tightly around her waist, shivering a bit as we maneuvered over to the shuttle pick-up lane. One of the employee buses had pulled up, and I motioned for her to get on ahead of me.

She hesitated for a moment, looking over at me with narrowed eyes, probably still wondering if I was a serial killer, but then she stepped up onto the shuttle. I lifted our suitcases into the luggage area inside and turned to the driver.

"B2, please," I said, taking a seat across from my feisty blonde companion as the door closed behind us.

The shuttle jerked forward, and I braced myself against the seat, studying her. She was still working to catch her breath, her cheeks a little flushed from our sprint through the airport. Her hands fidgeted with the tote on her lap while her gaze flitted about and she took stock of the situation. Finally, she inhaled a sharp breath and turned toward me.

"I guess since we're sharing a ride, I should introduce myself. I'm Noelle Nichols."

"Noelle?" I raised an eyebrow. "Like in the *Christmas Carol*? Were you born on December twenty-fifth or something?"

She rolled her eyes as her lips quirked in a subtle grin. "No, July third actually. I'm a total Cancer. My parents just loved Christmas."

I blinked. "A total what now? Cancer? You sick or something?"

She burst out laughing, as though she couldn't believe how clueless I was. The sound of her laughter was cute. "No, not that kind of cancer. The zodiac sign. Cancer. You know, astrology?"

I shook my head. "Can't say I do."

"Well," she started, leaning back into her seat as if preparing to give a lecture, "Cancers are known to be homebodies. Comfort, family—that's our thing. We're nurturing, emotional, fiercely loyal, and protective of those we care about." There was a hint of a smile on her lips as she continued, "Imaginative, maybe a little moody, and definitely not fans of change. I'm a textbook Cancer, through and through."

I listened as she rattled off this list, nodding occasionally, but my mind drifted a bit. All I really caught were the words "homebodies" and "moody." It was as though she was speaking a different language.

"I used to love riding horses," she continued. "A total Cancer thing, you know? Being outdoors but still craving the comfort of home. And I could spend hours in the kitchen, baking mostly—comfort food and things like that. My mom always said—" She stopped abruptly, as if someone had flipped a switch. The animation drained from her face, and she lowered her eyes. Her shoulders tensed, and she pressed her lips into a thin line. Something had hit a nerve. Her entire demeanor had changed, stopping whatever thought had started to slip out—a complete shutdown.

Then it hit me. It was the brief mention of her mom that had made her clam up. There was a story there; that much was clear. But based on the way she was crossing her arms and staring out the window, she wasn't about to share it.

She clenched her jaw and tapped her fingers nervously on her leg. I remained silent. I wasn't about to dig any deeper.

"So, Captain Vinter," she said after a long while, breaking the silence with that snarky tone I was learning was her go-to defensive mechanism. "Or is it Iceman? Do you have a first name?"

"Kol," I replied. "And my call sign is Icehawk. Iceman is from the movie *Top Gun*."

She stared at me for a second before bursting into a fit of giggles, her laugh echoing through the nearly empty shuttle. "Oh my God! Kol? Like what bad kids get in their stockings!? Talk about being perfect for Christmas! Did your parents know you were going to be a naughty boy?"

I smirked, trying to keep a straight face. "Real original."

"No, seriously!" she continued, her laughter only growing. "And Vinter? Winter in some language like Swedish, right? So you're like the coldest *coal* ever! What's next, Captain Frostbite?"

I glared at her, but she was on a roll.

"Wait, wait—Kol Vinter? So what, did your parents want you to be the Viking villain in some Christmas special? I bet you were born during a snowstorm, right?"

Wordlessly, I raised an eyebrow.

"Let me guess, your middle name is something like *Blizzard*. Do you have a cousin named *Storm*? Or, wait—are you secretly flying Santa's sleigh on the side?"

Glancing around at the other passengers, I crossed my arms and sat back. She kept going, each comment more idiotic than the last.

"I can just see it now," she said, "*Kol Vinter*: Santa's enforcer, delivering coal and icy stares to all the naughty girls. I mean, it all fits—a pilot who navigates through snowstorms, dropping coal from thirty thousand feet! I bet you've got the whole *cold-hearted captain* thing down. Did your parents plan this out, or did it just happen naturally?"

She was now practically in tears, doubling over with laughter, while I sat there, forcing myself to keep a straight face as she unraveled over her own jokes.

Finally, when she started to calm down and wipe the tears from her eyes, I asked, "You done?"

She rolled her lips in, another giggle slipping out, but she nodded.

I leaned in, saying in a low voice, "Because I can think of a few ways to put that smart mouth of yours to better use."

Her eyes went wide, pupils dilating. She froze, not making a single sound, as if she was holding her breath. Her reaction was priceless. I'd hit a nerve.

Before she could utter a comeback, the bus jerked to a stop, and the driver called out, "B2!"

Noelle blinked, breaking the spell. She grabbed her tote and stepped off the shuttle without saying a word, leaving me to grab our suitcases. I watched her saunter ahead with a little sway in her hips. What a damn diva.

I cleared my throat. "My truck's this way."

She flipped her thick, curly blonde hair over her shoulder, then turned and followed me. When we reached my Bronco, she paused, her eyes widening a bit. She appraised the vehicle, giving an appreciative nod.

"Nice ride," she said, running a hand along the hood. "I've always thought the new Broncos were badass. I like the color too. Race Red, right? And the lift kit—it's perfect for snow."

She'd noticed the lift. Not bad. "Yeah, I'm a fan. Gets the job done."

I tossed our luggage into the back and shrugged off my uniform jacket, throwing it onto the backseat, on top of my leather bomber jacket. I hadn't thought I'd need the bomber for this trip, but with the snowstorm turning into a real doozy, I was glad I had it.

As I rolled up my sleeves, Noelle opened the door and reached up for the inside handle. She wasn't tall enough to step up into the vehicle easily. Swiftly, I moved to her side of the vehicle and slid my hands around her waist, giving her a solid boost up into the passenger seat.

She blinked at me in surprise. "Didn't peg you for the chivalrous type, Mr. Captain."

I shrugged, giving her a slight grin as I let go of her waist. "My momma raised me right."

Chapter Three

12/23 midday

Kol's big red four-by-four Bronco roared to life, a deep rumble vibrating beneath me. I situated my tote and wiggled out of my coat, tossing it in the backseat. I glanced over at him as he threw the gearshift into reverse, getting a good look at his hands for the first time. They were so massive that it looked as if he could bend the thing in half if he wanted to. The guy was easily twice my size and built like a damn mountain. I'd been taken aback by how easily and carefully he'd helped me into his truck. It was ridiculously high off the ground, and being five-foot-three on a good day meant I practically had to claw my way up to the seat. I had to admit it: my boots, although stylish, weren't very practical for snow or big-ass trucks. Somehow, with Kol's help, I'd managed to get in without pulling another embarrassing stunt. I fumbled with my seat belt, and by the time I'd clicked it in place, Kol was already pulling out of the airport parking lot.

"So," he said as we turned onto Grand Central Parkway, "where exactly are you headed, Stinkerbelle?"

Stinkerbelle. I hated how easily that nickname rolled off his tongue, as if he had me all figured out. I refused to acknowledge it or, worse, let him think it bothered me. Besides, what could I say, given the situation? After overhearing my tirade back at Gate 73, he probably thought I was a bitter shrew. Clearly, my personal PR needed a serious reboot. If I let him keep seeing me as some high-maintenance diva, the next three hours locked in his car would be unbearable. I needed his help, and the last thing I wanted was for him to hate me. He was interesting, someone I actually wanted to talk to, but it was obvious he knew how to be a cocky asshole when he chose to be. I wanted to keep him on his toes—make him second-guess everything—so I could maintain the upper hand in this power dynamic. It was time to spin the narrative and show him I wasn't only some spoiled brat who threw tantrums at airport gates. For now, Mr. Captain could think he was in charge. I had at least four hours to change his impression of me, prove how great Noelle Nichols really was, and maybe even impress the man. Regardless, I didn't care what he called me, as long as he got me to Ms. Winters's office in time to sign those papers.

"Downtown Saratoga Springs, please," I said, reaching for my phone to find the exact address. "I have to meet with my aunt's attorney to sign some last-minute paperwork." His help was the first good thing to happen to me all week. I glanced over at him and gave him an effortless smile. "I really appreciate you doing this for me. Can I at least buy the gas?"

"Don't worry about it. Saratoga's not that far from my place." He reached over, pressed the nav button, and pointed for me to enter the address.

"Oh, where do you live?" I asked, leaning forward and tapping on the screen.

"Off I-90, near Rotterdam."

"Hmm, I know that area. I grew up just outside of Saratoga. I guess this is my lucky day—having the pilot of my canceled flight live so close to where I need to be and offer me a ride."

"You planning on staying long?"

"No." I bit my lip, thinking about the weather. "I'd planned on signing the papers today and going back to Atlanta tomorrow. But with this surprise snowstorm, who knows? You'd think with all the fancy equipment and technology, the weather gurus would have figured out how to make a reliable forecast."

He shook his head. "Well, Mother Nature is one mysterious woman—always keeping you guessing, just like women in general." He smirked. "Weather's tricky. It's not just about the clouds and temperature. You've got pressure systems, wind currents, moisture levels. There's a million moving parts. And even with all the technology, the forecast can be off because things change faster than you think. That's what keeps pilots on their toes. One minute, you've got clear skies, and the next, you're dodging turbulence. I've seen it change right in front of my eyes from the cockpit."

I nodded. "That makes sense. I guess that's why people always say pilots are great at flying by the seat of their pants."

"If you say so. But that's why I'll never trust a pilotless plane. The tech wizards say it's coming, but no machine can handle the weather, winds, and everything else that affects how an aircraft responds. A computer doesn't have instincts."

"I agree with you there," I said, a little shocked by the idea that one day there could be pilotless planes similar to driverless cars. If they couldn't get a car to work right on autopilot, how on earth did they think they could make a plane fly on its own?

I mean, I understood that drones didn't have pilots on board, but at least there was a pilot in a dark room somewhere ultimately responsible for it. "I would like an actual person in control when I'm thousands of feet up."

"You would be smart. Especially when the shit hits the fan."

At that, I smiled and turned to look out the window. I focused on listening to the steady hum of the engine and the tires whirring against the wet pavement as we inched our way out of the city. The traffic was practically crawling, and the dark clouds above warned that the weather was about to get a whole lot worse.

I glanced over at Kol, realizing he hadn't put any music on.

"So," I said after a few more beats of silence, "what kind of music do you usually listen to?"

Kol raised an eyebrow. "I'm a country music sort of guy— old-school stuff, like George Strait, Johnny Cash. Newer stuff too; Eric Church and Luke Combs are a couple of my favorites. What about you?"

I shrugged. "I like everything from rock to EDM to dubstep. Avicii's one of my all-time favorites, but I'm really into Tyler Childers these days too."

He shot me a surprised look. "Wait, EDM? Like, festival music?"

I grinned. "Yep, I've been to a bunch—Bonnaroo, Okeechobee, and Electric Forest—back in college. I love the entire festival experience. The energy, the lights, the bass drops. I haven't been to one since I started working at the Martindale Agency, though, for lots of reasons. I miss it."

Kol chuckled, shaking his head. "Hm, music festival junkie. I didn't see that coming. So, you're into camping with a bunch of hippie types?"

"Don't knock it," I teased. "It's fun, I'm telling you. And anyway, I listen to all kinds of music. I think it's always been my saving grace. It's the energy that matters. I mean, I get that festivals might not be everyone's thing, but music is music."

His gaze slid my way for a moment, and a barely perceptible smirk appeared on his face as he kept his attention mostly on the road. "I'm not sure I can picture you in one of those festival getups, dancing to whatever it is they play."

"Please, I've got range," I said with a laugh. "I listen to country too, so I'm not just some rave queen. Plus, Tyler Childers? He's so...incredible."

Kol snorted. "Okay, I'll give you that. Tyler Childers is solid. But I don't know about all that other stuff."

I wrinkled my nose, trying not to laugh. "Oh, so you only like *sad cowboy* music? Songs about trucks, heartbreak, and whiskey? That's your thing?"

His eyebrow shot up. "You mean songs with actual substance?"

"Substance? You've got to be kidding," I shot back. "Festival music is about more than just mosh pits and bass drops. It's about social change, diversity, people coming together to make something bigger than themselves. The artists I follow are out there pushing boundaries, speaking up about things, supporting equality, worrying about climate change, and advocating for mental health. Sure, the beats are great, but a lot of the messages are really solid."

"Sure, if you insist."

"But don't get me wrong," I continued. "I'm not saying country music doesn't have substance. Country's great for telling stories that hit home, you know? It talks about real-life struggles—family, love, loss, and where you come from. I think that's why I like Tyler Childers so much. His songs are real, and so are the issues he sings about. At the end of the day, all genres have depth; they just express it in different ways."

Kol nodded slowly. "All right, I'll give you that. But I'm still not convinced that camping with seventy thousand sweaty people sounds like a good time."

I laughed. "Hey, as long as you appreciate the message and don't deny that all music is good, I'll take it."

"Yeah, well, except when it's terrible." He snorted.

"See, that's the problem. People don't give stuff that's different a chance. It's what happens to Taylor Swift. Some people love to hate on her, say she sucks, but that's not fair. They just don't like her style of music. Doesn't mean she's not a genius."

He tilted his head and twisted his mouth slightly, clearly skeptical. "Taylor Swift? Genius—really?"

"Absolutely. She writes her own music, works her ass off, and never backs down. Even when Kanye was a complete dick to her, she was composed and kept going. You can't deny her talent or her business success."

"Kanye's a dick to everybody," he said with a laugh.

"Exactly! People just hate on things for the dumbest reasons or no reasons at all."

Kol grinned. "Okay, I can get on board with not bashing Taylor. But let's be real—something like... say, screamo is not gonna help us survive this drive. How about we stick with my playlist for now?"

I let out an exaggerated sigh. "Fine. I guess Skrillex might be a bit much for a snowstorm. We'll just stay in your country comfort zone. Go ahead and start your playlist. I'll save mine for later." I crossed my arms, thinking about all the songs I'd play.

"See? It's not so hard to let me take the lead, now, is it?"

I shot him a sideways glance, trying not to smile. "Don't push your luck."

For a few seconds, we just rode along, the city slowly falling away behind us as we crossed over the New Jersey state line.

Kol tapped his fingers lightly on the steering wheel, then cleared his throat, drawing my attention. "So," he began, keeping his eyes on the road, "what's the deal with the attorney? Family business?" He glanced at me briefly before refocusing on the highway.

"Yeah." I shrugged, staring out the window as the world raced by in a blur of gray. "My Aunt Mary passed away about a month ago. She's left me something in her will, and I need to take care of it."

"Is that what got you all worked up at the gate? Estate stuff?"

I huffed out a sarcastic laugh. "That, and my life being a total dumpster fire, but thanks for asking, Mr. Captain."

He grunted. "You can just call me Kol, you know."

"Yeah, but I think Mr. Captain is better. Fits your whole tall, dark, and serious vibe. Very Night Stalkerish."

His lips twitched as he reached out and turned up the heater a bit to fight the growing chill from outside. "So, why are you heading up there at the last minute?"

I sighed. "Long story short, I've been so buried in work that I put it off until I had no choice. I have to sign everything by the end of today or I won't receive what my aunt left me. Instead, it'll be donated to the church. And—no offense to the church—I'd really like to keep whatever she's giving me, because I'm going to need it at this point. The last month has been overwhelming, with her death and then everything happening at work—the biggest project of my career, going for a huge promotion. I just haven't had the time or...the emotional bandwidth."

He gave me a quick glance but didn't pry further. A big wet snowflake splattered against the windshield.

Kol turned on the wipers. "Speaking of time, this snow might slow us down," he said.

I peered out at the landscape as we drove north. The snow was starting to fall in earnest now. Flakes smacked the windshield like wet spitballs. The windshield wipers squeaked with each swipe, dragging across the glass as if reluctant to move. The wet snow was light enough that they didn't have much to push aside, so they made a faint, high-pitched screech on every pass.

I groaned. "Of course we're already running into snow. Because things weren't complicated enough."

I pulled out my phone and dialed Ms. Winters. It rang and rang before finally going to voicemail. "Hi, Ms. Winters. It's Noelle Nichols. I'm on my way, but I'm running behind because my flight to Albany got canceled. I'll get there as soon as I can. Please wait for me."

Hanging up, I dropped the phone into my lap and sighed. "Great. If we don't get there by five, I'm screwed."

"We'll make it." Kol's tone was confident, but his hands gripped the steering wheel a little tighter as more snowflakes started to fall. The road quickly became slick. He twisted the dial on the console, engaging slippery mode. I had wanted a Bronco for a long time, so I'd read about how these newer models could automatically adjust throttle response, transmission shift points, and traction control settings to improve performance on icy surfaces. This wasn't a good sign.

"I swear, this is all some cosmic joke," I said. "You ever have those days where the universe just piles everything on you at once?"

Kol glanced at me. "Yeah. Three tours in Afghanistan will do that."

I blinked, not having expected him to drop something so heavy into the conversation. "Well, I guess you win the bad-day contest."

He shrugged as if it wasn't a big deal, but I could tell by the way his jaw ticked that maybe it was.

The truck's tires squelched over the slush as we drove further into the storm.

Deciding to pry a little and learn something about this stranger sitting next to me, I asked, "So, what's the story with you and flying? Was it something you fell into through the military, or did you always want to be a pilot?"

Kol shifted in his seat, frowning for a second as though debating whether to respond. "No, not always. But once I joined the Army and started flying, I was hooked. Now, I can't imagine doing anything else."

He paused, a brief flicker of pride crossing his face. "After the Army, I knew I wanted to stick with it, so when I found out that there was a structured pathway to transition to fixed-wing aircraft, I jumped at it. I could earn my ratings all the way through to my ATP certification over the course of a year. Flying for National Airlines is just the next chapter. Civilian flying's a whole different beast, but the view from up there never gets old."

I tilted my head slightly, leaning in with curiosity. "So, not only do you get to see the world from the cockpit, but that's your office? That beats the little gray office with a view of the parking lot I had by miles. You're basically living the dream, aren't you?"

"Depends on how you look at it. Sure, flying is incredible. I mean, how many people get to say their office is thirty-five thousand feet above the ground? Watching the sunrise over the clouds, thunderstorms lighting up a cumulonimbus at night like a mythical war between gods, or catching the colorful waves of the aurora borealis—it's pretty damn great. But it's also a lot of responsibility. Most people can make a mistake at work and fix it. If I screw up, it's not just me—it's the lives of hundreds of passengers, crew, and even people on the ground that are at stake. Keeps me on my toes, for sure."

I examined his face a bit more closely. Apparently, he wasn't just flying for the thrill—he had people's lives in his hands every time he went up there. I shifted in my seat, tucking a curl behind my ear as I gave him a sideways glance. "Well, Mr. Captain," I teased, letting a smirk play on my lips, "I guess you're no stranger to high-stakes situations. A snowstorm must be a breeze compared to navigating the skies with a whole plane full of people counting on you."

Kol straightened up in his seat, flexing the muscles in his forearms as he leaned forward to assess the storm ahead. "You could say that," he muttered. The dark clouds seemed to be sinking lower, and the snow was picking up, swirling faster and colliding with the windshield more rapidly. His jaw tightened. The silence between us stretched as music played in the background. Though Kol didn't say a word, I could sense him scrutinizing every flake, every inch of the road, like someone trained to see danger long before it hit.

We'd just passed the West Point Military Academy exit, and I was already on edge and biting my thumbnail. The knot in my stomach tightened with each passing mile as the conditions got worse. I hated driving in the snow.

"Don't worry. This thing handles worse obstacles than this," Kol said, reassuring me with confidence. "It's made for going off-road and through mud slicks."

I wanted to laugh, but the sound that came out was more of a nervous hiccup. "I hope you're right. Dying in a fiery crash after flying off the highway isn't exactly how I pictured my day ending."

His focus broke for a moment as he turned toward me, the corners of his mouth lifting slightly, more in quiet encouragement than amusement. "We're not going to die, Stinkerbelle. I've got this. Just sit back and relax."

I slumped back in the seat, staring anxiously out the window at the increasingly white landscape. "I wish it were that simple."

As the snow began to blanket everything around us, I couldn't help but wonder if we would actually make it to Saratoga before the storm buried us. I chewed my lip and glanced at Kol again. The calm, assured look on his face eased my mind. I took a deep breath, trying to trust that he really did have everything under control.

This was going to be a long drive.

Kol Vinter

Chapter Four

12/23 late afternoon

The windshield wipers scraped rhythmically against the glass, battling the snow that seemed to be coming down harder. It swirled beyond the low beams of the headlights like a swarm of oversized gnats. Almost two hours had gone by since we'd left the city.

I focused on the road ahead while Noelle kept me entertained. For most of the drive, we'd listened to my playlist, with her singing along, mostly off-key. I didn't mind. It was interesting how uninhibited she was—not caring in the least what I thought. Most of the women I'd been with were too focused on appearances, trying to impress everyone around them instead of just being real. They were never able to relax and just be themselves. Noelle, though, was different. She was similar to my sisters, who would always sit in the backseat and belt out the words to whatever song came on, even if it annoyed me.

"I don't understand how you can only listen to country music all the time," she said as the fourth Blake Shelton song finished playing. "I mean, they're great songs, but don't you want more variety?"

"Variety? Country music has it all. You must not be paying attention."

She scoffed, reaching for her phone. "Okay, my turn. We need something fresh to keep us awake with all this never-ending snow. It's hypnotic and pulling me under. I can barely keep my eyes open."

She synced her phone up, and a mash-up of a cheer routine and an eighties bubblegum pop song began to play. Noelle laced her fingers together and pressed her hands to her heart. "I love me some Chappell Roan," she crooned, rocking side to side. I took note of how she belted out some line about calling her hot, not pretty. Yeah, I bet she'd get off on the right kind of praise. Next up was another song by the same girl—"Good Luck, Babe." The contrast in our taste in music was...jarring.

"You've gotta be kidding me," I muttered, shaking my head. "This is—hyper."

"Hyper? This is empowerment!" she said, her eyes lighting up as she cranked up the volume. "This song is all about moving on from toxic relationships and taking back your strength. It's a celebration of self-worth."

I raised an eyebrow. "It sounds as though someone's screaming into a karaoke mic after three too many tequila shots."

Noelle gasped dramatically. "Blasphemy! You just don't get it. It's fun, it's vibrant, it's...good times."

I let her have that one, focusing back on the road as she bobbed her head and sang along. Eventually, though, she scrolled a bit and tapped the phone to select something new. I was relieved when "The Nights" by Avicii started playing. The upbeat rhythm hit me right away, and I nodded along, appreciating the song's reminder to live life to the fullest.

"So you're an Avicii fan, huh?" Noelle teased.

"Yeah," I admitted. "This one's good. I like 'Wake Me Up' too."

"Finally, some taste," she said, grinning. But then her smile faltered. "It's so sad though, you know? That Avicii... Tim Bergling...died by suicide. He was so young. It was such a tragedy."

I nodded, the energy in the car shifting. "Yeah. Hell of a loss. It goes to show that you never really know what someone's going through."

Noelle became quiet, which I was guessing was a rare occurrence since she'd been such a chatterbox all night so far. Silence settled in, the playlist continuing, neither of us saying much. The storm had only intensified, but at least the music was keeping us distracted from how bad the roads were getting.

After a while, I glanced over and saw her resting against the window, her head tilted just enough that I could tell she'd drifted off.

Three hours had passed in a blur of music and conversation, and we were getting close to Albany. I shifted in my seat, keeping one hand firm on the wheel as the tires crunched over the snow-covered road.

"Hey, we're almost to Albany," I said quietly to see if she was awake, but she didn't stir.

Until now, she'd been a whirlwind of energy—talking fast, making sarcastic remarks, and throwing around opinions like confetti. But now? Her body seemed tense. Turning to get a better look, I realized that her hands were clenched into fists, and her brow was furrowed. Her eyes moved rapidly under closed lids—she was definitely dreaming. A few minutes later, she jolted awake, eyes wide, chest heaving. She looked around, trying to mask the fact that she'd reacted to waking up as if she'd been shot.

I glanced at her. "What's wrong, Stinkerbelle? Bad dream about missing your flight?"

She rolled her eyes, but it was half-hearted. It was clear she wasn't really in the mood for verbal sparring. "Funny, Mr. Captain." She repositioned herself in her seat, rubbing her temples as though she were trying to shake off more than just a nap.

I didn't push. People tended to spill when they're ready, and she didn't seem ready. Still, there was something gnawing at her—that much I could tell.

Fat snowflakes and small pieces of ice hit the windshield in thick, wet splats. The Bronco vibrated as it adjusted its grip on the slick road, but it didn't faze me. I was used to rough conditions. Hell, I'd taken this thing through rainstorms that had turned my property into a mud pit. Slipping and sliding through those trails was second nature at this point. But Noelle? She was wound tight.

I shot her a glance. "You look as if you're about to jump out of your skin. Everything good?"

She waved a hand dismissively, faking a smile that failed to conceal her discomfort. "Oh yeah, just peachy. Love driving in snow. It's my favorite thing ever."

I chuckled, shaking my head. "Is that sarcasm I hear?"

"You think?" Her response was sharp.

I pressed my lips together, watching her fidget with her hands. Something was up with her. I'd seen this demeanor before in guys I used to serve with—jittery, waiting for the other shoe to drop.

"You didn't strike me as the nervous type," I said.

She gave a half-shrug, keeping her attention on the storm outside. "I'm not. Just...snow and I have a complicated history. Snowstorms have a way of messing up things in the worst possible way." Her words were clipped, and I sensed she didn't want to get into it further. Fair enough. We all had our demons.

"Got it," I said, adjusting my position in the seat to ease the tension in my back. I made sure to keep my body relaxed, to show her that the storm outside didn't worry me in the slightest. Noelle was on edge for reasons she clearly didn't want to talk about. I hoped my composure would help her settle down.

"I can handle this," I said, glancing at her again. "Trust me—dodging enemy fire teaches you how to stay calm in situations similar to this."

"I haven't said a word about your driving, have I?" she asked defensively.

Now that I thought about it, she hadn't at any point seemed worried about my ability to drive in the snow. No, her issue was with the snowstorm itself. Whatever had happened to her, it ran deep.

"No, no, you haven't. But after listening to your diatribe at the gate, I figured you were thinking it."

She chewed on a nail, continuing to stare out her window. Tension rolled off her in waves. Normally, in this type of situation, I would stay quiet the entire drive—just do what needed to be done and move on. But most people didn't intrigue me in the same way she did. On the outside, she was a perfectly polished, overly confident city girl. But after spending some time with her, I could tell there was a lot more to her. There was a roughness there, similar to the blunt-talking, assertive women I'd known in the Army, the kind who had to deal with cocky men all day.

"You're not a fan of winter, huh?" I asked, trying to keep the conversation casual. My eyes flicked toward her.

She hesitated, tapping her fingers lightly against her leg. "Not really my favorite," she muttered. "I'm more of a summer girl. Give me beaches and margaritas any day."

I grunted, amused. "You and every girl I know."

She snorted, though she lacked her usual gusto.

The road stretched ahead of us. It was dark now, and the snow was falling even thicker. Noelle rubbed her temples again, this time with a little more force.

I didn't say anything for a while, just kept driving, watching the snow and trying to gauge how much worse it might get.

As we passed the exit for the Albany Airport, I couldn't resist teasing her a little.

"Well, Stinkerbelle, if your flight hadn't been canceled, you'd be in Saratoga by now, sipping hot cocoa or whatever you city girls do to unwind. But, then again, you wouldn't have had the pleasure of getting to know me for the last...what, almost four hours?"

Her scoff was immediate, and her lips curved up slightly in amusement. "Oh yeah, because driving through a snowstorm in the dark is *totally* worth getting to know you."

"Hey, I'm great company. Don't act like you're not impressed."

She shot me a sidelong glance and then relaxed her shoulders and sighed, dialing down her hoity-toity attitude a notch. "Okay, fine. But seriously, I am grateful. If it weren't for you, I wouldn't have had a chance getting to the attorney's office on time. I would have lost whatever my aunt left me in her will."

I shrugged, keeping one hand steady on the wheel and dropping the other to my leg. "Glad I could help, even if it means battling through a snowstorm. We're making decent time, considering the bad conditions. Normally it takes around three hours to get to Albany, and it's taken us not quite four. We should be in Saratoga in another hour and a half if we keep up this pace."

"Let's hope it doesn't take any longer than that," Noelle said, then picked up her phone and tried calling the attorney again. Like before, there was no answer.

The tires easily cut through the slush, but more and more slick spots formed as we continued north up I-87. Noelle hadn't stopped biting her nails since she'd woken up, and I figured it was time to get her mind off the storm outside. The last thing we needed was for her to have some sort of panic attack.

"So, what do you do for a living, Stinkerbelle?" I asked, keeping my eyes on the road, figuring that work talk was safe territory.

She huffed, crossing her arms as though she were getting ready for a fight. "Oh, I guess you didn't hear that part of my conversation with my friend at the gate. I *used* to be a marketing account manager at the renowned Martindale Agency in Atlanta. You've probably never heard of it."

Bitterness had crept into her tone. Shit, I'd picked a bad question but now had no other choice than to plow forward. "Used to? What happened? Couldn't handle the corporate ladder?" I joked, turning and giving her the best fake smile I could muster.

Her head whipped toward me, and based on the scowl on her face, she hadn't appreciated my attempt at humor.

"Relax, it was a simple question. We've already established I fly planes. I'm only trying to get to know you a little."

She fidgeted in her seat again, clearly not thrilled to be talking about this. "Okay, so it's a big marketing firm. I do campaigns for major brands—think national commercials, global outreach, the works. Or at least I used to. I quit."

"Quit?" I tilted my head slightly, intrigued. "A job of that caliber doesn't seem to be something you simply walk away from."

She let out an indignant laugh. "Oh, trust me. You would have, too, if you were me."

I waited as she fidgeted with the edges of her sleeves. After a few moments had passed and she was still silent, I nudged her gently. "What happened?"

"Blake Mercer is what happened—more like *Blake Merciless*. Let's just say my charming ex-boyfriend decided to stab me in the back, steal my work, and take the promotion I'd been working my ass off for. Then, for good measure, he dumped me as if I was some intern who brought him the wrong coffee."

I let out a low whistle. "You've got to be kidding."

She folded her arms, shaking her head. "Oh no, not kidding. The firm had everyone who was interested in the promotion prepare a pitch for this huge project, and of course, my aunt died right in the middle of it all. So while I was rushing to her funeral, he, unbeknownst to me, dug through my files, going through everything—my pitch, creative briefs, storyboards, the whole damn project." The volume of her voice was steadily rising. "Then, when I got back, he was all smiles, telling me how it'd be best if we didn't see each other the week before the presentation so we could *stay focused*. Meanwhile, I was working myself to death on that campaign—pulling all-nighters, skipping meals— just to make sure everything was perfect."

She paused, her lips tightening as she glanced over at me. "I knew it would be tough with us both competing for the same promotion. We're both super competitive, so that wasn't a surprise. But after dating for two years, I thought I meant something to him. Turns out, I was just convenient until I wasn't."

"That's some serious bullshit. What kind of scumbag does that?" I said, gripping the wheel a little tighter as I imagined giving this Blake guy a lesson in humility.

"Yeah, and get this—after I nailed my pitch, the clients were ready to sign on. They were thrilled until Blake swooped in with some *brilliant* new ideas. He undermined parts of my pitch, took credit for the ones the clients liked, and offered a couple of ideas that were unrealistic pipe dreams due to cost but that he knew they'd eat up. During his presentation, he mentioned a few things that I'd researched but hadn't had time to share during the meeting. That's when I realized he'd been through all my stuff. Suddenly, he was the genius, and I was just there for backup."

She took a deep breath and groaned. "To top it off, he convinced the higher-ups that I'd make a good assistant under his supervision. The partners agreed, gave him the promotion, and made him my boss."

The truck slid slightly on the snow, but I barely noticed as I watched her fume. "I take it you didn't just sit there and let him get away with that?"

She snorted. "What was I supposed to do? Call him out in front of the clients? The agency partners were already falling over themselves to praise his presentation. Right after the meeting, while I was still dumbfounded by what had just happened, he walked me to my office. He was smug as hell when he dropped the next bomb. He said he'd always known I wasn't on his *professional level* and that he needed a woman who could help him run his own agency one day. Then he casually added that now that he was my boss, we'd only have a working relationship. *'No hard feelings, right?'*" She shook her head, squinching up her face in a snarl. "I didn't even have the words to respond. He just left me standing there, as if I was nothing."

My hands itched to punch something. "So, he screws you over at work and then dumps you in the same breath. Class act."

"Yeah, real winner," she muttered, turning to stare out the window. "Yep. And after all that, I had no choice but to quit."

We were both quiet as what she said sank in. This guy hadn't just sabotaged her career—he hadn't even had the decency to end things with respect. After two years, she deserved more than a casual brush-off. If you were going to walk away from a woman, you needed to do it with honesty and care, not in a way that suggested she was some inconvenience.

A surge of protectiveness rose up in me. "You did the right thing, leaving. No one needs to put up with that kind of crap. If I ever cross paths with that guy, he's going to need a new set of teeth."

Noelle sucked in a breath, probably startled by my promise of retribution. "You'd actually punch him, wouldn't you?"

"I've taken on worse than some corporate douchebag. Trust me, he wouldn't be a problem." I shot her a sideways glance. "I'd love to see him get what he deserves."

She fell silent for a minute, then asked, "You don't think I'm just some whiny girl complaining about a nasty breakup?"

"Not even close." I shook my head. "What he did was beyond low. And your former bosses are idiots if they couldn't see through that. That kind of company? That kind of guy? They don't deserve someone like you."

She let out a quiet, surprised laugh. "Someone like me, huh?"

I shrugged. "You strike me as the kind of person who doesn't back down from a fight. You got screwed over, but it doesn't mean you're down for the count. People like you get back up."

She opened her mouth to say something but then shut it, chewing on the words for a second. After a couple of minutes, she twisted in her seat to face me, dropping her elbow onto the center console and resting her chin on her fist, studying me. "Thanks," she finally said, her tone a little softer. "I don't know what I'm gonna do now."

I nodded. "You'll figure it out. Sounds as though you've gotten some good experience. You're tougher than you give yourself credit for."

She raised an eyebrow, a hint of sass creeping back into her expression. "Tough? You think a girl like me is tough?"

Unable to resist, I turned a little and reached over to cup her cheek in my hand, brushing my thumb along it gently. She leaned into my touch. "You walked away from a job you busted your ass for because some jerk tried to ruin you. Yeah, that takes guts."

She blinked, seemingly caught off guard by the compliment. "Well, Mr. Captain, I didn't expect you to be so supportive."

I smirked. "What can I say? I've got layers."

She was about to respond when something caught the corner of my eye—red and blue lights flashing up ahead. Then a line of brake lights came into focus. My gut clenched.

"What the hell?" I muttered, dropping my hand from her face. I jerked back around and gripped the wheel with both hands, easing off the gas. But before I could fully process the situation, I realized we were coming up fast—way too fast—on a line of cars at a dead stop in the middle of the highway.

A jolt of panic shot through me.

"Shit!" My foot moved to apply light pressure to the brakes in an attempt to avoid a skid. The Bronco fought the slick snow, and the tires battled for traction. But it wasn't enough.

Everything morphed into slow motion as I aimed for the shoulder from the left lane—anything to avoid slamming into one of the cars ahead.

"Hold on!" I shouted, adrenaline surging through me. The truck slid sideways across the road.

Noelle's hand shot out, gripping the *oh shit* handle next to the door. "Oh my God!"

The truck fishtailed hard, the rear end swinging out. The snow-covered road beneath us was nothing but ice now, slick as glass. My heart pounded as the wheel jerked in my hands, the back end whipping violently from side to side. Even with four-wheel drive and the slippery mode on, we skidded off the shoulder, bouncing as tires tore over the rough, icy grass. For a split second, everything was suspended in time—the Bronco started to tip, and I thought we might go into a roll.

We were just along for the ride now, the vehicle lurching down a small embankment. The shocks groaned under the impact as we were tossed side to side. Noelle's scream cut through the chaos. My arms strained while I fought to keep us from flipping, and my teeth clenched so hard that the pressure radiated painfully through my face.

"This can't be happening! Oh God, I don't want to die—not like this!" she yelled.

The Bronco hit a rough patch. The tires lost contact, and for a moment, we were airborne. We hit the ground with a sudden, violent jolt that slammed us against our seat belts. Noelle's head hit the side window with a thud, and she gasped, eyes wide with terror.

"Not like that night! Not like four years ago!" she cried out, gripping the dash, her knuckles white. Her voice was raw, panicked, the words spilling out as though she were reliving a nightmare.

As we continued to bounce and shift back and forth, the Bronco's undercarriage scraped against hidden rocks until finally the tires found traction on the snow-packed earth.

"Hang in there!" I shouted, yanking the wheel. The truck finally skidded to a halt, the front end dipping into a snowbank, stopping us with a jarring bump that sent us both lurching forward again. Thankfully, we hadn't flipped over. I shifted into neutral so I could catch my breath.

Everything went dead silent. We sat there for some time, our breathing heavy and uneven, the snow swirling around us like we were in the middle of a snow globe that the evil Snow Miser had just shaken.

I flexed my hands on the wheel, my heart pounding in my chest, but I kept my voice steady as I asked, "Are you okay?"

She nodded, but her face had gone pale. Her eyes were wide and filled with something more than fear from what had just happened. There was clearly so much more to her story.

"I'm fine," she muttered, but it didn't sound convincing. Her hands were shaking, and from the way her body shuddered, it was obvious she was anything but fine.

I reached over, wrapping my hand around one of hers and giving it a squeeze. "We're okay. The Bronco's built for this. We're not stuck, and we're not going to die in this ditch. Trust me."

She let out a shaky breath. "I hate this," she whispered, more to herself than to me. "I hate everything about this."

I rubbed my thumb along the back of her hand, catching the slight tremble there. "Life has a way of blindsiding you," I said softly, trying to calm her down. I wasn't talking out of my ass—I'd been there, taken by surprise in ways that had shattered everything I thought I understood about the world. "It knocks you down when you least expect it, hits you right where you're most vulnerable. But that's when you find out what you're really made of. You have to keep pushing forward, even when it feels as if everything's been taken from you. You don't stop. You keep going, even when the pieces of your life don't fit the way they used to."

She stared at me, her eyes still wide, but now there was something else behind the fear—a hint of recognition. She understood I was talking about more than us nearly crashing.

"And when it feels as though you're out of options," I said, my hand tightening around hers just a little, "you dig deeper. Maybe it's for yourself, or maybe it's for someone you care about, but you keep pushing forward. Life's gonna test you, see how much fight you've got in you."

Her gaze shifted to our hands, and she curled her fingers around mine—not speaking.

Shit, why was I sharing all this? Why was I rambling? The words had come tumbling out as though a secret part of me had been unlocked. Why did this girl's feelings matter to me? I'd only just met her.

When she finally spoke, her voice was barely above a whisper. "I don't know if I've got anything left."

That hit me hard. I had a feeling she wasn't just talking about us nearly flipping over. There was something deeper, a wound she hadn't let heal. But pushing her to talk wasn't what she needed me to do. No, right now, she needed someone to help her see that life was worth living. And I wanted to be that person for her, even if I didn't exactly know how, even though my own heart was in a sorry state.

"You don't have to have all the answers right now," I said, giving her hand another squeeze. "You don't have to be strong every minute. Just take it one step at a time. One breath, one fight, whatever it takes. And you get back up, because lying down and giving up?" I shook my head. "That's not an option. Not for someone like you."

Her lips trembled for a second before she pressed them together. "Someone like me?"

"Yeah," I said with confidence. "Someone who's tough, intelligent, and beautiful inside and out. Who's been dealt a terrible hand but, deep down, knows giving up isn't an option. You're someone who's strong enough to fight back against whatever it is from your past that's making you think...you should have never been born."

She froze.

Releasing her hand, I took her chin between my fingers, forcing her to look at me. "You're a fighter, or else you wouldn't be driving through a snowstorm to take care of your family business. You'd still be on the phone whining to your friend," I said with a half smirk.

She blinked, as though she'd not expected me to speak such brutal truth to her.

The storm outside raged on, but inside the truck, it was quiet—just Noelle and me and the raw honesty hanging between us.

Her eyes narrowed. "That's pretty deep for a guy who just swerved us off the highway."

I chuckled. "I've seen a lot worse than this. You learn to roll with the punches. Life knocks you down; you get back up and ask for more."

For a moment, she didn't say anything. She just stared out at the falling snow like she was trying to make sense of what I'd said. There was a long pause before she nodded—slowly at first, then a little more firmly. "Okay. I get your point...I think."

"All right, Stinkerbelle. Let's get this thing back on the road," I said, using the nickname I knew she hated but refused to acknowledge.

She grunted, and that was enough to tell me she was regaining her footing again.

"Be happy we didn't hit any of those stopped cars and only took a little detour—a ride on the wild side," I said, grinning. "This thing's tough."

"Glad one of us is," she muttered, rubbing the side of her head. A small smile tugged at her lips. "And good thing I have a hard head."

Noelle
Nichols

Chapter Five

12/23 evening

Kol ensured slippery mode was still on, then engaged what he called the 4A setting, explaining that it was designed for low-traction surfaces like snow and mud. I braced myself, gripping the handle tighter as he shifted into reverse.

"Time to get out of this mess," he muttered.

He pressed down carefully on the accelerator, and the tires spun a bit before catching some traction. The Bronco inched backward, its massive wheels biting through the snow with a low rumble. Kol rocked us back and forth in short bursts, reversing just enough to break free from the bank and allowing us to move toward the highway. As the tires hit patches of uneven ground at different angles, we were tossed from side to side. Each bump caused the cabin to sway as the suspension worked to absorb the impact. All the while, Kol grinned, as if backing out of a snowbank and maneuvering over the dips and ruts was just another Monday for him.

When we were almost to the highway, we lurched over a snow-covered rock, jarring the cabin and rattling my bones. I clutched the handle, bracing for the next impact, holding on for dear life. Kol, on the other hand, was still gripping the steering wheel, calm as ever, like we were cruising down a sunny highway and not bouncing through a frozen obstacle course.

"How are you so calm?" I asked, my voice higher than usual. "It feels like we're about to tip over at any moment."

Kol smirked, keeping his eyes locked on the terrain. "You've gotta feel the ground through the truck. Plus, I do this kind of thing all the time. Off-roading is a blast."

"Off-roading?" I gave him a side-eye. "You actually do this for fun?" My knuckles were white now, but he didn't seem fazed.

He gave me a quick glance, his grin widening. "Yep, there's a Bronco club, and we have these Off-Roadeos all over the country. Mud pits, rocky slopes, you name it. Way more fun than what we're doing."

We hit another patch of uneven ground, and the Bronco jerked forward as Kol effortlessly steered us over it. "You should try off-roading sometime, Stinkerbelle," he said teasingly. "You might like it."

I shook my head. That was a hard pass. "Maybe next time, when I'm not fearing for my life."

But I couldn't deny that he was handling the Bronco like a pro. It was, well...impressive. I was maybe even a little jealous that he was so at ease while I was practically vibrating with anxiety.

We finally made it back to the highway, the snow-packed ground giving way to the pavement of the shoulder. Traffic remained at a near standstill, and now there were more cars backed up farther than the eye could see.

Still shaking, I latched onto the armrest to keep myself steady. I wasn't about to show Kol how freaked out I was. At least, I hoped I wasn't.

One of the cars gave us space to merge into the line of traffic. Kol chuckled and guided us back onto the highway. "No need to worry. This thing's built for survival. Just like me."

I forced a shaky laugh, trying to act like everything was fine, even though my pulse was still racing from flying off the road.

Kol shifted in his seat and glanced at the traffic ahead. "There's got to be a wreck on the bridge. They always freeze up first."

If that was the case, the flashing lights we'd seen earlier would make sense—it must have been an emergency vehicle rushing toward an accident up ahead. It would explain the backup. We were barely moving. Who knew how long it would take to get around whatever was up ahead? All the red taillights glowed brightly against the fresh white snow. Funny how they added a pop of holiday color to the otherwise dreary scene, like neon candy canes, making the situation feel a little less miserable.

I sighed, looking at the line of cars that stretched toward the Mohawk River. "Fantastic," I muttered. "Nothing like spending hours sitting in dead-stopped traffic."

Kol glanced at me, his brows bouncing as a half smile tugged at his lips. "Don't worry, we're not sitting here all night. There's an exit up ahead. Route Nine runs parallel to the highway. We can jump on that and get around this mess."

Before I could ask what he had in mind, Kol was guiding the Bronco onto the shoulder, easing us past the line of stopped cars. The other vehicles barely moved as we cruised along the edge, and soon the green exit sign for Troy Schenectady Road came into view.

Moments later, we veered onto the exit ramp, leaving the jammed traffic behind. Kol soon turned onto New Loudon Road, and we were immediately surrounded by strip malls, gas stations, and fast-food places.

"I think it's time we stop and get some gas," he said, glancing over at me. "Maybe stretch and grab something to eat? Couldn't hurt, right?"

My stomach growled in agreement, and I realized I hadn't had a real meal all day. Plus, I seriously needed to use the bathroom. "Yeah, that sounds like a good idea. I could definitely use a break."

Kol pulled into the first gas station we came across. After the long, dark drive, the brightness of the fluorescent lights made me squint. As soon as we pulled up to a pump, I wasted no time unbuckling my seat belt, grabbing my tote, and jumping out. My legs wobbled like Jello, and I nearly stumbled, but I quickly shook it off. "I'll be quick," I said, rushing toward the building, now desperately needing to go.

Inside the bathroom, I glanced in the mirror. I was glad I'd thought to grab my tote—I looked rough. I hadn't had a chance to clean up all day, and it showed. I dug through the bag, pulling out a compact, some wipes, and a hairbrush. It wasn't much, but it was enough. I managed to wipe away the smudges of exhaustion and tears from under my eyes, run the brush through my hair, and dab on a bit of tinted lip balm. At least now I looked somewhat presentable. I grimaced at my reflection, thinking of how haggard I must have appeared the entire drive.

I worked to pull myself together as best I could, then glanced down at my phone and realized I'd been in here a while. A twinge of guilt hit me for taking so long. With a sigh, I stuffed everything back into my tote and hurried out of the bathroom.

Kol was standing at the counter with a bag of snacks in one hand and two steaming cups of coffee on the counter in front of him. I quickened my steps, reaching him as the cashier was handing him a receipt. "Sorry that took so long," I said sheepishly.

He shrugged and gave me a little smirk, sliding one of the coffee cups over. "No problem. It took me some time to put the snow chains on."

I grinned. "Always the Boy Scout, huh? Prepared for anything?"

"Something like that." He chuckled. "After living in upstate New York for the last several years, I've learned to keep chains on hand this time of year."

I wrapped my hands around my coffee cup, the warmth instantly thawing my cold fingers, and raised it to my nose. Immediately, I recognized the aroma—peppermint mocha. "Mmm, this smells so good." I took a small sip, testing the temperature.

"I figured you'd appreciate something festive."

"It's my favorite," I said with a soft smile, glancing at him over the brim. "Especially around Christmas. How did you know?"

Kol shrugged and tucked his card into his wallet, which he then shoved into his back pocket. "Lucky guess."

I took a long sip of the peppermint-infused coffee. "You didn't have to, but...this is perfect. Thank you."

He handed me the bag of snacks. "I figured caffeine and sugar would help us survive the rest of the way to Saratoga," he said, grabbing a couple of bottles of water I hadn't noticed and tucking them under his arm. Turning to leave, he added, "I've got strong black coffee to keep me sane." He lifted the cup in a toasting motion before switching it to his other hand to swing the door open for me.

As I walked across the parking lot, I peeked in the bag and laughed. "Popcorn, candy—looks more like a night at the movies."

"You know, it's the whole salty and sweet combination. It's also easy to eat while driving."

Kol walked me to the passenger side, resting one hand on the small of my back. The motion was so natural, like he'd done it a thousand times before. Once there, he opened the door for me. It was such a gentlemanly thing to do. Blake had never once bothered.

Kol placed his coffee in the center console, then stuck the water bottles into the side pocket of the door before securing my peppermint mocha in the cup holder. He offered me his hand, helping me step up into the seat. The gesture threw me for a loop. This guy, with all his gruff exterior and brashness, had a soft streak.

He closed my door and returned to the gas pump, putting the handle back in its place. After shutting the fuel door, he rounded the front of the vehicle and got into the driver's seat. We both buckled up, and Kol eased us back onto Route 9. There was less traffic now, but more snow. The road stretched ahead of us in quiet, white-lined solitude.

After a few moments, Kol cleared his throat. "All right, Stinkerbelle, we need a distraction." His eyes stayed on the road, and his grip on the wheel relaxed, but I could sense he was up to something. "Let's get to know each other better—see if you're the whiny brat at the gate or the put-together marketing executive."

"Ah, you've got—" Before I could finish, he started firing off questions.

"What's your favorite color? And why?"

I whipped my head around, half-amused, half-offended by the sudden turn in the conversation. His curiosity caught me off guard yet again. There was something surprisingly appealing about how direct he was. Maybe I was winning this guy over a little. At the very least, he didn't seem to hate me as much as he had back at the airport. "Starting with the easy ones, huh?" I shrugged, pretending to think it over. "Fine. Cerulean. You know, that blue the sky turns just before it's completely dark and the stars start to twinkle awake."

He let out a small chuckle. "You get points for being specific. I'm more of a forest green guy. The color of a Colorado blue spruce, you know?"

I cocked my head to the side. "Not army green?"

He shook his head. "No, I've seen enough of that color to last a lifetime." Without missing a beat, he said, "Okay, next... Favorite dinner?"

"Lasagna," I replied straightaway, the word spilling out almost reflexively.

"Why lasagna?" he asked, tilting his head slightly toward me, his eyes sparking with genuine interest. The way he was watching me reminded me of Amanda's goldendoodle, and I couldn't help but chuckle.

"It's a comfort thing," I said, twisting around to study him, ready for whatever question came next. "My mom used to make it every Sunday. It's like a warm hug with layers of sauce, cheese, and noodles. Plus, who doesn't love carbs?" I quickly asked, "What's yours?" I wanted to get answers too.

"Steak and potatoes," he answered, licking his lips like the *meat-asaurus* he was. "But it's gotta be rare."

"Rare, really? You mean, still mooing?"

"Exactly," he replied, deadpan. "It's the only way to eat a good cut of meat."

"Not Philistine," I muttered, somewhat impressed.

Kol narrowed my eyes slightly. "Philistine? You gotta explain that one."

"It means someone who's, you know, uncultured, especially when it comes to art or food." I smirked, shooting him a sideways glance. "And you, sir, liking your steak rare, shows you might have the makings of an *epicure*."

He snorted before breaking into a full-blown laugh, the sound surprisingly warm. "Oh, jeez, you and your fancy words. I'll have to trust you on that." He tapped the wheel lightly, then glanced over. "Favorite dessert?"

I pretended to mull it over. "Probably tiramisu. I'm a sucker for anything with coffee and cream."

He nodded approvingly. "Solid choice. Mine's chocolate chip cookies. Nothing beats them fresh out of the oven."

A grin spread across my face. "You haven't had mine yet," I teased. "My secret cherry chocolate chip cookie recipe would blow your mind."

He let out a dry laugh. "Big words. I'll believe it when I taste it."

"Oh, you will," I fired back. "And it'll be life-changing."

I'd just promised to make this guy cookies even though we would never see each other again after he dropped me off at Ms. Winters's office. But hey, this little exercise was a good way to kill the boredom of the long drive.

His grin widened, and he returned his attention to the road. "We'll see about that."

Had he just shown an interest in seeing me again? My imagination went into overdrive, picturing what those massive hands and full lips could do to me. A sigh of desire slipped out. Oh, God, I hoped he didn't notice.

The game continued, him lobbing question after question without giving me a chance to ask any in return. Drinks, hobbies, dream vacations—it was like a fast-paced interview but less formal, more playful.

After a while, I decided to put my foot down and take the spotlight off myself. "Okay, new rule. I'll answer your questions, but you have to answer one of mine for every one of yours."

"Deal," he agreed with no hesitation. "So, tell me about your family."

My stomach tightened. That was one topic I wasn't ready to unpack. "My aunt passed away three weeks ago," I said, picking the safest part of my story. "She was my only relative, but we weren't very close."

Kol's grip on the wheel tightened, his lips forming a thin line as he nodded. His usual teasing smirk had vanished, replaced with a quiet seriousness. His eyes stayed on the road, but there was something different in the way he stared straight ahead. He seemed...affected by what I had said, like he cared.

"Sorry to hear that," he said. "Losing family's never easy, especially if you don't have any other family."

I was surprised by the softness in his tone. "What about you? What's your family like?"

"Big Catholic family," he replied simply. "Parents still married, one younger brother, two younger sisters, and lots of cousins. I'm the oldest. So, of course, I had to keep them all in line. It's always loud and chaotic whenever we're all together, just how my momma likes it."

"So, you're bossy. Good to know."

"Only when necessary," he said with a wink.

"What made you join the Army?"

He was quiet for a moment, his jaw tightening just a bit. "Family tradition," he said finally. "My dad was in the Army. My grandfather too. It just made sense."

I studied him. Based on his hesitation, there was more to it than that, but I didn't push.

We continued like this, peeling back our layers one question at a time. He talked about his military experience but kept it brief, skimming over the darker parts.

The mention of his grandfather had me curious, and before I could think it through, I asked, "What's your favorite childhood memory?" I immediately wished I could take the question back. What if he turned it back on me? It wasn't something I usually asked, mostly because I dreaded answering that sort of thing myself. Now I'd opened a door I wasn't ready to walk through.

He paused, rubbing his forehead. "Camping with my dad. We used to go every summer, just us guys. He taught me a lot about how to handle myself out in the wild."

"That sounds...nice," I said, my voice softer than before.

"Yeah, it was." His smile faded slightly. "What about you? Any favorite memories?"

I hesitated, that familiar ache creeping in. I wasn't ready to talk about my parents—not with him, not yet. "I'll have to get back to you on that," I said lightly.

I never shared my feelings about my past with anyone except Amanda. She had been there for me every step of the way after my parents died, a steady presence in the storm. Amanda understood the limits of my grief, that I could only face it in pieces. We'd spent countless nights talking it out, glasses of wine in hand, dissecting the pain and confusion. Still, there were things even she didn't know—the darkest moments I couldn't bring myself to voice. Those fragments of loss stayed locked away, buried so deep that not even Amanda's comforting words could draw them out. Sometimes, I worried that confronting those buried memories might break me all over again. So, I held back, keeping those parts hidden, even from myself.

Kol glanced over at me. "Fair enough, Stinkerbelle. You've got layers too."

Our conversation created a lighter vibe between us, making the miles slip by. We'd settled into a comfortable rhythm, the banter making the tension in my shoulders ease up. But then, in an instant, the calm vanished.

The Bronco's back end jerked to the side as we hit a patch of ice, and my stomach dropped faster than a roller coaster. My hand shot out to grip the handle, bracing for what might come next. Kol's hands moved quickly on the wheel, steadying the truck.

"Whoa!" I yelped, my heart in my throat.

Kol gave me a quick glance. "It's all good. Just a little fishtail. Nothing to worry about." His words were more of a command than reassurance. He wasn't about to let me spiral.

He let out a soft grunt. "Next question: Are you a virgin?" That had come out of nowhere, catching me completely off guard.

"What?" I spluttered, half-laughing at his audacity. "That's way too personal, Mr. Captain!" But, of course, backing down from a challenge wasn't my style, so I jutted my chin out and crossed my arms. "No, I'm not a twenty-six-year-old virgin. And now it's your turn to answer a question. How many women have you been with?"

He smirked and turned to study me, running his fingers over the scruff of his chin. "Fewer than ten," he replied smoothly.

"Seriously?" I arched an eyebrow, genuinely surprised. "I pegged you for a much higher number, what with your time in the military and your playboy pilot status. I figured you'd have women throwing themselves at you at every destination."

"Sorry to disappoint. I'm selective. Your turn. Same question."

As I started to formulate a response, I glanced at the road ahead. Suddenly something clicked. He'd thrown out the virgin question on purpose, hadn't he? It had been to distract me from the slippery roads and the hazardous conditions we were driving through. Clever. Kol had been doing that the entire ride—figuring out when I was getting too anxious. His ability to read me probably came from having two younger sisters. He was perceptive, way more than I'd given him credit for when we'd first met.

I tapped my fingers on the armrest, debating how much to share. "A handful," I admitted. "Dated a guy in college who I thought I might marry. That blew up in my face when he cheated on me with one of my sorority sisters." I let out a short laugh, though the memory still stung. "Cheating's my line in the sand. No second chances."

"Can't argue with that."

"Then there was Blake Mercer," I said, scrunching up my nose. "But we've already covered that disaster in detail, so no need to go down that road again."

Kol shifted his grip on the wheel. I bet he was as tired of sitting here as I was. Then he turned to me, giving me that smirk—the naughty one I was quickly learning meant he was about to ask something wholly inappropriate. "Okay, moving on. Condoms or bare?"

I nearly choked on my spit. Of all the questions... But I wasn't about to give him the satisfaction of seeing me blush. "Bold question, Mr. Captain," I shot back. "Bare, obviously, is better. Condoms can hurt, but the guy has to be clean as a whistle. What about you?" I crossed my arms, awaiting his response.

He chuckled, his eyes glinting with mischief. "Well, if the Army taught me one thing, it's to never trust a chick in the baby-making department."

My jaw dropped. "Wow, that's cynical."

He didn't flinch. "Nope, just survival tactics."

"Uh-huh," I scoffed. "People shouldn't be having sex if they don't trust each other, but for your information, I have an IUD.

Last thing I need right now is a baby," I said, giving him a pointed look. "Okay, so it's my turn."

Kol nodded, a hint of amusement still dancing in his eyes. "Go ahead."

"Are you married? Or have you ever been?" I asked.

"No." His response came quickly, with no further explanation. He kept his gaze on the road, his expression unchanging.

I waited, but when it was clear he wasn't going to offer up any more information, I asked another question. "Any kids?"

Again, just a simple "No." This time, though, his jaw tightened ever so slightly. I watched him for a moment, weighing whether to push. Something about his body language told me to let it go, so I did.

Kol stayed quiet for a beat. Then, casually, he threw out another question. "What about you? You want to do the whole marriage and motherhood thing?"

I smiled softly, staring out at the swirling snow before answering. "Yeah, I do. If I meet the right guy. It's a privilege, y'know? To have another human being's life in your hands, to raise them, guide them... It's an awesome responsibility. But I wouldn't rush into it."

He gave a slow nod, his features softening just a bit.

The silence stretched between us. As we continued along Route 9, the scenery gradually changed. The forest-lined road began to thin out, replaced by scattered homes and small businesses. It was subtle at first—just a lone building here, a cozy home there—but soon, the trees gave way to a mix of stores, restaurants, and neighborhoods. We were now in the heart of Saratoga Springs, where Route 9 seamlessly turned into Broadway, one of the major arteries of the city.

The city lights began to emerge through the snowfall, creating a warm glow that spread across the downtown area. The storefronts along Broadway were decked out in full Christmas glory—garlands wrapped around lampposts, wreaths hung on every door, and twinkling white lights draped like glistening icicles. Mannequins in the windows were dressed in holiday-themed outfits, surrounded by fake snow and model villages that were so detailed you'd swear you could hear tiny carolers singing from them.

Kol gave a low whistle, slowing down to take it all in. "Man, this place really pulls out all the stops for Christmas. Feels like we're in one of those holiday movies."

A pang hit my chest, but I forced a smile, not wanting him to pick up on my discomfort. "Yeah, Saratoga's famous for this. They make sure every corner is sprinkled with holiday magic. Normally, on Christmas Eve, Eve, the sidewalks would be crowded with people. But I guess, with the storm and the hour getting late, people are choosing to stay home."

As we cruised down Broadway, I spotted what had once been one of my favorite places to visit—a local bookstore. It was only one store down from a candy and ice cream shop. A slab of fudge and a new book, what could be better? In the bookstore's window display, a model train chugged along a miniature track, weaving between books dusted with glittering snow. It was a kid's dream world.

Across the street, a mom-and-pop market stood proudly on the corner of Caroline Street, illuminated by twinkling white lights. Out front was Saratoga Springs's official Christmas tree, situated next to Santa's Cottage. The whole scene was straight out of a Christmas card.

Kol's eyes roamed from side to side. "It's...something else," he murmured, his focus on Santa's Cottage and the glimmering Christmas tree in front of the market.

Everything here on Broadway was so beautifully familiar to me. Memories crowded in, bittersweet and tinged with heartache. The cheerful scene tugged at something deep inside me that I didn't really want to deal with. I hadn't been back to Saratoga during the holidays since...well, since everything had changed. The decorations, the lights—they stirred memories I'd been running from for years.

Kol unexpectedly enveloped my hand in his. "Did you use to come here a lot?" he asked gently.

"Every year," I replied, forcing a lightness into my voice. "My parents loved the holidays. We'd come to see the tree lighting and wander through all the shops. Oh my gosh—when I was little, preparing to visit Santa was such a big deal. I had to have the right outfit and the perfect letter to explain why I shouldn't be on his naughty list." I chuckled, remembering how my mother always said that *Danger* should have been my middle name.

His eyes flicked back to the road. "Well the city sure nailed the holiday magic."

I nodded, swallowing past the lump in my throat. "Yeah, they always do a great job."

Despite the tears stinging my eyes, I managed a small smile. "It's nice to see they haven't lost their touch."

We turned onto Caroline Street, transitioning almost seamlessly from the downtown area to a quieter, Victorian neighborhood. Rows of historic homes lined the street, their classic architecture made even more charming with Christmas lights and lanterns glowing warmly on porches and in windows. Each house had its own character—a wreath here, a giant Nutcracker statue there—creating a patchwork of holiday spirit.

When the navigation system told us we'd reached our destination, Kol slowed. We approached a house on the left, and I spotted a sign that said: Holly Winters, Esquire. It stood next to the driveway of a beautiful Victorian home, the porch of which was strung with lights flickering beneath a growing layer of snow. The porch itself was adorned with rocking chairs and garlands, exactly like something out of a Christmas storybook.

Kol parked the Bronco, grabbed his leather flight jacket from the backseat, and exited the truck. He pulled on the bomber jacket as he rounded the car, and before I could even gather my things, he'd already made it to my side of the truck. I'd barely managed to unclasp my seatbelt before he was there, opening the door for me.

"C'mon, Stinkerbelle. Those boots aren't made for walking in eight inches of snow." He extended his hand, and I took it, sliding down from the high seat, my heels crunching into the snow.

I turned back and picked up my Dior tote from the floor and grabbed my coat, not bothering to put it on. "They're perfectly fine boots," I quipped, even though he was right. The ridiculous spiked heels were no match for the snow.

"Sure," he said, wrapping an arm around me to steady me as we made our way up the driveway. "They're great if you want to end up on your ass."

I wanted to snap back at him, but the warmth of his touch threw me off, so I slid my arm inside his coat and around his waist and settled for an eye roll. "Duly noted, Mr. Captain."

He chuckled softly, guiding me carefully up the porch steps until we reached the front door. Then he let go of me so I could knock. My breath fogged in the air as I waited, heart pounding. I hoped Ms. Winters was still around even though it was well past closing time.

Noelle Nichols

Chapter Six

12/23 evening

The door swung open, revealing Ms. Winters. She looked much the same as I remembered from church years ago, except for a few more lines around her eyes. She wore a light blue sweater with a snowy scene on the front, the white of her perfectly coiffed gray bob matching the snow in the design. As always, she was impeccably polished and put together.

"Noelle! I'm so glad you made it!" she exclaimed, pulling me into a stiff hug. The embrace lasted longer than I liked, her hands brusquely patting my back before releasing me. "Come in, come in. It's freezing out there!"

I stepped inside, with Kol trailing right behind me. Ms. Winters's gaze shifted to him. She eyed him up and down. "And who do we have here?"

"Ms. Winters, this is Captain Vinter. He was one of the pilots scheduled for my flight from New York to Albany before it was canceled." I smiled at Kol, and my face flushed from embarrassment as I recalled my colorful conversation with Amanda. "He overheard how desperate I was to make it to your office today and kindly"—I shot him a rueful glance—"offered to drive me since he lives nearby."

"It's nice to meet you, Captain Vinter," she said, stretching out her hand.

"Likewise, ma'am," he said politely, shaking her hand. "Please call me Kol."

"What a delight to have you both visit on this snowy Christmas Eve, Eve," she said. "Oh, and please, call me Holly. *Ms. Winters* is far too formal, especially since Noelle and I are practically family." She gave him an approving nod.

"Yes, ma'am," he replied respectfully, but I caught the hint of formality in his words.

Holly's eyes darted to his uniform, and she gestured toward his jacket. "So, who do you fly for?"

"I'm a pilot with National Airlines."

A slow smile spread across Holly's face as she glanced back and forth between us. "Is that so? Well, you two make quite the lovely couple. It's nice to see there are young men who are still chivalrous." She folded her arms, her eyes gleaming with amusement.

My cheeks burned. "Oh, no, we're not a couple. We literally just met. It was only a ride. Kol lives in Rotterdam."

"Rotterdam, huh?" Holly's eyebrow quirked up. "That's almost an hour away, even on a good day."

Kol shrugged, unfazed. "Yes, ma'am."

Holly's eyes crinkled as she let out a knowing chuckle. "Mm-hmm." She turned back to me, her expression softening a little.

"Well, it's good to have you home for the holidays. It's been so long since you've spent any time in Saratoga. I assume work keeps you busy?"

I forced a small smile. "You could say that," I muttered. A pang of shame shot through me, and my eyes darted to Kol. I half-expected him to spill the beans about my current jobless state. Thankfully, he kept his lips sealed.

Holly waved a hand as if swatting away an invisible bug. "Oh, and I must apologize for not getting back to you earlier, Noelle dear. I was down at the church helping prepare for tonight. We were setting up beds and getting hot meals ready for folks who need a warm place to stay during the storm." She glanced out the window. The snow was falling in thick, heavy flakes. "It's shaping up to be a monster of a storm, and we want to make sure no one gets stuck out in it." She turned back to me, a tight smile on her face. "Time got away from me. By the time I checked my phone, well...here you are."

"I'm just grateful you were able to see me after your normal hours."

"No worries. Come on in and warm up," she said, ushering us further into the house. "How about some tea? I've got a delicious holiday blend, cinnamon and cloves. Perfect for this weather."

"That sounds great," I replied, eager to have something to do with my hands other than fidget nervously.

Holly bustled off toward the kitchen, leaving Kol and me standing in the living room, surrounded by her Christmas décor. I laid my tote and coat on the sofa.

Several walls of the room had floor-to-ceiling bookshelves, all of which were lined with tiny collectible figurines. And each and every one of them was decked out in holiday cheer. A towering Christmas tree draped in Victorian-style ornaments and twinkling lights dominated the corner. The whole place screamed Christmas. Kol walked over to the tree, examining the intricate glass ornaments and ribbons that were woven through the branches.

Holly returned, setting down a tray on the coffee table. On it were two steaming mugs and a plate of cookies. "Here you go. This will chase the chill away," she said cheerfully, handing me a mug.

"Thank you," I said, taking it and wrapping my hands around the cup. The warm, spiced scent curled up to my nose, comforting in a way I hadn't expected.

"You've got quite the collection here," Kol said, joining us from across the room.

Holly's gaze drifted to Kol. "Yes, it's been a work in progress for ages. I adore the holidays, and this has been a longtime hobby of mine. Now, make yourself at home," she said before turning to me. "Noelle, shall we step into my office?"

A knot formed in my stomach, but I nodded. "Of course."

Kol stepped aside. I glanced at him, then awkwardly held out my hand for a shake. "Thanks for bringing me. You can leave my suitcase here in the living room. I really appreciate you driving me all the way here; you were a lifesaver."

He stared at my hand, an odd expression crossing his face, like I'd just spoken in a foreign language. Then his eyes met mine, questioning, but he said nothing.

My stomach did a funny little flip. Of course he'd be eager to get out of here. Why wouldn't he be? I was sure he had better things to do than babysit some girl who had been stranded in the middle of the airport. A guy like him—airline captain, military pilot, someone who looked like he'd just stepped out of a magazine—wouldn't want to waste any more time on me. He was probably just doing his good deed for the year. It wasn't like I was his type; that was for sure.

Holly's lips twitched in amusement. "Take your time, Kol. Enjoy the tea." Her tone made it clear she wasn't in a hurry to see him leave. "We'll just be a minute."

He gave a small nod, and Holly guided me toward her office. As I closed the door, I noticed Kol's gaze lingering on me.

The office was cramped, with all the antique furniture and Christmas trinkets Holly had stuffed in here. She gestured to a chair across from her desk and sat down, flipping through a stack of papers. I settled into the seat, glancing at the shelves, which were lined with old books, porcelain figurines, and a few framed photos. She cleared her throat, glancing up at me over the rims of her glasses.

"As you know, Noelle," she began, her tone firm, "I sent you a certified letter two weeks ago explaining that your aunt Mary's will specifically required you to be here in person to accept the assets she left you. I'm glad you made it today because this is the last day the probate court will allow for the estate documents to be signed and notarized. If they're not finalized today, it will be assumed that you've declined the inheritance, and the assets will automatically go to the next in line—the church."

I nodded. "Yes, and I came as soon as I could with work and all." My eyes drifted to the stack of legal documents on her desk. "What exactly did she leave me?"

Holly sighed, leaning back in her chair. "Before we get into that, Noelle, I need you to understand how deeply Mary was affected by the loss of Joy and Shep. She was distraught, and not seeing you after they passed hurt her terribly. She wanted to give you time, but being all alone made it difficult. Even so, Mary knew you needed space to grieve."

A heavy lump formed in my throat. Guilt crept in, winding its way through me. Holly kept talking, her words chipping away at the walls I had built around those memories.

"I know your parents' deaths must have devastated you," she continued, her voice gentle, "but Mary just wanted to be there for you. She waited, hoping one day you'd come back, visit the house, or at least give her a call."

I stared down at my hands, trying to ignore the stinging in my eyes. By avoiding Saratoga, I'd been ignoring everyone connected to my parents, including Aunt Mary, hurting them in the process. Facing that reality twisted my stomach into a painful knot.

A wave of shame crashed over me. Holly was dredging up memories I'd shoved deep down. "I was busy with work and trying to cope after losing both my parents," I replied, more defensively than I'd intended.

"Of course you were," Holly agreed, her gaze softening for a moment. "But Mary just wanted to protect you. She worried about you making impulsive decisions in your grief."

"What do you mean?" I asked, completely confused.

Holly adjusted her glasses, picking up the top document. "The terms of her will are simple yet strict. She left you her entire estate."

My head snapped up. "Wait, what?"

"But on one condition," she added quickly, holding up a hand. "You must live in Saratoga Springs for at least one year."

I opened my mouth, but nothing came out. Live here? For a year? The news knocked the breath out of me, leaving me reeling.

"So...you're saying she left me her house? Here in the city?" I managed to croak out.

"Yes," Holly confirmed. "Her house and all its contents." She paused, fixing me in her steady gaze. "But keep in mind, if you don't meet her one requirement, the entire estate will be donated to the church."

My heart pounded as my mind tried to wrap itself around this unexpected revelation. "Oh my gosh. I can't believe this," I mumbled, running a hand through my hair. "So if I don't live here, the church gets it all?"

"That's right. Living here is Mary's one stipulation." Holly's expression remained unchanged, almost as if she was challenging me to say more, but I just sat there, dumbfounded.

She cleared her throat, shuffling some of the papers on her desk. "And, Noelle," she started, leaning toward me, "there's more."

I braced myself. "Go on," I said, trying to keep my voice even.

Once more, she adjusted her glasses, peering at the documents. "Mary didn't just leave you her house in Saratoga," she began slowly, her eyes flicking between the papers and me. "She also left you your parents' property out in Greenfield."

That hit me hard. My mind went blank for a moment before the questions came tumbling out. "Excuse me. Run that by me one more time. Greenfield? My parents' property? I thought...I thought after Mary took all of it when my parents died, she sold it like she did the horses."

Holly shook her head, a hint of impatience in her expression. "No, she didn't. Your aunt held onto it, Noelle. She never sold the property."

I stared at her, clenching the arms of the chair. "Why?" I asked after a beat, the doubt spilling out, raw and unfiltered. "Why did she keep it? I thought she hated my dad. I thought she took everything out of spite after my parents died."

Holly shook her head and sighed. "Mary didn't hate your father, Noelle. There were misunderstandings and hurt feelings, yes, but she never hated him. They had their differences, but that didn't mean she wanted to punish *you* for them."

She pushed the documents to the side and leaned forward, folding her hands on the desk. "You have to understand that Mary was ten years older than Joy and a devout Catholic. When Joy married Shep, an atheist, outside of the church, outside of the sacrament of marriage, Mary was beside herself—it was sacrilegious. It took Mary and your parents many years to reconcile. It wasn't until after you were born, and your parents agreed to raise you in the Catholic church, that they were able to overcome most of the hard feelings."

I sank back into my seat, staring at the edge of Holly's desk, confusion swirling inside me. Why hadn't anyone ever told me these things? I'd never known my father was an atheist. I'd spent my whole life in the dark about who he truly was. We'd always attended church, just like so many other families. Had he changed his beliefs, or had he just been playing along all those years to keep the peace with Aunt Mary? It shattered me to think I'd never really known what was in his heart...how little I knew about my parents in general. I'd never gotten to know them as individuals, never understood why things were strained with Aunt Mary. As a kid, I'd picked up on the dynamic but had just accepted it as the way things were.

Tears blurred my vision. There was so much I would never learn. Had coming here been a mistake? Maybe I was better off in the dark, pretending I understood them. What I didn't know—what I refused to face—couldn't hurt me, right?

Holly scooted a box of tissues toward me. I pulled a couple out and dabbed at my eyes. Twisting them in my fingers, I took a breath and regained a bit of my composure.

"So, she took everything to...protect me?"

Holly nodded. "She was worried about you. You were young, grief-stricken... She thought you might do something impulsive, like sell the farm, or worse, marry someone who'd manipulate you out of your inheritance."

I sat there trembling, still trying to make sense of what Holly was telling me. "So she's been holding on to all of it for me this whole time?"

"Yes. She didn't want to burden you with it until she felt you were ready. She wanted to give you time. Time to grieve, to grow up a bit, to find your own way. But you never visited, never spoke to her." Her words cut deep, each one landing with a sting. "She always planned to give it back to you, Noelle. She even sold the horses to a nearby farm to ensure they were well taken care of, knowing you weren't in a place to make those decisions. Sadly, she just didn't live long enough to make things right in person."

The room spun slightly. "She did all that? For me?" I whispered, more to myself than to Holly. A wave of emotions hit me, the grief I had buried so deep breaking through.

"Yes," Holly said gently. "She wanted you to have a place to always call home, to have something to fall back on no matter where life took you."

My mind swirled with memories of the farm, the horses, and my parents. It was too much, all hitting at once. I brought my hand up to my mouth.

Holly tapped her fingers on the desk, regarding me kindly. "Noelle, she loved you in her own way. She wasn't perfect, and maybe she should have reached out to you and explained sooner. But now she's giving you a choice."

My chest tightened, the pressure building until I couldn't hold it in any longer. Tears spilled over before I could stop them. A sob tore from my throat, raw and jagged. Holly rose from her chair, moving around the desk to pull me up into a hug. I didn't resist, just stood there letting the tears flow, releasing years of pent-up hurt and misunderstanding.

"She only wanted the best for you," Holly whispered.

I buried my face in her shoulder, overwhelmed by the truth of it. All this time, I had believed the worst of my aunt, pushed away any thought of reconciliation. And now, it was too late.

Holly rubbed my back, offering what comfort she could. Then she pulled away slightly, keeping her hands on my shoulders. "But there's something you need to understand clearly," she said, her tone firm. "Mary set up the estate so that you can only have it if you move back here. You need to live in Saratoga Springs for at least a year, or everything goes to the church. You will have full access to both properties and may choose where to live. Basically, it will be as though you're living rent free in a fully furnished home. Also, there is a life insurance policy. Those monies were designated to be paid into a trust. You will receive an allowance each month you live here, and money may be withdrawn for approved care and maintenance of the properties by the trustee until and at which time you complete the living requirement. At the end of the twelve-month period, the trust will be liquidated. If you have met the requirements, then that too will be yours."

"Who is the trustee?"

"Me."

I stared at her, the reality of the situation starting to sink in. Moving back here—to the place I'd been avoiding for so long—felt impossible, but now it seemed like the only option. It also meant I would get a chance to hold on to a piece of my past—a chance I hadn't realized I might want until now.

Holly's hands loosened from my shoulders, and she took a step back, letting out a quiet breath before returning to her side of the desk. I stayed rooted in place, fighting to calm the storm inside.

I sniffed, reaching for a couple more tissues from the box, dabbing at my eyes and blotting my nose.

I needed to pull myself together.

Taking a deep, unsteady breath, I relaxed my shoulders and sat back down in the chair. Holly sat down, keeping her eyes steady on me, and waited. My hands felt clammy as I rested them on my lap. Now wasn't the time to dwell on emotions. We had business to finish.

Holly once again shuffled through the documents on her desk, tapping them into a neat stack before setting them in front of me and placing a pen on top. The ball was now in my court.

I stared down at the papers, my fingers toying with the pen. Could I really do this? Could I move back to the farm and face all those memories?

The ink on these documents represented so much more than property. My parents had built the farm from the ground up. It was where I had learned to ride, where I'd spent hours mucking stalls and feeding horses. But going back meant facing everything I'd lost, and I wasn't sure I could do that.

Holly shifted in her seat, a hint of impatience crossing her face. "Noelle, I didn't mean to overwhelm you. I just thought you'd be...happy about all of this. I understand this is a lot to take in. You grew up on that farm; it's part of who you are."

Happy? That word seemed so far away from what I was feeling.

I clenched my jaw, glancing up at her. "It's not that simple, Holly." The words came out harsher than I'd meant them to, but I couldn't help it. My emotions were all over the place, and I felt cornered.

She didn't know that I'd just quit my job in Atlanta, or that my life was a complete mess. The fact that this was my only option—unless I wanted to start over, looking for a job doing who knew what, who knew where—was a harsh reminder of how much of a failure I was. I could imagine my old coworkers at the agency and my sorority sisters from NYU whispering about how I'd ended up back in Saratoga. A total loser. God, it was all so embarrassing and unfair.

Growing up, I had always taken a back seat to all the rich girls who could afford two-hundred-fifty-thousand-dollar warmbloods with which to compete in the AA horse shows. It was then I swore to myself that one day I would make the kind of money that would allow me—or maybe my daughter— to compete at that level. I'd learned early on in life that having money gave you power and allowed you to have all the best things. I'd worked hard to earn a scholarship to NYU, and I'd managed to get into one of the best sororities, where I'd studied and emulated the wealthiest girls. I'd learned to walk, talk, and act like the elite pony girls whose shadows I'd grown up in. I'd obtained my MBA and secured a high-paying job at one of the most prestigious marketing agencies in the country. I'd been so close to realizing my ambitions when that fucking Blake had ripped them away. Senior account manager would have been just one stepping stone away from partner. Now, I was starting all over again—alone.

Holly cleared her throat, bringing me back to reality.

"That farm was my...my parents' dream. I'm not sure I can live there without them."

Her eyes softened, but only a fraction. "I understand," she said. "But this is a gift, Noelle. Your aunt left you everything she had, including the farm. It's an opportunity, not a burden."

Opportunity. There it was, that word that made it all sound so easy, so black and white. "And what if I change my mind after I sign the papers?" The question slipped out before I could stop it, and I braced myself for the answer.

Holly sat up straighter, running her finger over the edge of the documents in front of her. "The will is very clear, and Mary set strict terms. You have to live in either of the properties for at least forty-six weeks of the next year. If you fail to meet that condition, the assets go straight to St. Peter's Church."

Forty-six weeks. It seemed like a lifetime. I nodded slowly. This wasn't just some property to flip or a temporary escape. It was a commitment. "I understand," I said, lifting the pen. My hand hovered over the first signature line. A war was being waged inside me. I was full of uncertainty. But what choice did I have?

I swallowed, trying to ignore the lump forming in my throat.

My hand trembled slightly as I scrawled my name on each document, the pen scratching across the paper like nails on a chalkboard. When I finished, I pushed the stack toward Holly and sat back, staring blankly at the desk.

It was done.

"Good. This is good," she said, gathering the documents and assembling them neatly. "You made the right choice, Noelle. Your parents would be proud."

I didn't respond, too drained to argue or even acknowledge what she'd said. Standing up, I forced a tight smile onto my face and followed her out of the office. When we stepped into the living room, I froze. Kol was still there, sitting on the couch, his eyes glued to his phone. I had assumed he would be long gone. But no. There he sat.

He glanced up, and his expression softened the second he saw me. Then he stood, his gaze narrowing as he glanced between Holly and me. His jaw tightened, like he was ready to go into battle. It was the same expression he'd worn when he first approached me at the airport—except this time, it was directed at Holly, and there was nothing friendly about it.

Apparently oblivious to the coldness in his stare, Holly turned to me, placing a hand on my shoulder. "You know where to reach me if you need anything."

I nodded, unable to form any more words. Kol watched me, his expression unreadable, but I caught the way his eyes crinkled ever so slightly, like he could sense that something life-changing had happened in that office.

Kol Vinter

Chapter Seven

12/23 night

When Noelle stepped out of Ms. Winters's office, her eyes were red and puffy. She'd been crying. Every instinct in me screamed to protect her, even though I barely knew her. Something inside me flared, a need to be the one who wiped those tears away.

She tried to cover up her emotional state with a forced smile, but I wasn't buying it. I shot Ms. Winters a quick scowl. Whatever they'd talked about had clearly upset Noelle, and she didn't seem the type to cry easily. I bit back my questions though. Noelle would tell me if or when she was ready.

We'd spent the majority of the past four hours talking—mostly lighthearted stuff, but I'd gotten a few glimpses into the serious parts of her life and had learned a lot about her. Being cooped up with someone in a snowstorm brought out the truth faster than any candlelit dinner. It was a great way to learn what a woman was really like, outside the pretentiousness of the dating scene. From what I'd gathered, Noelle was an open book—most of the time. She didn't bother hiding who she was, and I respected that. But the topic of her parents? That was a door she kept bolted shut. It stirred up in me an instinct I didn't usually have for strangers—to defend her from whatever hurt lay behind that door. It wasn't the same as looking out for my brother and sisters, or even the guys in my unit. This was different. More visceral. I wanted to shield her from whatever caused her pain and make it right.

"The storm is getting worse," I said, showing them the radar on my phone. "We need to get going if we're gonna make it anywhere tonight."

I picked up Noelle's coat and bag and stepped closer to her.

Ms. Winters turned toward Noelle. "Where are you staying tonight, dear?"

Noelle glanced at me before responding to Ms. Winters. "I, uh, had a hotel booked in Albany for tonight," she stammered. "I thought I'd fly into Albany, grab a rental car, drive to Saratoga, and head back to Atlanta tomorrow." She paused, a hint of pink spreading across her cheeks. "But...everything got thrown off when the flight got canceled. I haven't made any new plans yet." She bit her lip, her shoulders slumping. "I guess I should've thought this through earlier. God, I feel so stupid—"

I interrupted her before she spiraled any further. "You're not stupid," I said firmly. "I figured you'd need a ride somewhere, so I stuck around." I glanced out the window at the swirling snow, then back at her. "It's not like anyone's getting around in this storm without four-wheel drive and snow chains. And right now, my Bronco's the only thing that can cut through this."

Her eyes widened, and she blinked at me for a second. "You stayed because...?"

I rubbed the back of my neck, trying to play it off. "Yeah, well, you didn't think I'd leave you to fend for yourself, did you?" I pointed out the window, at the snow that had built up on the porch railing during the short time we'd been here. "Even with four-wheel drive, we're not getting far. This storm's only gotten worse since you went into your meeting."

Ms. Winters pursed her lips, worry creasing her forehead as she glanced from Noelle to me. "It looks rather bad, doesn't it? Are you sure it's safe to drive at all?"

"It's worse than bad." I sighed, consulting the weather app on my phone again. The radar showed nothing but a sea of white. "We'll have to take it slow. But yeah, I can get us somewhere here in town."

Ms. Winters clasped her hands together and leaned forward. "Well, Noelle, why don't you stay at your aunt Mary's place now that you own it? It's exactly as she left it the day she passed. I even hired a cleaning service to go by each week. Oh, and if you want to keep that up, let me know, and I'll give you their number."

Now that she owned it. Hmm, interesting development. It made me wonder if she had plans to move back to Saratoga.

Noelle's mouth twisted like she'd bitten into something sour. "I don't know... It feels weird, staying in a dead person's house."

Ms. Winters waved it off. "Oh, nonsense! It's your house now. And don't you worry about Mary's place being haunted or anything like that. It's just a house. You'll be just fine. But if you're uncomfortable, you and your...friend here could stay with me."

I caught the slight wince on Ms. Winters's face. Clearly, she didn't actually want houseguests, but she felt obligated to offer.

"Thank you, but—" Noelle started, and then the lights cut out, leaving us in pitch black.

Ms. Winters yelped and immediately began scurrying around, shuffling across the hardwood floor. "One second, I've got a flashlight around here somewhere!" She rummaged through a drawer as I switched on my phone's flashlight to help light up the room.

"Oh no! I wonder how long the power will be out," Noelle said. "I doubt any crews can get out during this mess."

"Ma'am, will you be okay here by yourself if we leave?" I asked, shining the beam around.

"Oh, I've been through my share of outages," Ms. Winters said with a huff, finally finding her flashlight. She flicked it on, casting a shaky beam of light. "I'll be fine. A long time ago, I had all my fireplaces converted to gas, so they don't need electricity. There's nothing to worry about."

"How far is it to your aunt's house?" I asked.

"Mary's place is only down the street. Not far at all," Ms. Winters said, waving her hand dismissively. "If you're bundled up, it's an easy walk. But with all the snow piling up, you might want to take that big red sleigh of yours that's parked out front."

I almost laughed. "Sleigh?"

Ms. Winters chuckled. "Santa's sleigh, Bronco—it's all the same in this weather, isn't it?"

I rolled my eyes.

"The Bronco can definitely handle a couple of blocks, even in this weather," I said, shaking my head. *Santa's sleigh*, huh? Never thought of my truck that way, but I guessed it fit.

"Well then, it's settled," Noelle said, exhaling slowly. "We'll stay at Aunt Mary's."

"Ma'am, if you need help, just call Noelle, and I'll come," I offered, turning toward the door.

"Oh! The keys!" Ms. Winters hurried over to a drawer, pulled out a keychain, and passed it to Noelle.

Noelle held the keychain in her palm, staring at the key fob for a second, which had a horse etched onto it. Her thumb brushed over the horse, and something softened in her expression. She nodded, slipping the keys into her tote.

"Thanks, Ms. Winters. For everything," she said.

"All right," I said, placing a hand on Noelle's back and guiding her toward the door. "Let's get moving before the storm picks up more."

With her tote looped over my arm, I paused by the door and held her pretty red coat up, waiting. Noelle's brows arched in surprise. A small smile tugged at the corners of her lips as she stepped forward, sliding her arms into the sleeves. I eased the coat up over her shoulders, taking an extra second to pull her hair out from under the coat and smooth the collar. She tilted her head, a look of surprised gratitude flickering across her face as she glanced back at me.

Noelle glanced over at Ms. Winters. "Thank you for everything. I'll talk to you soon."

Ms. Winters gave her a quick hug. "You take care now, both of you. And drive safely in that sleigh of yours!"

We stepped outside into the biting cold. The only light came from the flashlight on my phone and its dull reflection off the snow. There weren't any electric lights on for as far as we could see. I hooked an arm around Noelle's waist as we shuffled down the slippery sidewalk. Her boots skidded on the ice, and she grabbed onto my jacket, muttering something about her impractical footwear.

"Easy," I murmured, guiding her toward the Bronco. I opened the passenger door, holding her steady as she climbed inside. Once she was settled, I moved around to the driver's side, snow crunching beneath my boots with each step. The cold hit me, a gust of frigid air rushing across my face.

I jumped inside and quickly cranked on the engine. The Bronco roared to life. Its headlights pierced the swirling snow, illuminating the curtain of white that danced in front of us. I flipped on the defrost setting, watching as our breaths fogged up the windshield.

"Where to now?" I asked, turning my attention to Noelle.

Narrowing her eyes in thought, she stared out into the storm. "I think it's about eight houses up." She pointed in the direction opposite the way we'd come earlier.

I nodded and noticed how sad she still seemed, haunted by whatever had happened in that office with Ms. Winters. I rotated toward her, cupping her cheek and running my thumb along the soft curve. Her skin was chilled, but the contact sent a pleasant warmth through my palm. "We'll be there soon," I said quietly, offering her a small smile.

She gave a half-nod, pressing her lips into a thin line. This wasn't the same Noelle I'd met at the airport, the one who had come off as spoiled and brash. Then, she had put on a confident front, all wild laughter and unfiltered remarks. Now I was witnessing a deeper, more cautious side to her—someone who held her true feelings close and carefully guarded the parts of herself that had been hurt.

"You okay?" I asked, still cradling her face in my hand.

"Yes," she whispered, though her eyes remained despondent.

"Liar," I whispered, but I decided to let it go for now. I brought my hand back to the steering wheel and eased the Bronco out of the driveway. Ice crunched under the tires, a sound that promised nothing but trouble if I wasn't careful. The snow swirled thick around us, turning everything into a blur of white. I had to grip the wheel tightly to keep us moving straight backward. Even with four-wheel drive and chains, the tires slipped a few times as we were getting out of the driveway, threatening to drag us into a snowbank.

The houses on either side of the street were practically indistinguishable under the thick layer of snow deposited by the storm. "Sure it's up this way?" I asked, straining to see through the windshield. The tires fought for traction as we crept forward. It was like navigating through a whiteout, the snow so thick it blurred out the edges of the road. I kept the beams of the headlights low, trying to make out anything beyond the hood, but the swirling flakes made it nearly impossible.

Noelle sat forward in her seat, scrutinizing the row of darkened Victorian homes. "It's hard to tell..." she muttered. "They all look the same."

I scanned the houses as well, even though I didn't really know what I was looking for. Each roof was piled with snow, icicles dangling off the edges. They all seemed more or less the same to me.

"Wait...there!" She pointed, excitement creeping into her tone. "That's it! The lamppost with the horse."

I spotted it—a vintage lantern with a silhouette of a racehorse perched on top. It wasn't lit, of course, thanks to the power outage, but it was the only thing distinguishing this driveway from any others. I maneuvered through the snowbanks and turned into the driveway. The tires spun for a second before catching, jerking us forward. Once we had made it all the way up, I shifted into park and engaged the parking brake.

Noelle grabbed her phone and squinted at the screen. "Power's out all over the city," she said, exhaling sharply. "They're saying it might be a while before it's restored."

"Figures," I muttered, staring out into the darkened street. This storm wasn't letting up any time soon.

Noelle hopped out of the Bronco before I even had a chance to shut off the engine. Independent as hell, that girl. Not used to a man treating her like a lady either. I climbed out, chuckling as I shut the driver's door and made my way around the front; in those boots, she wouldn't make it far on the ice-covered ground.

"Seriously?" I called out, watching her teeter as she slowly made her way forward.

She turned, shooting me a defiant glare. "What? I'm fine!" She took another step, her boots skidding across the slick driveway, her legs wobbling like those of a newborn deer.

I crossed my arms, bracing myself for what came next. Sure enough, she flailed, trying to regain balance. For a second, it looked like she might pull it off. But then her heel caught the edge of a brick flower bed, and it was game over. Her feet flew one way, her blonde curls whipped the other, and her arms windmilled. She lost her grip on the tote bag, and it went flying, getting snagged on a low tree branch nearby. The entire scene played out like a cartoon, ending with her face-planting in the snow.

I bit back a laugh as I jogged over to the heap that was Noelle. "You really need a lesson in *wait for the guy to help you out*, don't you?" I teased, crouching down next to her.

She spit out a mouthful of snow, propping herself up on her elbows and shooting me an indignant glare. "Not. A. Word. I have it under control." She kept scowling as she attempted to stand.

"Right," I said. "Totally under control."

I plucked her tote out of the tree.

When she endeavored to rise from her knees, she yelped and fell back onto the snow, turning to hold her ankle. She looked up at me through her eyelashes. "It's just a little sprain," she said unconvincingly.

"Uh-huh," I said, bending over to help her up into a standing position. "Let's see if you can walk." As she gingerly attempted to keep her foot off the ground, I gestured toward her ankle.

"I'm fine," she hissed through clenched teeth, but when she attempted to put weight on it, she winced and nearly toppled over again.

I caught her before she face-planted a second time. "Yeah, you're fine," I said dryly. Handing her the tote, I shook my head and grinned.

"Come on, hold still." I crouched down, slipped my arm between her legs, hooked it around her thigh, grabbed her forearm in my other hand, and ducked my head under.

"What are you—" She gasped as I swung her up and over my shoulders, securing her in a classic fireman's carry. "Kol! Put me down!"

"Not a chance."

I had tried to lift her up in a somewhat dignified manner, but she was squirming too much, making it difficult.

"Damn it, Stinkerbelle. You're not making this easy. Now behave." I smacked her ass for good measure.

"Ugh! You brute!" She huffed, though her tone had carried a hint of laughter.

"Yep. We're doing this my way now. Otherwise, you're going to end up breaking something." I stomped up the porch steps, keeping a firm grip on her though she kicked and wiggled the whole way.

"Kol!" she squealed, half-laughing, half-protesting as her tote swung wildly and nearly clocked me in the head.

"You always this stubborn, or is it just a special occasion?" I asked, trying to keep a straight face while she groused.

"Depends on the company," she shot back, her voice muffled from being upside down.

At the door, I set her down gently but kept my arm wrapped around her waist to support her as she balanced on her good leg. She dug into her tote, fishing for the keys.

"Need me to help with that too?" I teased, arching an eyebrow.

"Ha, ha," she muttered, finally yanking the keys free. She slid the key into the lock and pushed. The door creaked as it swung open.

Kol
Vinter

Chapter Eight

12/23 night

I pulled my phone out of my pocket, tapping the icon to activate the flashlight. It cast a small beam ahead, lighting the way to the living room. We stepped inside. Noelle limped beside me, grumbling about her twisted ankle, but she let me support her as we walked.

Once we got to the living room, I led her to a sofa and helped her settle onto it. "Looks like I'll be staying a while," I said, peering around the room. "No way I'm driving out in this blizzard. And I can't leave you alone and hurt." I shot her a sideways glance, trying to gauge her reaction. "Hope you don't mind having me around."

"Oh, joy," she quipped, rolling her eyes. "I guess if I must endure your company, I'll survive." She cracked a smile, clearly pleased with her own joke.

"Glad to hear it." I found my way to the kitchen and rifled through a few of the drawers until I found a chunky flashlight. Flipping it on, I returned to the living room and set it on a side table, letting the beam bounce off the ceiling so it cast a dim light over the room.

"It's freezing in here," Noelle said, rubbing her arms. "They must've had the heat turned way down for it to be so cold this soon after the power went out." She huffed out a few times, her breath forming little puffs of condensation in the air.

"No surprise there," I muttered, surveying the room. "A house this old probably doesn't keep warm too well. I'm sure Ms. Winters didn't want to pay any more for utility bills than absolutely necessary." My eyes landed on the fireplace tucked in the corner.

Noelle followed my gaze. "Victorian homes always have at least one fireplace, so that's good. But since there's wood stacked beside it, I'm guessing Aunt Mary hasn't converted over to gas yet like Holly did."

"It won't be a problem if there's more wood out back. I can get a fire going," I said, stepping closer to inspect the hearth. A decent stack of logs sat next to it, but it wasn't nearly enough to last through the night. "I've got some skills when it comes to starting fires. Military and camping experience comes in useful, you know."

"Well, aren't you handy to have around? Always the Boy Scout."

"Stay put," I ordered, pointing a finger at her. "I'll take a look outside and see what I can find."

As I turned to head for the back door, my stomach let out a loud growl, which echoed through the room. Noelle snorted, covering her mouth with her hand. "Sounds like someone's hungry."

"I hope there's some food in this place," I said, rubbing my stomach. "I'll handle the wood first, and we can worry about dinner later."

I made my way through the kitchen to the back door and pushed it open, stepping out onto a large screened-in porch. A gust of icy air hit me hard, the screens doing little to block the wind. I moved through the storm door and descended the steps, my boots sinking into more than a foot of snow.

The backyard stretched out in front of me, a dim, shadowy blanket of white. My view of it was further muddled by the falling snow. My phone's flashlight struggled to light the way, but I trudged toward what appeared to be a storage shed attached to a carport. Next to the shed, under the carport, sat a decent stack of cut wood and an old car. It was resting under a tarp, but the edges glistened with ice. It was damp—no doubt about it—and would need to dry out before we could use it. As I uncovered it, I discovered that it had been cross-stacked, allowing for air circulation, so hopefully, it would be dry enough to use by the time we burned through the wood inside.

I hauled the first load to the porch, setting it down near the door before heading back for another. The cold air cut right to my bones as I moved about, my breath fogging the air with each exhale, but I welcomed the activity. After sitting most of the day, the workout felt damn good. With a few more trips, I had a decent pile stacked up on the porch, ready to bring inside.

I braced the door open with a piece of wood and grabbed an armful of logs, hefting them against my chest while still holding my phone to light the way. The cold air from the porch followed me inside as I made my way through the kitchen and into the hallway. The old wooden floors creaked with the weight of my footsteps as I passed a broad staircase that led up to the next floor.

When I reached the living room, Noelle was sitting on the sofa, as I'd instructed her to do, like a good girl. She turned to me with an amused grin on her face and reached behind her, tugging one of the afghans from the back of the couch. She spread it over her legs, curling her hands around its edge. "How's it coming?" she asked, settling back into the sofa.

"Better than expected," I grunted, maneuvering the logs to the hearth. "Your aunt must've really enjoyed using this fireplace. She stored the wood under the carport in a way that kept it as dry as possible. That takes some planning."

"It's hard to imagine how she kept up with this place all by herself. She never married, and as far as I know she lived alone. This house must've been a lot to handle for one person. I don't remember her ever asking for help though."

"She must have been very independent," I said, arranging the logs into a neat pile. "This wood looks like oak, which means it should burn for a long time and provide a decent amount of heat."

When the pile was arranged, I turned around, and she smiled at me, a hint of affection in her eyes as she drew the blanket up around her shoulders. "Well, I'm definitely grateful for you helping me. And don't worry," she added with a flirty edge, "I'm thinking of ways I can say thank you for all this hard work."

I paused for a second, considering that. Was she flirting with me because she actually wanted to or because she felt like she owed me something for helping her out? It had been clear to me from the beginning how fiery she could be—brash and quick with her words. Normally, I went for quieter women. The wild ones were just out for a good time, and that wasn't where I wanted to end up. I wasn't into random hookups. But I didn't quite know what Noelle's intentions were. She was different. She had a wild edge, but there was a layer underneath it, almost like she was hiding some kind of brokenness that lay deeper than whatever that idiot Blake had done to her.

Maybe it was her emotional depth that drew me in. It was the kind you didn't often find in someone her age. She was beautiful—drop-dead gorgeous, in fact—and here she was, in her bright red coat and casual clothes, shivering under a blanket that was pulled up to her chin, looking more captivating than any woman I'd ever met. Was it her deep blue eyes, or was it the intensity behind them that had me hooked? Either way, there was something about her I couldn't ignore, even though I had no intention of pursuing her. I wasn't about to hit on her just because I'd given her a ride in a snowstorm. I had done that because it was the right thing to do. She needed help, plain and simple.

I stood. "It's no problem. I'm just doing what needs to be done." With that, I headed back out for the next load of wood.

I got into a good rhythm as I went back and forth hauling wood from the porch to the hearth. Noelle remained huddled under the blanket on the couch while I brought in each armload and placed it carefully on either side of the fireplace.

"So, do you always stack it like that?" she asked when I was almost finished.

"Yup. Cross-stacking," I explained as I set a couple of logs down in a crisscross pattern, leaving gaps between each piece. "This way, it allows for ventilation, which'll help it dry out faster. Plus, it keeps the pile sturdy so it doesn't topple over when I reach for more later."

She nodded, seemingly impressed. "You really are a multi-talented outdoorsman, huh?"

"You have to be, living out here in the backwoods," I said, standing and heading out for another load.

Once I had all the wood from the porch spread out over the hearth, I shrugged off my jacket, tossed it onto an armchair, and started arranging the dry logs that were already inside in the fireplace. This wasn't one of those shallow, decorative fireplaces found in modern houses. This one was a beast. It had a big, deep hearth with a thick stone base meant to hold logs as wide around as my thigh.

I layered the wood in a pyramid before placing some smaller kindling on the bottom to get things going. The cross-stack I'd set up would allow for air to flow between the logs, feeding the flames as they caught.

Once the setup was ready, I struck a match and lit the kindling. For a second, nothing happened, and then a small flame flickered to life, spreading across the dry tinder. I leaned back on my heels, watching the fire grow. Soon it was crackling softly as it licked up the edges of the oak logs. Within minutes, the flames caught the larger pieces, and warmth was radiating out into the room.

Noelle limped over and sat next to me, extending her hands toward the fire. "You sure know your way around a fireplace."

I gave her a sideways glance. "You know, back in the day, these fireplaces had to heat the entire house. The bigger the hearth, the bigger the fire, and the more rooms it could keep warm. That's why you see these massive fireplaces in older homes. Smart design, if you ask me."

"This is cozy," she replied, sighing contentedly as the heat started thawing out the room. "Definitely beats freezing."

We spent a few minutes in companionable silence, enjoying the fire, and then Noelle shifted beside me before slowly rising to her feet. She winced as she put weight on her ankle but waved me off when I opened my mouth to offer help. Shrugging out of her coat, she crossed the room and hung it on a coat rack near the front door. "It's so dark in here without electricity," she remarked, glancing out the window into the pitch-black night. "I wonder how long the power will be out? Hopefully not for days."

She carefully made her way back across the room. Once she reached the area between the sofa and the fireplace, she sat down on the floor again, crisscrossing her legs.

The flames became quiet, so I adjusted the logs with the poker, making sure they'd continue to catch evenly. The fire roared to life. "There. That should keep us warm for a while," I said, settling back and taking a knee beside her, watching the flames dance along the oak logs. The heat continued to fill the room, and for a moment, we were both content. This old place might have its quirks, but with the fire blazing, it seemed perfect.

I turned to Noelle. The firelight washed over her face, illuminating her features in a soft, golden hue. It struck me how naturally beautiful she was—long, curly blonde hair tumbling over her shoulders, deep blue eyes reflecting the flickering flames, and flawless skin with a few freckles sprinkled across her nose. She wasn't wearing a stitch of makeup, just sitting there in front of the fire in a simple gray sweater dress and black leggings, still sporting those fancy boots. There was a serenity about her that hadn't been there before. Some of the tension had finally melted away. It threw me off for a second.

Without thinking, I lifted my hand. The urge to touch her—to kiss her—rose like the heat from the flames. I moved closer, my fingers itching to brush against her cheek, but I stopped myself, pulling back just as she glanced up. Clearing my throat, I dropped my hand, grabbed the poker, and prodded at a log.

"I should, uh, go grab the suitcases," I muttered, trying to sound casual. I stood up and set the poker back in its stand. "Be right back."

She nodded, her eyes drifting back to the fire as I stood. When I stepped outside, the cold nearly took my breath away. In my haste to leave, I'd forgotten to put on my jacket.

As I crossed the porch, I pulled out my phone and tapped on the flashlight. Once again, I noticed how beautifully this old Victorian had been maintained. Even with snow piling up, the house stood strong against the harsh elements. Its decorative trim and tall windows spoke of a time when homes were built to last, crafted with a level of care you just didn't see anymore.

I quickly navigated the slippery steps and went to the truck, hauling the suitcases out of the back. Then I hurried back up the steps. Pausing, I glanced at the intricate carvings on the porch columns. Noelle's aunt must've really loved this place. It was a stroke of luck that she'd left it to Noelle in her will at a time when Noelle's life was—how had she put it?—a "dumpster fire." Hopefully, Noelle would keep it and maybe even consider moving to Saratoga. The thought of her here, living in this house, was appealing to me in a way I couldn't explain.

But then my thoughts shifted back to how upset she'd been after the meeting with the attorney. Why was she so sad? Her aunt had left her this incredible home. I was curious, but it still didn't seem like the right time to ask her about it. There were certain things you just didn't pry into unless invited.

I pushed the door open and stepped back into the warming living room. "Noelle?" I called. The firelight threw a glow around the room, but there was no sign of her, so I made my way into the kitchen.

There she was, hobbling around on her good foot. I crossed my arms, raising an eyebrow. "I thought I told you to stay put."

She spun around, a wide grin plastered on her face. "There's food! Like, a lot of food. It's so weird, Kol. It's like no one's touched this place since..." Her voice faded, her eyes flicking away from mine.

"Since she died," I finished for her, and she nodded.

The kitchen did, in fact, appear as though it was simply waiting for its owner to stroll in. Utensils sat in a jar on the counter, a cookbook was open on a stand, and a kitchen towel hung folded over the oven handle. It was like time had been frozen.

She pointed the flashlight at the pantry door. "There's a ton of food in there. I can't believe no one cleaned it out. It's like everything's just been left exactly how it was three weeks ago. I guess the cleaning service Holly mentioned only does the basics to keep the place up. Lucky for us, they didn't throw out all the food."

"That's good. Now sit," I ordered, pointing to the kitchen chair. "Let me take a look at that ankle before you make it worse."

"Oh, come on, it's just a sprain," she protested, but I didn't wait for an argument. I grabbed one of the chairs and set it down behind her, pressing a hand onto her shoulder to ease her downward. She pouted but obeyed, dropping into the chair.

"Give me some light," I said, nodding toward the flashlight in her hand. I lowered onto one knee in front of her. Gently, I pulled off her boots, then slipped off her socks, tucking them inside her shoes and pushing them under the table. My fingers slid up her calf as I adjusted her leg to check her ankle. She shivered slightly at my touch. Examining her ankle, I didn't see anything that would indicate she had broken it or had much of an injury, but damn did her skin feel good in my palm.

I dragged my fingers down to her arch and massaged her cold foot. I caught her sharp intake of breath, and my pulse jumped. For a split second, my mind raced to other places I wanted to touch, places that had nothing to do with her ankle. All I could think about was how those legs would feel wrapped around me. Heat shot through my gut, pooling lower. I adjusted my position and stood, trying to ignore the tightness in my jeans.

I jerked my hand back, clearing my throat. *Focus.*

"Looks like you've got a mild sprain," I said, trying to sound clinical. "A little swollen, but nothing too serious."

"Oh, good," she muttered, rolling her eyes. "I was worried I'd be crippled forever." She moved to stand, but I pressed my hands down on her shoulders, pushing her back into the chair.

"Nope," I said firmly. "You're not going anywhere."

"Bossy much?" she said.

I leaned in closer until my face hovered inches from hers.

The sudden nearness of her made me pause. Her eyes locked onto mine, and I had the insane urge to close the gap, to taste that sass on her lips. My heart rate kicked up a notch, but I pulled away and straightened, taking a deep breath.

"I'll make us some food," I grumbled, scanning the kitchen.

She let out a shaky laugh, then folded her arms and leaned back. "There's some canned soup, pasta, and...I think I found rice?" She wrinkled her nose. "But some stuff's gone bad. It's hard to tell what's good in this darkness, so double-check everything."

I walked over to the sink and turned the handle, curious to know if the water heater was gas-powered. The pipes groaned for a second before a steady stream flowed. I waited for a minute, and sure enough, warm water rushed over my fingers. That was a relief. At least we'd have hot water for a shower. I gave my hands a quick wash and moved to find something to eat.

The pantry was well stocked, and the fridge was fairly full. "We'll make it work," I said, my mind half on the food, half still stuck on that damn near-kiss a minute ago.

"Well, lucky me," she teased from behind. "Stuck with a man who might even be able to cook."

I had a shred of hope when I caught sight of the old gas stove; it might not rely on an electric ignition either. I twisted the knob, and after a second, a blue flame flickered to life. I leaned in closer, noticing the small pilot light under the burner—keeping the stove ready to go even without power. Another good thing we had going for us. I glanced over at Noelle, who was watching me from the chair, her ankle now propped on another seat. "Thank God for old-school stoves," I said, pointing to it and smirking. "We're not going hungry tonight."

She gave me a mock round of applause. "Bravo, survivalist. Show me what you've got."

I snorted and turned to the pantry, digging through cans and boxes. There was nothing fancy, but I did find some staples: canned beans, rice, and a few spices that might have been older than me. The fridge was a similar story: eggs, cheese, pickles, various drinks, and other condiments—the basics.

While checking expiration dates, I called out, "So, you and your aunt Mary, were you close?"

She adjusted her leg on the chair. "Not really," she admitted. "Mary was ten years older than my mom, and there was this big falling out before I was born. It was...complicated. We were polite, I guess, but not close."

I grabbed some eggs and other good finds, shut the fridge door with my hip, and set the food on the counter, listening. "Still, it must be hard," I muttered, finding a bowl and cracking a few eggs into it.

Noelle's shoulders rose in a small shrug. "Yeah, it is. It's hard to believe she's gone. One minute, she's bustling around, running the church bake sales, and the next... Well, she died in such an odd way and so unexpectedly—she fell down some steps at the church. Fitting, I guess, since she practically lived there." She threw out a small, bitter laugh. "Kind of poetic, in a dark, twisted way. Devout Catholic, right to the end."

"Catholic, huh?" I asked, whisking the eggs. "Me too. Raised that way, at least. Don't do church much anymore though."

"Same," she muttered. "Guess we've both lapsed then." She shook her head, as if she was shaking off an old memory. "I don't go much anymore either," she whispered. "Too many... reasons not to."

"I get that," I said, keeping my tone light. Her comments resonated with me. We didn't even need to swap stories. I understood what it was like to have doubts, to step away from the faith that I had grown up with.

I grabbed a pan and set it on the stove, letting it heat for a minute while I found a cutting board on which to chop up some precooked bacon. "All right, let's see if this ancient stove can work some magic." I tossed in a bit of butter, watching it melt. "Tonight's menu: breakfast burritos."

"Oh, that sounds good. Anything warm will be so much better than gas-station junk food and airport wine." She grinned.

I had found some tortillas in the fridge that looked safe enough, so I tossed a few into another pan and covered them with a lid to warm them up.

"Yep," I said, pouring the eggs into the pan and stirring slowly. "It's all about improvisation. We might not have any fresh tomatoes, but I did find a can of diced tomatoes with green chilies."

It made me happy to be able to cook a nice little meal for her, here in the midst of the blizzard. I glanced over at the fridge, remembering something I'd spotted there when I'd rifled through it earlier. Along with the eggs and bacon, there had been several bottles of wine nestled on the bottom shelf. It appeared her aunt had good taste. I opened the fridge, grabbed a bottle of pinot grigio, and set it on the counter. Why not make this meal a little more civilized?

I returned to the pan, mixing in the chopped bacon with the eggs before sprinkling a generous amount of shredded cheese on top and letting it melt. I grabbed the warmed tortillas from the other pan and spread them out on top of a large cutting board, my stomach growling again.

As soon as the cheese was thoroughly melted, I spooned the mixture onto the tortillas, adding a scoop of diced tomatoes and chilies before rolling the burritos up tightly. Not bad, considering our limited supplies. I plated the burritos and set them on the table. Then I grabbed two glasses from the cabinet, popped the cork on the wine, and poured a generous amount into each glass, setting them beside our plates.

"Let's get you turned around," I said, walking over to Noelle. I rotated her chair and eased her closer to the table.

"Thanks," she said, her eyes drifting to the burritos and the wine. "Looks impressive."

I grinned and sat down across from her, pushing one plate closer. "Told you I had some survival skills. And I figured we could make this a little more...gratifying." I raised my glass slightly in a mock toast. "Dig in."

Noelle didn't need to be told twice. She picked up a burrito and took a big bite, letting out a contented sigh. "Oh wow, this is really good." Her eyes widened in surprise and appreciation. "First proper meal I've had all day."

I chuckled, taking a bite of my own. "Glad it's hitting the spot."

I washed the food down with a sip of the wine, which had a nice, crisp finish.

This, I figured, was as good a time as any to steer the conversation back to her aunt. "So, you didn't get to stick around after your aunt's funeral?"

She shook her head, sighing softly. "No. I had to fly back for work. Like I told you, I was competing for that big promotion." She took a couple of deep swallows of her wine, then added, "I feel bad about not coming to see her more." Her tone had softened. "I mean, after everything that happened... Well, it doesn't matter now. Bottom line, I should've made more time to see her—talk to her. She was all alone here."

I nodded. "Life gets in the way," I said simply.

We fell into silence after that—not an awkward one, just the kind that comes when you're too hungry to keep talking. We focused on the food in front of us, devouring the burritos without much more conversation. Between bites, we took slow sips of the wine, savoring it as much as the meal. By the time our plates were empty, she had finished off her glass. So I poured her another, which she accepted with a small smile.

"Thanks. You're surprisingly domestic," she said.

"Don't spread that around." I winked.

I gathered up the empty plates, balancing them in one hand. "Stay put," I said, pointing a finger at Noelle before she could even think about getting up. "I've got this."

I turned toward the sink, setting the dishes on the counter. When I went to toss the bacon box and tomato can into the trash can under the sink, something caught my eye. An emergency radio hand-crank solar lantern sat nestled between the bags and cleaning supplies. I pulled it out.

"Well, look at this," I said, inspecting the gadget, curious about how much light it would emit and hoping it was charged up. "This is a cool little device. I'm surprised your aunt would have one of these."

Noelle raised an eyebrow in mild interest. "What is that? Some doomsday prepper thing?"

"Better," I said, turning it over in my hands. "It's got a solar panel, a hand crank, and even Bluetooth, so that means I can connect it to my phone and...play some music." Without waiting for her response, I pulled out my phone and linked it up. In a few seconds, a Christmas song filled the room.

Noelle burst out laughing. "You, Mr. Captain, have a Christmas playlist?"

I shrugged, taking a sip of my wine. "What? Who doesn't like Christmas music this time of year?"

She smirked, and the gleam in her eye told me I was about to be roasted. "It's just not what I expected."

As "Jingle Bell Rock" revved up, she grabbed my phone and started scrolling through the playlist. "Oh, this is funny," she said, scanning the list. "'I Saw Mommy Kissing Santa Claus.' Seriously?"

"What? It's the John Mellencamp version." I smirked and left her to her fun, returning to the sink to start washing the dishes.

The song changed to "All I Want for Christmas Is You," and Noelle snorted with laughter. "I can't believe this," she muttered, scrolling through the list and biting her lip in fascination as though each title held some secret about me.

As she sat there laughing and making comments, I scrubbed the plates and utensils, rinsed them off, and placed them in the drying rack.

"You got something against Christmas classics?" I asked after the last plate was clean, tossing a glance her way.

"No, but this?" She held up the phone, waving it in the air. "I just didn't peg you as the 'Deck the Halls,' kind of guy. I thought you only listened to...country music?"

I chuckled, tossing a dish towel over my shoulder. "You've got a lot of opinions for someone who barely knows me. Maybe you shouldn't make so many assumptions. There's more to me than meets the eye."

Her lips curled into a smirk. "Oh, really?"

"Yeah, really," I replied, wiping off the counter. "I mean, just because I like country music doesn't mean I fit into some cookie-cutter mold you've got in your head."

I placed the last item in the pantry and turned around to see her hobbling toward the fridge. "What did I say about staying put?" I grumbled.

She flashed me a playful grin, the wine making her all the more bold. "Relax, I'm looking for dessert." With that, she yanked open the fridge door and leaned inside, digging through its contents.

My eyes drifted to her curves. Her tight leggings framed one hell of an ass. I swallowed the urge to cross the room and pull her up against me.

Noelle squealed, startling me from my lascivious thoughts. She pulled out a large tin decorated with a festive candy cane pattern, her face lighting up like a kid on Christmas morning. "Aha! These always have the best goodies!"

She popped the lid and gasped. "Peanut butter fudge and chocolate fudge!" When she whipped around to show me, she grimaced—her ankle clearly giving her grief.

I shook my head at her enthusiasm. "You're like a kid in a candy store," I said, striding over. "But also, you're a stubborn one. I told you to stay off that ankle."

Before she could protest, I scooped her into my arms, making sure to steady the tin with one hand. She let out a soft yelp but then settled against my chest, clutching the tin like it was the Holy Grail.

"You're ridiculous," I muttered, carrying her to the living room and setting her down in front of the fireplace. The fire had burned down, with several of the logs reduced to embers. It was time to add more wood to keep it going.

She smiled up at me, her eyes sparkling. "You know, if getting bossed around means I get the royal treatment, I might start liking this whole military commander thing you do."

I let out a laugh. "You'd better be careful what you ask for, Stinkerbelle."

I turned to the hearth, grabbing a couple of logs to feed the fire. "Now, sit tight while I make sure we don't freeze in here."

Noelle Nichols

Chapter Nine

12/23 night

Kol tossed another log onto the fire, the flames licking at his hands as he nudged it into place with the poker. "I'm building it up so it'll burn through the night," he said. "If I stack it right, it should last long enough to keep the room warm until morning. But with this blizzard, we'll need to do more than just rely on the fire. I'll try to seal off the room the best I can by shutting the doors to the rest of the house and closing all the vents, blinds, and curtains. We've got to conserve the heat as much as possible."

I scooted next to him. "Just don't burn the house down on the first day I own it, okay?"

He glanced at me, one eyebrow bouncing, but didn't crack a smile. "No worries, Stinkerbelle."

His voice held the same no-nonsense tone of authority he'd used all day—when we'd flown off the road, when he'd navigated the backroads, and when he'd scrounged up a meal in the kitchen without electricity. And now he was managing a fire like it was no big deal.

I moved away from the fireplace and stretched out my legs, watching the flames curl around the fresh logs as he went about sealing off the room.

While he worked, I followed his movements, trying to figure out how someone could be so damn sure of everything all the time. It was infuriating, honestly. The way he just said things with absolute confidence, like the world would bend to his will if he simply told it to. Nothing I ever threw his way seemed to faze him—no teasing, no playful jabs. Kol was always in control.

"I'll help you in the morning with whatever you need to get sorted before I get out of here," he said from the other side of the room.

Something about the way he said it hit me in the chest. *Get out of here.* He'd said it like he couldn't wait to leave, as if this whole day of being stuck with me in a snowstorm was an inconvenience he was ready to move on from, as if he was eager to be done with his good deed and get on his way.

It shouldn't have stung, but it did. Just as we were starting to get to know each other, he was already talking about leaving.

"You're really in a hurry to *get out of here*, huh?" I couldn't help the little edge of sarcasm that crept into my voice.

Kol shrugged nonchalantly. "I'm trying not to overstay my welcome. I'm sure you have places to be for the holidays." He said it like spending the day with me had meant nothing at all.

Did he ever second-guess himself? Did he ever lie awake at night, doubting his decisions like I always seemed to? Probably not. He wasn't the type to get stuck in his own head, chewing over every little thing. He acted, he moved forward, and that was that. Simple. Direct. No looking back.

Part of me admired it. Hell, part of me wished I was the same. Must be nice. I had to admit; it was comforting, in a way, having someone like that around—someone who always seemed to have it together. But at the same time, it drove me crazy. What would it take to crack that cool, calm exterior just once?

"So, did you have any idea your aunt was going to leave you this place?" he asked.

I reached over and picked up a nutcracker sitting on the side table next to the sofa, fidgeting with it. "Nope. No clue about the house, what was in her will, or anything else for that matter. It was a total surprise." Restlessly, I snapped the nutcracker's mouth open and closed, letting its wooden jaws bite down as though it was taking a chomp at the ultimatum in the will. The thought of having to move back here to Saratoga was freaking me out. I didn't think I could do it.

Kol poked at the fire again, then glanced over his shoulder at me. "You've gotta be excited though. A house like this? Especially considering your current circumstances... Seems like a pretty sweet deal. Are you planning on living here permanently?"

My stomach tightened. If I couldn't make sense of what I was feeling, how could I explain it to him? I scooted back so I could lean against the front edge of the sofa, biting the inside of my cheek. "It's complicated," I said, twisting the nutcracker between my fingers and messing with its little levers—anything to keep my hands busy. "Giving up my life in Atlanta wouldn't exactly be easy."

Kol sat down between the fireplace and me, extending one leg casually while keeping the other bent, draping his forearm over his knee. He waited for me to speak, though I wasn't sure where to start.

Taking a deep breath and gathering my thoughts, I moved the nutcracker's legs, making him march across my lap. "I liked my job and was good at it, but most days, it was as if I was just... marking time, you know? Like everything was on autopilot—not bad, not good, but I was just doing what I was expected to do. And then, one day, fate reached over and shook my personal snow globe, flipping my life upside down." I shrugged. "I went from a career that was on track, a boyfriend who I thought was total husband material, and a past that was neatly tucked away where it belonged...to this." I glanced around the room, laughing bitterly. "Jobless, single, hitching rides with strangers. And a past that is now the only future I have." I laughed, but there was no humor in it. "Sometimes fate is a little bitch."

I pressed my thumb against the nutcracker's handle, making it bite down again. Fate really had dealt me a twisted hand. And for good measure, the gods had thrown a tall, dark, and handsome Night Stalker squarely in the mix just to mess with my emotions.

Kol stayed quiet as he studied me. I was grateful for the silence.

After I'd watched the flames flicker and spark for a few minutes, my thoughts started spiraling in a completely different direction. I couldn't stop thinking about the way he'd looked at me earlier in the kitchen—like he wanted to devour me.

He was temptation wrapped up in all the things I shouldn't want but did. Desperately. And maybe that was exactly what I needed—a one-night fling. Although, I doubted he'd be interested in that sort of dalliance considering how eager he seemed to be to leave in the morning.

What I wanted right now wasn't complicated. I just needed to forget everything, even if only for a night.

Kol got up and stirred the fire again until the embers glowed brightly. His hands moved with precision—hands that were probably just as capable of lighting *me* up if he wanted to. God, I wanted to be reckless. I wanted to throw myself at him, let him burn away everything I'd been holding on to for far too long.

Tonight I wanted to be wrecked, to be so consumed by someone that I couldn't remember my name, much less all the screwed-up things life had thrown at me. Kol was the kind of man who could do that; I could tell just by the way he moved. I wanted him to worship every inch of me, to let him light up every one of my nerves like a Christmas tree.

My eyes trailed over Kol's broad shoulders, watching the way his muscles shifted beneath his uniform shirt. He was the kind of man that came with warnings—older, never married, a jet-setting airline pilot. He probably had a different woman in every city. But then again, he was the ideal catch for a line of women a mile long. There was no denying he was a drop-dead gorgeous, badass Army Night Stalker, and wealthy enough to own his own home and property, where he could take his brand-new Bronco out mudding for kicks.

He was also exactly what I needed—someone who could break down every wall I'd built, who could unravel all the carefully spun control I'd tried to wrap myself in over the last four years.

Right now, I wanted danger. I craved the thrill of being with someone who could take me apart and put me back together in all the wrong ways.

I wanted to be the girl with her hair down, flying in the wind as the thoroughbred beneath her galloped full speed across the fields without a care in the world. God, I wanted to find a man who wasn't fragile, one who I could ride hard and wouldn't break if I pushed him.

"Ahem." Kol cleared his throat, and from the sound of it, not for the first time. "Earth to Stinkerbelle," he teased, crossing his arms over his chest, waiting for me to snap out of my fantasies.

Startled by the not-so-innocent place to which my thoughts had strayed, I blinked, my face heating as I realized how close he was now—standing just in front of me.

"Sorry, I guess my mind drifted for a sec," I said, dropping my head back to see him better.

"Judging by the look on your face," Kol said with a chuckle, "wherever it went must've been really good."

I shot him a playful grin, shrugging off the embarrassment. "Someone as straightlaced as you might not want to go poking around in a mind like mine. I've been pent up for way too long."

Kol's eyes flickered. For a split second, I thought he might take the bait and respond to my insinuation, but instead, he just stayed quiet and sat down on the floor in front of me, with one knee up, leaving some space between us. He turned his attention back to the fire like nothing had happened.

Seriously, what was his deal? I wasn't blind. I saw the way he had checked me out. But it was like he was holding back, and I didn't get it.

I stretched my legs out, my frustration bubbling up. Every time I threw him a line, he didn't bite. Not that I minded the chase, but damn, it seemed he wasn't interested at all. Why did he always have to act so unaffected?

"You don't seem too thrilled about living here in Saratoga," Kol said, leaning back a little and tapping his hand on his thigh to the rhythm of the song drifting from the kitchen. "I take it you've gotten used to the big-city life—shopping, hitting up the latest foodie hotspots, all that."

I shrugged. "Yeah, something like that."

Kol angled his body toward me. There was a hint of curiosity on his face. He was clearly not buying my casual brush-off. "Hmm, funny. I'm the opposite. Left the Bronx for the quiet upstate life, and I love it out here. But I guess you could always sell the place or rent it out if it's not your thing."

Both of my options—living here or selling the house—felt wrong. How could he possibly understand? I honestly didn't know what I wanted to do—and having to move here and stay for at least a year was the last thing I'd expected when I'd met with Holly.

"Maybe I should sell this old house and backpack across Europe," I said. "Or, better yet, convert an old school bus and drive until I run out of road. You know, live in the moment, throw caution to the wind. Just me and some stray dog—no people, no worries—not caring about tomorrow." I rolled my eyes, knowing full well that I sounded idiotic.

The fire cracked loudly, almost like it disagreed with my idea. Perfect. Even the house was judging me.

Kol pressed his lips together and narrowed his eyes. "That would be a stupid mistake." His words were harsh, cutting through my cynicism. "You can't be serious about walking away from a beautiful Victorian home worth a mint in your hometown when you don't even have a job. What? You're just going to quit life and drift around? Maybe you just need to suck it up. How bad can it be?"

I ground my teeth, irritation simmering under the surface. He didn't get it. Kol had no idea what being in this town did to me or what memories haunted me here. The last thing I needed was his judgment about how I was handling it.

Scowling at him, I straightened up. "You don't know a damn thing about me. Or what I've been through. So don't act like you've got all the answers."

If he thought walking away from this house was stupid, he'd think I was completely insane to walk away from my parents' property too. There was no way I was telling him about that. And now was definitely not the time to dump my whole tale of woe on him—tell him about how my parents had died in a storm not too different from this one, about how Aunt Mary had left me more than just this house. He wouldn't understand, and even if he did, I didn't want his pity.

"Maybe you shouldn't be making so many assumptions," I said, throwing his own words back at him. "There's more to me than meets the eye." I lifted my chin, quoting him again with just the right amount of bite.

He didn't respond right away but merely watched me with that same infuriating calm. The challenge hung there between us, my dare for him to push back.

But instead, he sighed and turned to stare at the fire. He didn't argue, didn't push me as I'd expected. And that, more than anything, frustrated me to no end.

"Besides, I can't sell the house," I blurted out, tossing the nutcracker onto the table harder than I'd intended. The clunk of the wood meeting the table got his attention.

Kol's brow furrowed, confusion spreading across his face. "What do you mean? Ms. Winters said it was yours."

"It's not that simple." Although I wasn't in the mood to explain how my life had turned into a real-life Monopoly game with rules I didn't like, I did want him to understand the situation was more complicated. "There's a clause, and no, not the jolly man from the North Pole—more like a giant lump of *coal* in my stocking."

A tight line formed between his brows at how I'd said "coal." But he ignored my snark and moved on. "Clause? Like, what kind of clause?"

119

"A clause that requires me to do something impossible," I muttered. "It's an ultimatum—one that's completely unfair. So tonight, I'm going to enjoy having a free place to stay. Tomorrow, I'm walking away from it all. This town, this house...none of it's for me." I told him all this with confidence, but in actuality, I didn't yet know what I wanted to do.

Kol scooted back a little so he could see me better, then stared at me like I'd grown two heads. "You're acting like a spoiled brat, you know that? Too stubborn to see what's right in front of you. How bad can it really be?" he asked bluntly. "You don't strike me as the type to quit...but then again, you did quit your dream job."

His comments hit me like a slap across my face. I bristled, and a surge of anger flared up inside me. "I'm not spoiled," I snapped. "You don't have any fucking idea what you're talking about or who I am." My hands clenched into fists in my lap. "That job wasn't my dream. It was a means to an end. It was a paycheck, a way to make money and play the stupid game. You know, the *American dream*. But it was never my dream."

Kol didn't say anything, but his judgmental expression made his thoughts clear enough. Stoically, he waited for me to explain myself. So I did.

"Like it or not, the reality is that money might not buy happiness, but *not* having it sure as hell makes life harder. Rich people, they have opportunities handed to them. There are so many people out there who have more talent, more intelligence, and a better work ethic but are never given a chance because they don't have the money to be seen. They don't have to prove themselves twice over to even get a foot in the door. So yeah, I left the small town to chase the dream. I wanted my shot at making something of myself." I scoffed. "And before you snap back about the value of this house, it could be worth a million bucks, but what good would that do me if it shatters me in the process? I'll find another job."

The moment he started to speak, I cut him off.

"And maybe, you're the one who's fucking spoiled," I threw at him. "Maybe you've always had money and a perfect family. All the pieces easily falling into place for you. Who knows?"

I sucked in a breath and exhaled sharply, my chest heaving after the rant I hadn't planned to let loose. The silence that followed my words made me want to crawl out of my skin.

Kol grunted. "A classy woman doesn't need to talk like a sailor."

I snorted. "Who says I'm classy?"

He shook his head slowly, muttering under his breath, "This girl has no idea who she is. She's so—lost."

That stung in a way I hadn't expected. But instead of lashing out again, I bit my lip, letting the crackling of the fire fill the silence.

Kol sat back, watching me like he was sizing me up. "You're right. We are pretty much strangers, and I don't have a clue what makes you tick." He paused for a moment. "And just so you know, I was raised in a typical middle-class family by some of the greatest people you'll ever meet, and they love me. We weren't rich, but we had everything we needed. When I was eighteen, I didn't know what I wanted to do with my life, but I felt obligated to serve, like my father and his father before him. Best decision I could've made, but it left its scars."

He leaned forward, resting his elbows on his knees, gazing into the fire. "If I've learned one thing, it's that life isn't about what I have or what the other guy has. It's about experiences and the people you're close to. I don't live just to earn a buck. I don't value stuff or have any desire to acquire material things. Life's too short."

"Trust me, I know," I said, my voice barely over a whisper. I picked up the nutcracker again, running my fingers over its uniform. Kol's comments about me being a spoiled brat hurt more than I wanted to admit. He wasn't even close to understanding who I was or the reality of the situation, but there was no way I could tell him that. The truth wasn't something I could share— not with him, not with anyone.

Kol didn't respond right away, his dark eyes watching me in that calm, unreadable way that had been driving me crazy since the moment we met. Part of me hated how he could stay so composed, holding all his cards close to his chest, while I just tossed mine on the table without a second thought.

I squirmed uncomfortably and focused on the old nutcracker in my hand. I twisted it around, running my fingers along the sharp edges of its wooden hat. Kol probably thought I was a holy mess of bad decisions wrapped up in a high-maintenance package. And he wasn't entirely wrong. I *was* a mess, but not for the reasons he thought.

Here I was in front of this dream of a man, someone strong, calm and protective—a man who made me feel safe without even trying—and I was flying off the handle at a few pointed comments. No wonder he thought I was a stuck-up girl who valued things over people.

"I'm sorry. I didn't mean to be rude," I finally said. "You've been nothing but kind to me. You gave me a ride even though I was acting like an imbecile at the gate, and you drove through a snowstorm for hours just to get me here, to this house my aunt left me, only for me to turn around and say I don't want it. I wish I could explain my behavior, but the truth is...I can't. For the last four years, I've been desperately trying to catch all the snowflakes in my own snow globe, holding on to them, hoping they'd stay still. But it keeps getting flipped upside down. You're right...I am lost."

I didn't even try to stop the big fat tear that rolled down my cheek.

As the pressure built inside me, I stared down at the nutcracker in my hands. The truth was, I had a desperate need for connection, for someone to want me, to comfort me, for the giant hole in my heart to be filled.

The house was quiet now. The music in the kitchen had stopped playing momentarily, and the fire was oddly silent. It was as if the house was holding its breath.

"It's okay, Stinkerbelle. We all have our crosses to bear. I see you." Kol's voice was softer now, carrying something deeper—something raw. The steady control he always held onto seemed to waver, just for a moment.

Then he added in a rougher tone, "I've been where you are. Some things..." He paused, glancing into the fire for a few seconds before continuing. "Some things get stuck inside you. You carry them because you have to, because if you let go, your world flies apart. And I know what it's like to be in that whirlwind. You think if you hold tight enough, you can keep it all from spinning out of control."

Caught off guard, I blinked slowly as I absorbed what he was saying. He wasn't saying this to me out of pity. This wasn't mere sympathy. He was being genuine and sharing something he'd learned from his own pain. His quiet strength faltered for just a second, and I knew then—he understood.

The nutcracker's mouth snapped shut with a loud pop as I squeezed the lever unintentionally, making me jump. A low chuckle rumbled in Kol's chest. I froze, then set the nutcracker down, heat creeping up the back of my neck.

He was a tough nut to crack, but in that quiet moment, something changed between us, an unspoken understanding settling in.

Kol leaned back on one hand. There was a subtle tension in his body. He didn't say a word, just kept watching me, and it took every ounce of self-control not to let that silence eat at me.

Noelle Nichols

Chapter Ten

12/23 night

The fire crackled loudly, as though it were trying to fill the heavy silence. I wasn't about to get into all the things he might want to talk about—my life, my mistakes, and whatever emotional black hole I was currently orbiting. So instead, I decided to shift gears.

I pushed myself up using the edge of the sofa, trying to shake off the new awkwardness that had settled between us. I need to say something—anything—to change the subject. Kol remained quiet as I limped over to the tree in the corner. Aunt Mary had gone all out in her Christmas decorating, as always—she'd never done things halfway.

The fire burned steadily now, lighting up the space. I turned in a slow circle, finally taking in the full view of the room for the first time. It was like stepping into Santa's workshop. Unlit string lights framed the windows, a nativity scene stood on a small table by the front door, and a collection of vintage nutcrackers stood at attention on a nearby shelf. An antique wooden sled decorated with a bright red ribbon leaned against the far wall. The couch was sprinkled with festive throw pillows, each one embroidered with holiday patterns. On another table, a bowl filled with candy canes and glittering ornaments sparkled in the firelight. The Christmas tree shimmered with dozens of beautiful, tasteful ornaments.

"Look, there's an angel on the top of the tree," I said, limping back toward the sofa. "Of course she'd have an angel. It's perfect."

Kol had gotten up and stacked another log onto the fire. He nodded as he secured the fire screen.

"It's been years since I celebrated Christmas," I said, the words slipping out before I could stop them. My throat tightened as soon as they left my mouth. Damn. The last thing I needed was to get sentimental tonight. Our conversation had swung wildly from playful to heavy, but I needed to bring it back to something simple. I wanted him to see me as more than just a train wreck—as someone he'd actually want to be with tonight. "But, yeah, anyway it's a beautiful tree. The ornaments are all so unique."

Kol glanced over at me. "Since I joined the Army, holidays haven't really been my thing either. Not opposed to them, but they haven't been much of a priority. I've spent so many of them away, doing other things. I guess I let a lot of things lapse, like going to mass."

I made my way back to the sofa, tossing the pillows onto the floor—doing my best to act casual. "No heat means we'll have to camp out in here," I said. "We're going to freeze if we don't huddle up in front of the fire. This house is so old, the cold's creeping in from everywhere."

"You're right," he said, coming over to help me arrange the pillows and dig out a few more thick quilts and afghans from the hope chest. "The fire's helping, but this place still feels like an icebox."

A gust of wind slammed against the windows, rattling the glass. Kol stepped closer, his large frame suddenly making me nervous. We worked in silence, spreading out the blankets to make a comfortable pallet between the sofa and the fire. I smoothed the last blanket and stepped back—only to catch my foot on the edge of the rug...

Kol's arms wrapped around me, catching me mid-fall. His hands, strong and sure, gripped my back, pulling me against his chest, and for a second, we were way too close. His body was all heat and hard muscles as he held me suspended above the floor, dipping me like we were in a fancy ballroom dance.

"Again?" he asked. His teasing grin pulled me back to reality. "That's the third time you've tried to take a nosedive today. You trip more than anyone I've ever met, Stinkerbelle."

Heat surged through me—not only from embarrassment but because of how his powerful hands stayed locked on my waist, like he was in no hurry to let me go. The way his fingers pressed into my back made me wonder what else those hands could do. My mind raced, imagining them exploring my body, holding me, guiding me to try things I'd only imagined. He was so close now that the heat between us burned hotter than the fire behind him. My heart pounded in my chest. An undeniable current of attraction ran through us.

"Maybe I like it when you catch me," I said, my voice coming out lower than I'd intended.

His face didn't react, but his grip on my waist tightened just a little before he finally eased me down onto the pallet. His hands lingered longer than necessary before he stepped back. Silently I cursed him for letting go and always stopping just short of where I wanted him to.

As the firelight flickered around us, all I could think about was how much I wanted to provoke him—make him lose control.

Kol's eyes caught mine, a glint of mischief flashing just before he turned to get the suitcases by the door. I could tell he was up to no good. He dragged them over to the now-cushionless sofa and set them down without a word.

I tried to play it cool, like I wasn't all that interested, and pulled my phone out of my tote to check my socials and emails. But I didn't have any service. Damn storm. So I opened a game, eager for anything to keep my eyes busy on something other than Kol. But when he toed off his boots and unzipped his suitcase, my curiosity got the better of me. I leaned back against the sofa, taking a peek as he pulled out a pair of sweatpants and a T-shirt. Then he started peeling off his pilot uniform, and the sight of it was like a car crash—I couldn't help but watch. He was really going to change *right here*. Of course he was. Mr. Captain did what he wanted, and this was the only room in the whole house that was even barely warm. I tried to act like it was no big deal, casually glancing his way as he undressed.

First, his watch came off—a bulky, expensive-looking thing he tossed into the suitcase like it was nothing. Then he unbuttoned his uniform shirt, sliding it over his broad shoulders, down his muscled arms, and revealing a white T-shirt underneath. The way the fabric clung to his chest showed off nearly every detail. My breath hitched as he pulled it over his head, exposing a body that was basically carved from stone. His muscles flexed enticingly with each movement. His wide-set shoulders tapered down to a set of abs and a *V-cut* that had me almost reaching out. There was ink on his chest too—a tattoo of a pair of wings with some script woven between them, black and bold, covering his right pec and continuing over his biceps.

I swallowed hard and tried not to stare. Except I was definitely staring.

He glanced my way for a second, his lips curving into a smirk like he knew exactly what was going on in my head. I looked away, pretending to busy myself with my game. I couldn't let myself ogle him like a total creeper.

He tossed the T-shirt aside and unbuttoned his navy-blue uniform pants. They slid down, revealing boxer briefs that left little to the imagination. And by little, I mean his cock, which was large and very hard to miss. My face burned, but I couldn't stop sneaking looks, my gaze drifting down and back up again as he bent to pull off his socks.

He caught me staring and shot me that cocky smile. "What? Haven't you ever seen a man before? I thought you said you weren't a virgin."

I raised my chin, refusing to let him have the upper hand. "Oh, I'm no virgin. I just appreciate a man confident enough to change in front of a stranger. Clearly, you wanted me to enjoy the view."

His grin widened, but he didn't say anything, just turned and grabbed the pair of sweatpants he'd pulled from the suitcase. He yanked them on, then tossed on an old Army T-shirt. The firelight flickered over him, casting shadows that emphasized every line, every curve of muscle. It was like watching a Greek god getting dressed. He was strong, powerful, and annoyingly self-assured.

Without another word, Kol wandered off, rummaging through the house, leaving me alone by the fire. With my mind whirling in a frenzy, I sat there staring into the flames. I had assumed something was about to happen there, but no. Every time I thought I'd get a little more from him, he pulled back. It was driving me insane.

But I wasn't going to let him off so easily. Kol might be trying to keep things in check, but I wasn't in the mood for restraint. Not anymore. One way or another, I was going to stoke that fire and see just how hot things could get between us.

A few minutes later, Kol strolled back in with a big grin, holding two bottles of wine and a couple of glasses. "Turns out your aunt had great taste. All good Catholics like their wine, am I right?" He wiggled the bottles at me and set them down on the table along with the glasses.

I chuckled at the sight of him—this big, serious guy was getting excited about two bottles of fancy wine. "I wouldn't have guessed you'd be a wine guy, Mr. Captain."

"Storybook Mountain, 2019 Estate Reserve Zinfandel," he said, holding a bottle out. He made it sound like he was offering me a precious artifact instead of wine.

While he twisted the corkscrew, I studied his movements.

"You'd be surprised," he said. "Since becoming an airline pilot, I've had the chance to hit up some pretty amazing wine destinations. I kind of got into wine tasting."

I tried not to laugh, but a little giggle slipped out. "You? Wine tasting?"

He shot me a mock-offended look as he poured. "What? A guy can't enjoy a good glass of wine?"

I held up my hands in surrender. "Hey, I'm not judging."

Kol handed me a glass, and I took a sip. It was smooth and rich, with a little bite to it. "Not bad," I admitted, swirling the wine in my glass like I had a clue what I was doing.

"Yeah, as far as hobbies go, wine tasting is a particularly fun one," he said, swirling his own glass and taking a long sniff. "It's called oenophilia. Basically, it means I'm a wine nerd."

I almost choked on my sip. "Wait, you're serious?" I had to laugh. "I pegged you more for a beer and whiskey guy."

"I enjoy those too, but wine tasting is...different," he replied, all serious. "There's a whole method to it. You analyze the appearance in the glass, then the aroma, the sensations in your mouth, and finally, the finish." He settled beside me on the floor, stretching his long legs out and leaning back against the pillows he'd propped up next to the sofa.

"You're really into this, aren't you?" I asked, still in disbelief.

He gave a small shrug, but the smirk on his face told me he enjoyed surprising me. "Wine's more than just a drink. It tells a story. Every vintage, every bottle, is different. It's about complexity, character, and even flaws. Kind of like people."

I rolled my eyes. "That was almost poetic. Who are you, and what did you do with my captain?"

He chuckled, taking another sip. "So you assumed I wasn't a guy who appreciates the finer things?"

"Definitely not wine."

"I've been to some of the best wineries," he continued, undeterred. "France, Italy, Napa. Flights are cheap when you're a pilot."

"Okay, Mr. World Traveler," I teased, leaning back and taking a slow drink, allowing the flavors to linger on my tongue. "Where would you go for an ideal wine trip?"

He didn't even hesitate. "Tuscany, for sure. Late summer. We'd start with the vineyards, of course. The hills, the sunsets—nothing like it. Then we'd eat way too much pasta, drink way too much wine, and forget what day it is."

"That sounds suspiciously romantic," I said, giving him a side-eye. The way he'd said *we* so casually made me all fluttery inside. I liked this game.

"Life's about experiences," he said with a shrug. "Not just work. And trust me, Tuscany's the best experience."

I swirled my wine again, and this time it wasn't for show. "All right, I'm sold. We could definitely do Tuscany. But what about something a little less...refined? Maybe a backpacking trip through New Zealand. Wine tasting after hiking up some crazy mountain?"

Kol grinned, leaning back on his elbows. "Now you're talking. Finish the day with a wine tasting at some obscure vineyard in the middle of nowhere? Could be the perfect balance of rugged and refined."

I laughed, enjoying this unexpected side of him. "Who knew you would be so interesting, Mr. Captain?"

Kol sat up and poured me another glass of wine, the rich red swirling in the firelight. When he handed it to me, his fingers brushed mine just long enough to send a spark through my arm.

I opened the tin of fudge, offering him a piece.

"This should pair nicely with the wine," I said, popping a square of fudge into my mouth. The combination of rich chocolate and smooth wine was perfect. Kol raised an eyebrow, scrutinizing me as he took a bite.

"Okay, you got me. Fudge and wine. Not bad," he said.

I smiled, relishing the warmth from the fire and the slight buzz from the wine. "If you could go anywhere in the world right now, where would you go?"

Kol leaned back, narrowing his eyes thoughtfully. "Northern Sweden," he said. "Somewhere up above the Arctic Circle. We'd stay in one of those glass igloos, go ice fishing, and watch the Aurora Borealis dance across the sky. They've got these luxury resorts now where you can go dogsledding during the day and drink hot chocolate by a fire at night."

"That sounds magical," I said, raising my glass in appreciation. "Watching the Northern Lights from bed? Count me in. It would sure beat sitting in this cold, dark house."

"Would it?" he asked, cocking his head to the side. The gold flecks in his eyes glimmered in the firelight, and my tummy did a little flip. He grinned, and for the first time tonight, it seemed as though his guard had lowered a little. "You know, up near the North Pole it's quiet, peaceful. The kind of place where the world slows down, and it's just you, the snow, and the stars. Not so different from us sitting in the dark in front of the fire."

As I watched the flickering light from the fire dance in his eyes, I imagined going on a romantic trip with him. Actually, he was right about sitting here in front of the fire. This was pretty romantic.

"We'd have to try all the Scandinavian food. Reindeer steaks, maybe?" he said. "I hear they eat that a lot in northern Scandinavia."

"What! Eat Rudolph on Christmas? No way—hard pass." I shook my head and squinched up my nose.

Kol laughed loudly. "They've got a thing for wild game, but I guess I agree it might be in poor taste to eat reindeer on Christmas. So how about we go to a local place and feast on a smorgasbord? That way, we could taste a little bit of everything those Swedes like to offer. Then, when we can't possibly eat another bite, we'd get back to that glass igloo and watch the stars and Northern Lights."

"Not bad, Captain. Not bad at all. So, what's next on the travel itinerary?"

He tilted his head. "Machu Picchu in April. That's the best time to hike the Inca Trail, right before the tourist season really kicks off. We'd start at the base of the mountains, hiking through ancient ruins. By the time you reach the summit, it's like standing on top of the world. The clouds roll in over the peaks in the distance, and you feel you're on another planet."

I smiled, leaning in closer to him. "And after hiking for days, what do we do next?"

"We'd spend the night at a cozy lodge. Warm food, a hot shower, and maybe a bottle of Peruvian wine to celebrate." Kol's voice dropped a little. "Then we'd watch the stars from the rooftop terrace, knowing that'd we'd done something special that most people never get to do—together."

We locked eyes, and my pulse quickened. "You know, you're really good at planning dream vacations."

Kol shrugged. "I love to travel. Planning the trip is half the fun, you know. I've got a long list of places I want to visit."

I reached for a piece of the peanut butter fudge and held it out to him. His gaze flickered down to my hand before he leaned in to take a bite. His lips brushed against my fingers, and an electric current coiled between my thighs.

"What do you think?" I asked, watching him closely.

His eyes darkened, and for a moment, I thought he might close the distance between us. But then he swallowed, moving back a little. "Not bad, but I like the chocolate better."

I wasn't about to let him off that easily. I scooted a little closer, my knee brushing against his. "You know, for a guy who spends a lot of his time in the air, you're pretty grounded."

Kol chuckled softly, though his body tensed. "Gotta stay grounded. Keeps you from floating off."

"Is that why you keep pulling back?" I teased, resting my hand on his thigh. His muscles tightened beneath my touch, but he didn't pull away. "Afraid you might fly too close to the sun?"

His jaw clenched, and an internal battle played out behind his dark eyes as he gazed down at me. He exhaled slowly, as if trying to calm whatever was stirring inside him. "Noelle..."

"Kol," I whispered, leaning closer until our faces were mere inches apart. "What are you waiting for?"

His breath hitched, and for a second, I thought he might finally give in. The tension between us was thick, and I could practically feel the heat rolling off him. But then, right before our lips could meet, his resolve snapped back into place. He pulled away, clearing his throat and reclining back against the pillows.

"Stinkerbelle, you're playing with fire."

Crawling closer to him, I brushed my lips along his ear. "Good thing I'm not afraid of getting burned."

Kol Vinter

Chapter Eleven

12/23 late night

Noelle took a sip of wine and then stretched across me to place her glass on the side table, bracing herself by pressing her hand on my belly. It was warm, even through the fabric of my shirt. She couldn't quite reach the table, so I sat up slightly, taking the glass from her and setting it down myself. Her freed hand settled onto my thigh, a connection that was far from accidental.

She must have had enough of the back-and-forth that had been driving us both crazy. We'd been at each other's throats when we first met, the intense undercurrent of attraction between us undeniable but complicated. Her smart-ass comments and quick wit clashed sharply with my more reserved, no-nonsense nature. I'd not exactly been thrilled with being stuck in a car for hours with a woman who was loud, bold, and always pushing my buttons. But somewhere along that icy road, things had changed. Beneath all the teasing and sarcasm, we'd started to find common ground. Jokes had turned playful, and conversations about life had gotten a little deeper. The attraction between us had been simmering all day, and as much as I tried to keep it in check, she had a way of slipping under my skin.

I had kept her at arm's length, trying to convince myself it was for the best. Maybe I didn't want to deal with her complicated past, or maybe it was my own damn baggage that made me hesitate. Either way, I'd been hot and cold with her, and she wasn't blind to it. But now, with the fire, the wine, and the close quarters, I could see it in her eyes—she was done with the games. The teasing, the flirting, the tension building between us—it had all led to this. She wanted more, and hell, I did too.

When she'd put her hands on me just now, that hadn't been accidental. There was intent in the way her fingers molded to the hard lines of my abs and grasped my thigh with purposeful pressure. The heat between us was rising with every slow movement. And the way she moved closer to me made it clear she wasn't going to let me push her away this time. Noelle was tired of waiting, and I was done holding back.

"Thanks," she murmured, her eyes locking onto mine with an impish glint.

Damn, this girl was feisty. If she only knew the fire she was playing with, maybe she'd think twice about stoking my need like this. But then again, maybe she knew exactly what she was doing.

Just as I turned back to face her, she swung a leg over and straddled my hips. Her hands slapped my chest, shoving me back onto the pillows. She took my face in her fingers and kissed me hard. Her lips were warm and impossibly soft against mine, moving with a fervor that caught me off guard. Her tongue brushed along my lips, teasing them apart before slipping inside. The subtle taste of wine mingled between us, adding a sweet tang. The sensation was electric—her tongue exploring mine, tentative yet bold, igniting the fire that had been smoldering all day.

An electric charge ran through my veins, settling low and stirring a desire that was quickly becoming impossible to ignore. Her hips sank down, firmly settling onto me, and her body aligned with the growing hardness beneath my sweatpants. I wrapped my hands around her waist, sinking my fingers into her gentle contours as I struggled to maintain control. Her petite frame made her seem delicate and fragile somehow, which surprised me, especially since her big personality made her seem larger than life.

Her lips were demanding, and when she twisted her fingers in my hair, I couldn't help letting out a grunt. She moved with a confidence that was both surprising and intoxicating. For a moment, I let her set the pace, and her lips claimed mine with a need that rivaled my own.

She pulled back a little, giggling softly, before leaning forward again. This time, she captured my lower lip between her teeth and slowly dragged back, sending a jolt of current straight to my dick. My restraint was hanging by a thread.

I slid my hands down her sides, wrapping my fingers around her curvy ass and digging into her flesh. I ground her up and down the length of my shaft, eliciting a breathy groan from deep within her chest. This girl was definitely a firecracker, and the wine had only made her bolder. I couldn't let her play this game without consequences. She'd better not be teasing me without expecting to get wholly and completely fucked. A man like me could only hold back so much.

I wondered then if I should shut this down before things went too far. She didn't need some guy taking advantage of her while she was feeling defeated and unloved, and I sure as hell wasn't going to be a regret for her in the morning. I pulled away from those addictive lips, grabbed her wrists, and yanked her hands down, pinning them between her thighs.

She let out a gasp, her eyes widening at the force of my action. For a moment, she seemed taken aback. Then, a sly smile played on her lips, which were swollen from our demanding kiss. As she caught her breath, her chest rose and fell, drawing my gaze to the enticing curves hidden beneath her sweater.

The challenge in her eyes was clear. I had to set some things straight if we were going to keep playing this game.

"Listen, I'm no college boy or uptight ad executive," I said, locking eyes with her. "When I want something, I take it—no questions, no games." A dark hunger stirred to life as my grip on her wrists tightened. A shudder ran through her body, and her playful smile faltered. Her lip quivered ever so slightly before she steadied herself, defiance flashing in her eyes.

"Noelle," I growled, "I want you to understand something. I don't do playful. When I fuck a woman, it's not something she'll forget anytime soon." My eyes bored into hers, my words hanging in the air between us.

Her eyes grew big at my declaration. A spark of something wild lit up in them, and her lips stretched into a devilish smirk.

"Yes, sir," she purred, drawing out the *r* at the end and daring me to do my worst. That *sir* stirred something inside me.

I hadn't expected this side of her. The playful, wild child—yes, but not the woman looking to sate her untamed desires. The need to possess her surged through my veins. I hoisted her to her feet with little effort. Her lips formed into a surprised little *o* as she found herself staring down at me, her feet now planted on either side of my hips.

"Strip," I ordered, my tone brooking no argument. It was time for her to see who she was truly dealing with.

Instead of obeying, she stood motionless before me, her back straight, her chin up. There was a playful defiance in her eyes, as though she relished the forcefulness in my voice. Was this girl for real? I'd never met anyone quite like her. And that was saying something, after all the places I'd been and the women I'd known. Noelle was a challenge I couldn't refuse, an adventure that would either be the best damn thing I'd ever experienced or would blow up spectacularly in my face.

I waited silently. She was loving every second of having my full attention.

But she didn't know who she was dealing with. I didn't give orders lightly, especially to a slip of a girl like her. My body was coiled tight as she took her sweet time, relishing the power she held in this moment.

She reached up under her soft gray sweater dress and grasped the waistband of her leggings. Slowly, she slid them down, inch by tantalizing inch, first one side, then the other, over her hips and down her thighs. She teased me, knowing good and well that the dress fell over what I longed to taste but couldn't yet get a glimpse of. The sight of her fingers tracing the curves of her body had my cock throbbing.

This little elf thought she had me figured out. Every move she made was intentional, calculated to drive me mad, and it was working—damn, how it was working.

Noelle twisted a little to the side, her blonde curls bouncing with the movement. She placed the toes of her foot—the one with the twisted ankle—lightly on my stomach, using me for balance. Then she bent down, carefully tugging her leggings off. For a second, I worried about the pain she must be in, but she didn't slow down. This girl was determined, and I wasn't about to stop her.

She stepped back, wincing as she repeated the move with the other leg, quickly pulling the leggings free. Then, with a quick motion, she hooked them around my neck and pulled me up to her for a quick, hard kiss before abruptly letting go, sending me back onto the pillows.

Damn, she was audacious. I tucked my hands behind my head, sizing her up. "Well, keep going," I said, my voice coming out rougher than I'd expected. Need coursed through me. "Don't keep me waiting."

Noelle hesitated, toying with the hem of her sweater dress as I scrutinized her. She was a vision, standing there, with her blonde hair cascading over her shoulders and her eyes locked onto mine. But a flicker of uncertainty had replaced her previous petulant confidence.

Just when I thought she had chickened out, she moved her feet to straddle my hips once again. Carefully, she lowered herself onto her knees and then sat squarely on top of my cock. The heat of her core was a silent entreaty for something more, but she just sat there, keeping her eyes locked on mine. I remained still, waiting.

"You're not finished," I said.

For a moment, we just stared at each other. I could see the wheels turning in her head, conflict flashing in her eyes, but she remained stubbornly clothed.

I let out a disappointed huff, shaking my head as I moved my hands away from where they rested behind me. But she wasn't having it.

"No." The word was rough, commanding, and completely unexpected from her. Her hands shot out, pinning my forearms so I couldn't move my hands from behind me. I relaxed, and she let go, returning to her perch on top of me.

Then she brought one hand up to her mouth and, with the flat of her tongue, licked a line from her wrist to the tip of her middle finger. She sucked two of her fingers into her mouth all the way down to the third knuckle and slowly slid them back out, all the while keeping her eyes on me. She did this two more times, and when her fingers left her mouth the last time, they were glistening wet.

I swallowed hard, my throat suddenly dry. I had a feeling I knew where this was going, but I wasn't prepared for the sight that greeted me next. She used her other hand to lift her dress, giving me a peek at her dark pink lips. My cock twitched beneath her, aching to get inside that tight, wet heat.

She then dragged those wet fingers down the hollow of her folds, and my dick jerked again. Fuck, this girl was killing me. She slid her fingers to the tight little bundle of nerves at the apex of her pussy and, with agonizing slowness, drew small circles around and around. Her head fell back over one shoulder, and her eyes became hooded, but she didn't ever fucking lose eye contact with me, even as she started to squirm under the pressure of her own fingers.

"That's it. That's the last of my fucking control," I said. My hands slapped down on her thighs, startling her from her sensual display, and she gasped. In one fell swoop, my hands flew under her dress and raked up her sides, taking the sweater up with them. I shoved the dress up her arms and over her head, then tossed it aside.

Her hair tumbled down around her shoulders, a wild, curly halo that framed her flushed face perfectly. And then I saw the most delicious sight.

"What? No bra all this time?" I said, my eyes roaming over her bare chest. Her nipples were pebbled into tight buds, begging to be teased and tasted. "Damn, I never would have guessed."

Noelle regarded me with a wicked look on her face, her confidence returning in full force. "Maybe it's your lack of experience with women," she teased, her fingers idly tracing patterns on my chest.

At that, I laughed—a genuine laugh that seemed to reverberate through the room. If only she knew how long it had been since I'd laughed wholeheartedly. "Oh, Stinkerbelle," I said, shaking my head. "You have no idea what you've just done."

I had to hand it to her—not many women could get under my skin. But this little wildcat had. She'd made me crazy from the moment I'd laid eyes on her at the airport. From that sassy mouth to the curve of her hips, she had me entranced, and there was no going back now.

Without thinking, I threw my arm around Noelle's waist and twisted. Using our momentum to my advantage, I slammed her back onto the thick pallet. She let out a startled yelp. Before she could utter a single word, I was on my feet, looming over her. This was a game to her, one she was intent on winning. But nobody got the better of me, especially not when it came to matters of the flesh.

I ripped off my T-shirt and tossed it aside. Her gaze flicked over my bare chest, taking in the tattoos that snaked across my skin, before settling back on my face.

My heart hammered in my chest, pulsing with the need to have her, to brand her as mine, but I held back the fierce urge to take her hard and fast.

"Take them off," I demanded, pointing to my sweatpants.

Noelle sat up, keeping her dark blue eyes on mine as she got onto her hands and knees. She crawled over to me, each movement deliberate and slow, before kneeling at my feet and dropping her head. The sight of her, submissive and waiting, sparked something primal within me, a raw need to make her wholly and completely mine.

"Oh, so you can be submissive when you want to, hmm?" I asked. I wasn't buying her act for a second, but I had to admit, she played the part well.

She remained still, keeping her head bowed, and for a moment, I thought she might defy me and refuse to do what I'd asked her to do.

I reached down and grabbed a fistful of her thick hair, pulling her head back so she had no choice but to look up at me.

"I said take them off." I tightened my grip just enough to let her know I meant business.

Slowly, she dragged her eyes away from mine, letting them travel down my body. They lingered on the large bulge in my pants, a smirk playing on her lips as she took in the sight of my arousal. She was enjoying this, enjoying the power she wielded over me at this moment. But she was about to discover that I was no one's plaything.

She rose up on her knees and reached for my waistband. Slowly, she dipped her thumbs under the fabric, running them along the edge to the back of my pants until her arms were wrapped around me. Then she splayed her fingers across my lower back. She was careful to never make contact with my cock.

With a rough tug, she dragged my pants and boxer briefs down, exposing the curve of my ass to the cool air of the room. Her fingers then slid back around to the front, pulling both the briefs and pants forward and down, more than clearing my rock-hard dick. It sprang free, standing at attention and aching for her touch.

Her eyes widened slightly as she looked up at me with an approving grin, then bit her lower lip.

This little elf was playing with fire, and I was going to give her more than she expected. Let her have her fun for now.

Suddenly, she yanked my pants all the way down to my ankles, quickly tugging them off each foot before shoving them aside. And then, just like that, she returned to kneeling submissively at my feet. Her push-and-pull behavior said it all. She wanted to be in charge, but she also didn't want to disappoint me.

For a few heartbeats I stood there, naked and hard, looking down at her. The curves of her body were highlighted enticingly by the warm glow of the fire.

Finally I reached down and cupped her chin, lifting her face so that our eyes met. "You want to play games, Stinkerbelle?" I asked, my voice low and dangerous. "I can play."

Her breasts rose and fell with each breath, her nipples tight and begging for my touch. Her eyes flashed with defiance, but she didn't pull away from my touch. Instead, she leaned into it, her lips parting ever so slightly. It was an invitation, one I wasn't about to refuse.

My cock was hard as steel, aching for her. I'd been itching to say it all night, and I couldn't hold back any longer. "Noelle, I want that sassy mouth of yours wrapped around my dick now."

Her hands found my ankles, and she teasingly tugged them toward her, forcing me to close the gap between us. She placed her palms on my calves, gliding her fingers up and down, skimming my skin with featherlight touches. My muscles twitched with anticipation as her fingertips traced along the sensitive skin at the backs of my knees and left trails of fire blazing in their wake. With each pass, her touch became more demanding. And then, with an impish glint in her eyes, she trailed one finger between my legs, barely brushing against my balls.

A bolt of electricity shot through me, and I sucked in a sharp breath. Her mouth was so close to my cock but never touched it. The little minx was pushing me to my limits. Without warning, she cupped my ass, digging her fingers into my flesh, heaving my thighs against her boobs while I fought to maintain my stance.

It was too much. I'd been holding back all damn day, and if she didn't get to the main course soon, I was gonna blow before she even got going.

"You teasing little—" I sputtered, reaching down to tangle my hand in her hair. With a firm tug, I brought her chin to my cock, leaving no room for protest or argument. And of all the damn reactions she could have had, the little vixen let out a giggle.

A soft moan slipped past my lips as her breath tickled my skin. I twisted a fistful of her thick, curly hair and yanked her head back, narrowing my eyes as I glared down at her.

"Mm-mm," I growled as a warning. Her boldness and untamed spirit were undoing me, but I wanted her to know she was playing with fire. No more games. No more teasing. It was time for action.

Her playful smile faded to a look of pure want. Pulling back slightly, she rolled her lower lip into her mouth as if to stifle another giggle, and the action robbed me of what little restraint I had left. Keeping my fingers entwined in her hair, I guided her back to what I wanted.

Finally—*finally*—she wrapped her hands around my aching shaft. And she began to caress me. Her fingers barely closed around me, her grip tightening just a fraction as she explored my length.

The warmth of her hands and the softness of her skin made me sigh with pleasure. It was the best kind of torment. I could already imagine how her mouth would feel on me—tight, wet, and perfect.

The first touch of her tongue on my cock had me biting back a groan. She started at the root of my shaft, dragging the flat of her tongue up along its length. The sensation was almost too much to bear. I let out a low moan, my hips involuntarily bucking toward her mouth.

When she reached the head, she swirled her tongue around the sensitive tip, flicking it back and forth across the frenulum. Her tongue gave me a searing rush of pleasure—swirling, licking, sucking.

I couldn't take it anymore. I needed to be inside her mouth, to feel the tightness of her throat as she took me in. With a groan, I guided her closer, my hand still tangled in her hair.

Her touch was maddening, her tongue nimble as it teased. When she finally took me in, I couldn't stop the groan that ripped from my throat. "Mmm, fuck. That's good."

Noelle rose on her knees. She was just tall enough to take me deep. Her lips slid down, and she pulled back, going down again with a slow roll of her head. She shifted her stance, planting one foot on the ground for leverage, and suddenly, the crown of my cock slipped past the ridge of her throat. Her lips slid down nearly to the base of my shaft, and I swore I saw stars.

I couldn't take my eyes off her. Her head bobbed back and forth, slow and steady. She took her time. Goddamn, she had a mouth on her, and she knew how to use it. This little elf was a hellcat in disguise, making my legs shake. I fought to hold back, to maintain control, but as the muscles of her throat tightened around me and she struggled to take more of me, it was almost too much.

Fuck, I couldn't believe this seemingly delicate creature could fuck me this hard with her mouth. She was perfect—

everything I had ever wanted and more. Gripping the tendrils of her hair tighter, I took over the rhythm, guiding her up and down my shaft with increasing speed.

Within seconds, I started to thrust my hips, losing myself to the rush of this carnality. She met my thrusts with eager moans, the vibrations shooting straight through my cock. Her tongue slid over the sensitive skin, teasing and drawing out every ounce of pleasure. Gripping her shoulder, I thrust hard and deep. She took it all with an eagerness that was my undoing.

Knowing I couldn't hold on much longer, I reached down and wrapped my hand around the back of her neck to gently urge her back. I eased out of her mouth, my cock wet and shiny with her saliva. She looked up at me, her eyes glazed with lust. A glistening strand of my pre-cum connected her lips to the head of my dick. The sight nearly finished me.

My chest heaved as I fought for breath and tried to calm the storm of need raging through me. Noelle's eyes sparkled with mischievous delight. With a sinful smile, she lowered her head, her tongue darting out to lick the salty residue from my cock. My balls drew up, a clear sign I was close, so fucking close. Her hot mouth closed over the tip, sucking hard, and that was it. I was done.

Pleasure ripped through me like a tsunami, an explosive rush that stole my breath. My hips jerked uncontrollably as I let out a guttural groan, the sound reverberating off the walls of the room. My orgasm ripped through me, a wave of pleasure so intense it bordered on pain. The muscles of her throat tightened around me as she struggled to swallow my cum that was jetting down her throat.

And with that, I was spent. My vision blurred as I relished the last aftershocks of my orgasm. I stood there, bracing myself against her shoulders, trying to catch my breath and waiting for my heart to slow its frenzied pace. Noelle's eyes shimmered with a mixture of triumph and desire. She'd done this—pushed me over the edge—and if the smug look on her face was any indication, she was damn proud of herself.

Her tongue swirled one last time, a last lick that sent a shudder through me, and then she released me with an audible pop. I stepped back, giving myself some space, needing a moment to process what had just happened. I had to admit that I hadn't seen that coming.

Noelle sat back on her heels, satisfied with the result of her efforts. She had taken control and shown me she could handle anything I threw her way.

And in that moment, I knew I was in deep trouble. This girl was more than just a passing fling. She was a force to be reckoned with, a wildfire that was quickly consuming me. I had to tread carefully, or I might just find myself falling for her—harder and faster than I'd ever thought possible.

But for now, I would enjoy the ride, savoring every moment of our time together. Because one thing was certain: Noelle Nichols was unlike any woman I had ever met, and I had a feeling she was about to turn my world upside down.

"I knew you had a mouth on you," I said finally, "but never in my wildest imagination would I have guessed what it was capable of. Damn, Stinkerbelle, you're just full of surprises."

Noelle looked up at me with a proud little smile, her lips still glistening. I grunted, shaking my head in disbelief. Hell, she should be proud—she'd certainly blown my mind. "I don't even want to know how you learned skills like that."

She laughed, a sound that was quickly becoming one of my favorites, and I figured some smartass comment was about to follow.

"Oh, God, you're going to tell me anyway, aren't you?" I said, not even bothering to hide the amusement in my voice.

She grinned, and there was a naughty glint in her eye. "Well, now that you mention it..."

I held up my hands in surrender. "No, that's okay. I don't need the details."

With a mock-pout, she rose to her feet. "Fine, I'll spare you the story."

I shook my head, grabbing my sweatpants off the floor and pulling them on. I needed a moment to regain my composure, to reset before I did something I might regret—like letting her into my heart. I turned and walked toward the kitchen. The familiar strains of Christmas music were playing. I'd left my phone connected to the camping radio, and Bing Crosby was crooning about a white Christmas. This was definitely a far cry from the usual music I listened to, but it was a holiday indulgence.

I grabbed a couple of bottles of water, as well as my phone and the radio, before heading back to the living room. As I rounded the corner, my breath caught in my throat at the sight that greeted me.

There Noelle stood, in front of the fireplace, jabbing at a log with a poker. She had my uniform shirt on, barely buttoned and hanging halfway down her thighs. She looked fucking incredible, and for a moment, I forgot how to breathe.

I cleared my throat, trying to get my heart under control. "Here," I said, holding out one of the water bottles. "I thought you could use this."

She took it with a smile. "What? No more wine?"

"I think you've had enough," I said, though the words tasted like a lie. The truth was, I liked seeing her let loose, liked the way her eyes sparkled when she was being cheeky.

"Pish," she said, waving a hand dismissively. "That's not any fun. Come on, we still have one more bottle to go." She limped toward the table, taking a big swig of the water. Picking up her wine glass, she swung it back and forth. "How about you pour me another glass, Mr. Wine Connoisseur...I mean, Mr. Captain."

She laughed again, and damn if it didn't do something to my heart. I liked the happy Noelle, the one who wasn't anxious and wound up by her past or the uncertainty of her future. I moved to stand beside her, setting my water bottle, phone, and radio on the table. "All right, Stinkerbelle," I said, "but only because you asked so nicely."

I poured what was left of the first bottle into her glass and then opened the second. I had to admit, it really did have a nice fragrance, and it had paired well with—of all things—chocolate fudge.

Glasses in hand, we propped up against the sofa. For a while, we sat there listening to Christmas songs, eating fudge, drinking wine, and watching the fire. Noelle had her elbow propped on the edge of the sofa and was turned halfway toward me. One of her legs was extended on the floor toward the fire, the other was bent, and my shirt was open just enough to give me a peek of her glistening folds.

I was already getting hard again, but I didn't want to disturb the peaceful moment. There was something about the way the firelight flickered across her skin and something about the serene expression on her face that made me want to capture the image and hold onto it forever. While she gazed into the fire, she played with a tendril of her hair, wrapping it around her finger and letting it spring loose over and over. After a little while, she glanced over at me and smiled, and it was like a punch to the gut.

God, what a beautiful woman. I could envision her welcoming me home from every trip.

That thought had come unbidden, and for a moment, I allowed myself to entertain it. Noelle was unlike anyone I'd ever met, a whirlwind of energy that had blown into my life and threatened to turn everything upside down. She was vibrant and sassy, with a zest for life that was infectious. And yet, there was a sadness to her, a vulnerability that she tried so hard to hide behind her laughter and her sass.

I found myself wanting to know more about her, to uncover her secrets and truly see the woman within. What had made her the way she was? What dreams and fears lurked beneath the surface? And more importantly, why did I care so damn much?

I took a sip of my wine, letting the rich, complex flavors wash over my tongue as I watched her. Noelle was completely at ease, completely herself, and it was a sight to behold. She caught me staring and raised an eyebrow in question. "What?" she asked, a playful smile tugging at the corners of her mouth.

I shook my head, grinning. "Nothing. Just enjoying the wine and the company. This was definitely not the day I'd envisioned when I woke up this morning."

She laughed. "Well, you're not the only one." She reached out and took my hand, intertwining her fingers with mine. "You know," she said, turning to face me fully, "I've been meaning to ask you something."

"What's that?" I asked.

"Why *Icehawk*?"

I smiled at the mention of the call sign I'd earned during my time in the military. "It's a long story, but the short version is that it's a play on my last name, Vinter. Swedish for *winter*, right?"

She nodded, listening intently.

"Well, in the military, *hawk* is often used in call signs. It's meant to signify keen observation and the ability to swoop in for the kill. So, I was given *Icehawk*. It seemed fitting, given my specialties."

Noelle's eyes sparkled. "That's so interesting. I've always wanted a cool nickname. The best I've gotten is *No-torious*, which my friends used to call me when I was a kid because I was so damn stubborn."

I laughed. I'd gotten a good demonstration of her obstinate nature earlier. "I can see that."

She gave me a playful punch on the arm. "Hey, I'm not that bad."

"No, you're right. You're worse." She stuck her tongue out at me. "Yeah, I think Stinkerbelle is fitting too."

"You know, I was hoping if I ignored that ridiculous name, you'd drop it. *But no.* Even when I'm giving you the best blowjob you've ever had, you still have the audacity to use it. Now, Mr. Captain, you tell me who the stubborn one is."

I laughed. "You're funny." God, this girl lit me up. Her mouth wasn't the only thing I wanted to fuck. No, I wasn't nearly finished with her.

Chapter Twelve

12/23 late night

Man, oh man, how I wanted to run my fingers over his muscular bare chest and trace the lines of his tattoos with my tongue. I'd never been with a man like him—strong and domineering. All the guys I'd been with had been...well, average. I doubted Kol had any genuine interest in me. I was betting he only saw me as some immature girl who was fun to hook up with. And I was definitely not the type of woman he would choose to date. He'd claimed he was selective, which made me want to prove I was good enough. I laughed internally, still buzzing from the thrill of how I'd just impressed the big bad *Night Stalker* himself with my ability to take him deep into my throat.

Fighting a laugh, I thought about how I'd learned to control my gag reflex. Should I tell him? Maybe he wouldn't find it as funny as I did. I debated it for a moment. The mischievous part of me won out, and I started to giggle, unable to contain it any longer.

Kol brows scrunched together. "All right, just tell me. Whatever it is, get it out of your system."

I shook my head, still laughing. "Well, I was just thinking about how you said you didn't want to know how I learned to take a man into my throat like that." Kol pulled his hand from mine and let it fall onto his thigh. Frowning slightly, he fidgeted as though he was uncomfortable with where this conversation was going. "No, really, it's not what you're thinking."

He gave me an annoyed look. "Really, I don't need the mental image."

"Oh my gosh, you're being ridiculous." I huffed. "Just let me explain. It's something I learned when I was hanging out with my friends, not some guy. You see, when you grow up showing horses, you spend lots of time at the barn riding any horse or pony you can get your hands on. You even do homeschooling during show season. This means you also spend lots of time with people of all ages—mostly girls. Trust me, you will get a well-rounded education at a show barn."

I rolled my eyes, memories of those days flashing through my mind. "Let's just say once you've seen horses get it on, there's not much left for the imagination." I took a breath, my laughter bubbling up again. "So anyway, barn girls are known for their bravery and competitive spirit, even when it comes to who knows the dirtiest of secrets."

Kol's expression softened with amusement as I continued to babble on about riding. "There's something about bonding over the day-in and day-out dangers of riding the type of ponies that will jump a three-foot oxer with a bunch of crazy-looking flowers blowing in the wind all around the course. Horses get freaked out by anything odd or different. So a big part of showing is proving that your horse is trained well enough not to react and still be submissive enough to follow your lead. Riding is a humbling sport—everyone gets their turn hitting the dirt."

Listening intently, Kol tilted his head and ran his hand over his chin. He seemed surprised by the little bit of my past I was sharing.

"Well, anyway. Getting back to on topic," I went on, "one of the rites of passage was learning to get over your gag reflex by *swallowing* a banana. It's a miracle one of us didn't choke to death." I shook my head, thinking back to all the insane things we'd done while hanging out at the barn. "Our parents would just drop us off and assume we were too busy to get into much trouble. If they only knew." I laughed at the memories that seemed so distant now.

"So, has your little party trick impressed all the guys you've hooked up with?" he asked, his voice laced with sarcasm, but I could detect the jealousy pricking at his words.

"Like I told you," I reassured him quickly, "I haven't been with very many guys. And Blake didn't have any interest in me doing anything like that to him or in going down on me. He wasn't much of a kisser either; he was more of a hop-on-hop-off kind of guy."

Kol grunted, his eyes darkening. "Sounds like a wuss. Totally self-absorbed. I don't see you dating a guy like that."

"He looked good on paper. You know, perfect resume, driven to run his own agency one day. He comes from money, has a trust fund, wears bespoke suits. At first"—I sighed—"I was impressed by his credentials and work ethic. That is, until I realized he had absolutely no artistic vision or creativity. But he was excellent at schmoozing, and he knew everything about everyone in the industry."

Kol studied me momentarily but remained silent.

"He is history," I said firmly, frowning as memories surfaced again. "Honestly, there's nothing about him to miss...except the promotion that should have been mine. Ugh! Let's not talk about this. All I wanted tonight was to not think about my train wreck of a life. I just wanted you to fuck me until I couldn't remember my name...but no, here we are, rehashing why Noelle Nichols is the biggest loser."

Kol whipped around and grabbed my face, turning it toward him and squeezing my cheeks between his fingers.

"You listen to me, and you listen good," he said in a low growl, which got my attention real quick. "You're not a loser, Noelle. Things in your life might not be going the way you had mapped them out, but that doesn't mean you give up. Have you ever thought that maybe the direction you were headed was the worst thing for you in the long run? Stop and think about what your life would have been like if you'd ended up with that arrogant prick, Blake—shallow and unfulfilled."

His grip tightened just enough to make me focus solely on him. "You need to keep in mind that, on your worst day, you've got it better than eighty percent of the people on this planet. Life's always going to throw you in the dirt, just like those ponies you used to ride. Tell me, what did your trainer make you do when that happened?"

With my face still squished between his fingers, I mumbled, "Get back on."

"That's right," he said, releasing my face and leaving a ghostly imprint of his touch. "You're too capable to take the lazy way out. Whatever happened in your past to make you think you shouldn't have been born is something it's time you got over."

"You know," I whispered, "I never thought I'd end up here. Not just here, in this house, but here, feeling so...lost."

Kol regarded me seriously, the firelight flickering in his eyes. "Lost isn't always a bad thing. Sometimes, it's just a step on the path to finding yourself."

I swallowed hard. "I didn't mean for you to hear what I said at the airport. I guess I've just...I've felt that way a lot lately." The admission weighed heavily on my chest. "Everything keeps going wrong, and I'm tired of trying so hard for nothing. It feels like nothing I do matters."

Kol's jaw clenched. "I don't know why the hell you'd think something like that, but you're wrong. You have no idea how much your life matters."

I shook my head, biting my lip. "You wouldn't understand."

"Maybe not," he said, his eyes hardening with resolve, "but that doesn't mean you're not wrong. You think you don't matter? You think the world would be better off without you? That's bullshit, Noelle."

His words hit me like a slap, and my heart stuttered. I couldn't respond.

"You don't even see it, do you?" Kol cupped my cheek and said emphatically, "Every person you meet, every conversation, every moment you share—it all matters. Everyone has a purpose, whether or not they know it."

I blinked up at him, the lump in my throat growing. "But what if I never figure out what that purpose is? What if I just keep screwing up, one bad decision after another?"

Kol let out a long breath, his eyes never leaving mine. "Everyone screws up. Life's full of bad decisions. Hell, I've made more than I can count. But you don't get to check out just because things aren't going the way you planned." His voice softened just a bit, a note of sincerity threading through as he said, "You're stronger than that."

I bit my lip, trying to keep the tears at bay. "I just don't know what I'm supposed to do anymore. It's like no matter how hard I try, nothing ever works out."

"Maybe that's because you're chasing the wrong things," Kol said, sitting back slightly. "Maybe all this time, you've been focusing on what you think you're supposed to want instead of what really makes you happy."

My throat tightened again, and I thought about that as I stared at him. "And what do you think would make me happy?"

He shrugged. "I don't know. But I do know this—whatever's making you think your life isn't worth living, it's not who you are. And it sure as hell isn't where your story ends."

I nodded, taking a deep breath. "I guess I've been so focused on what I thought I wanted, I forgot to think about what I needed."

"And what do you need, Noelle?" Kol asked, stretching his arms along the edge of the couch.

"I don't know."

"Then it's time you figure that out."

He was being blunt, but not in a way that offended me. It was a wake-up call I hadn't realized I needed. For a few moments, I sat quietly, absorbing his words and processing the feelings they had stirred up within me. I'd been avoiding the truth for far too long.

Tossing back the rest of my wine, I simply replied, "You're right."

Without a word, I reached for the bottle and poured myself another glass, the rich, red liquid sloshing against the sides. As I brought the glass to my lips, I marveled at the man sitting beside me.

Wow, this guy not only understood me in a way no one else did, he didn't take any of my bullshit either. He spoke his mind and didn't mince words. His brutal honesty was refreshing—so different from the veiled politeness and backstabbing gossip I had become accustomed to since I'd moved to Atlanta and started working at the Martindale Agency.

Actually, Kol reminded me of my father—a straight shooter who had never lied or taken advantage of anyone. How had I lost my way so badly? Why had I wasted so much time and effort on a jerk like Blake? Somewhere between striving to keep up with girls who had everything handed to them and chasing a career that didn't feel like mine, I'd lost sight of what made me happy. Why had I felt it was so important to go off to a school like NYU, earn a master's in marketing, and pursue a job that was more about the paycheck than the passion? Had I been trying to prove something to people who didn't even matter? Those girls, with their perfectly trained, expensive horses, never knew the joy of working with an off-the-track thoroughbred, a horse discarded like garbage because it wasn't the fastest. But I did. I loved training them, watching them transform into incredible hunters and jumpers. They were horses with heart and grit. Maybe that was what I was missing. Maybe that was what I was meant to do—work with horses like my parents had. The realization hit me hard, like a punch to the gut. Kol's words had been a much-needed reality check.

I drained my glass fast and set it down with a decisive clack. Kol had turned toward the fire, and I felt that I should say something to him, react in some way to what he'd said, but all I could do was sit there...

For the first time in a long time, I felt a glimmer of hope—a sense that maybe I could find my way back to the person I used to be, the person who wasn't afraid to get back on the horse, no matter how many times she got thrown off.

I tucked my legs under me and turned to face Kol. I couldn't resist the urge to poke at the confident exterior he wore like a second skin. "Are you always right?" I asked.

He quirked an eyebrow, not even bothering to look at me as he replied, "Usually."

A burst of laughter escaped my lips. "Good to know you're so humble."

Kol rubbed his fingers over his mouth, a small smirk playing on his lips. He rocked his head to the side, turning to consider me. "I guess we should call it a night," he said, getting up and heading over to the fireplace. He added a couple of logs and poked at the others, rekindling the fire with ease.

As he moved, I admired the sight of his muscular back and broad shoulders. Then I stood up, unbuttoned his shirt, and slid it off.

When he turned around and saw me standing there, completely naked and holding his shirt, surprise registered in his eyes, quickly replaced by a mix of desire and conflict.

Chapter Thirteen

12/23 late night

I tossed his shirt at him and demanded, "Get your ass over here, Mr. Captain." I wasn't willing to let this opportunity slip away.

He walked over to me, looped the shirt around my neck like a scarf, gave me a chaste kiss, and took a half-step back. "Sorry, pretty lady, but we're done for the night."

Guilt was etched on his face, as if he regretted allowing things to become sexual between us. I knew what was coming before he even said the words: "I don't want to take advantage of you, Noelle. We've both had a lot to drink, and I don't think it's a good idea to cross that line right now."

I opened my mouth to argue, but he cut me off. "And besides, I don't have any condoms on me. I doubt your aunt Mary has any lying around."

I huffed, irritated by his sudden change of heart. "I told you, I have an IUD, and Blake required we have all the tests done and then some. I'm completely healthy. What about *you*?" I challenged, my eyes locking onto his. "I just swallowed a half gallon of your cum. You'd better be clean."

Kol chuckled—a low, rumbling sound that sent little flares and sparks zipping through me. "There's that mouth again," he said, a hint of amusement in his eyes. "But yes, I'm clean. I get an FAA medical every six months, and like I told *you*—I'm very selective."

I rolled my eyes. It was clear he was trying to let me down easy, but his insistence only fueled my determination. "So I get it. It's not really the lack of condoms. You're implying I'm not good enough. Oh, and that as long as *you* got off, everything is good?"

Inside, I was seething. But damn, he was hot, and after the shitty day I'd had, I deserved some satisfaction too. The wine had made me brave, and I wasn't about to back down now. "Besides, I never take the lazy way out." I threw his words back at him like a dagger.

I could tell by the blow job I'd given him earlier that he prided himself on being dominant, and my words would either incite him into action or send him packing. Either way, it was time for him to put up or shut up.

Kol's eyes narrowed, conflict raging within them. He was used to being in control, to calling the shots, and clearly my defiance was throwing him off his game.

"You're a lot of work, but I'm still willing to give it a go," I said smugly as I jammed my fist on my cocked-out hip. "Talk about high-maintenance," I said, letting out a dramatic breath.

I was pushing him to the brink, but I didn't care. I wanted him, and I was tired of playing games. But one thing was certain—I wouldn't make it easy for him.

"Fuck me, Kol," I demanded. "I'm not going to tell you again."

The air between us crackled as we stood there, locked in a silent battle of wills. The way he watched me hungrily left no doubt in my mind that he wanted me as much as I wanted him. But would he give in to his urges, or would he continue to hold back, driven by some misplaced sense of chivalry?

My heart pounded against my ribcage, matching the rhythm of the snow and ice falling against the windowpanes. Kol's nostrils flared, and his eyes turned black as his pupils blew wide. I'd poked the bear, and now he was awake.

In a flash of motion, his hand snapped around and fisted the hair in the back of my head. He yanked me toward him, our lips crashing together as he wrapped his other hand around my waist and pulled me against his hard shaft. A thrill shot through me; I'd finally gotten through to him.

I wrapped an arm around his neck, and using my good leg, jumped up and locked my legs around his waist. He caught me by the ass, his fingers gripping my cheeks tightly. As I squirmed against his shaft, his shirt wafted to the floor. A deep growl rumbled in his throat. The feral sound vibrated through me, igniting every nerve ending with raw need.

Kol walked us over to our makeshift bed on the floor and laid me back, never breaking the kiss. We melted into a tangle of hands, lips, and tongues, frantically devouring each other. He had one hand under my head and the other under my lower back, keeping me pulled close against him. My legs stayed locked around his waist as I ground against the bulge in his sweatpants. He kissed me like a man starved, as if he was depending on me for his very survival. And God help me, I wanted to be his to feast upon.

Yes, yes, this was exactly what I wanted, to lose myself in the moment. All action, no thinking. Only carnal pleasure. "Kol, I need you inside me now," I begged between kisses. "I want you hard and fast."

He pulled back, his lips leaving mine, and inhaled deeply. Looking down at me, he gave me a little kiss on my nose and then on my forehead. "I think it's time you learn a little patience," he teased.

He pushed up onto his elbow, leaving his fingers tangled in my hair. Then, using the other hand, he slowly traced a line from my chin down my throat, over my collarbone, and then lower, his touch setting off explosions along my hypersensitive skin.

His fingers continued their journey, skimming over the swell of my breasts, down my belly, and stopping just before he reached the place where I craved him most. The contact ignited a shiver across my skin, causing me to arch my back in a silent plea for more.

But then, without warning, his touch vanished. A cool rush of air replaced the heat of his hands as he pulled away. He rolled to the side and stood, leaving me cold and aching. Disappointment flashed through me, sharp and unexpected.

"Come back. Where are you going?" I asked, confused. Was he having second thoughts?

"The more you demand, the longer you will have to wait," he warned, making my insides clench with anticipation.

"So bossy," I whispered under my breath, earning a *tsk* from him.

He shook his head and strode over to the Christmas tree, taking his time to untangle one of the large red velvet ribbons draped over its branches. At the sight of it in his hand, my mind raced with possibilities.

When he returned, he kneeled beside me, gently taking my hand and helping me to sit up next to him.

"Close your eyes," he commanded.

I pursed my lips skeptically, exhaling a dramatic sigh.

"Noelle."

The way my name rolled off his lips had me obeying without further argument.

Kol brought the ribbon to my closed eyes, wrapping it behind my head and tying a firm knot. The ribbon pressed securely against my eyes, blocking out every hint of light. I tried to peek, but he had tied it expertly, leaving no room for cheating. He guided the ribbon's tails to the front under my chin, tying the strands into a snug bow against my throat—not too tight, but enough to ensure there was no chance of it slipping loose. The ends of the ribbon dangled loosely over my collarbones, brushing against my skin like a teasing caress. He seemed to have done this a million times, his fingers deft and sure as they manipulated the ribbon, and I couldn't ignore the flicker of jealousy that thought induced.

The lack of sight and the ribbon's restraint left me at Kol's mercy, a dangerous place I never thought I'd be. My pulse quickened in my throat, my breath catching slightly in anticipation of what might come. The loss of control was both exhilarating and terrifying.

As if sensing my trepidation, he took my hand in his. "Hey, it's just you and me here, Noelle. No rush, no pressure. This is all about you, about your pleasure. I want you to feel everything, to experience it all without any distractions." His fingers brushed against my cheek. "Trust me, I know what I'm doing."

I took a deep breath, forcing myself to trust him, even if only in this moment. Kol wasn't like Blake or any of the other guys I'd been with. His focus was entirely on me. No other man had ever taken the time to explore my body. But Kol...was a different breed altogether. He was a confident man who knew what he wanted and wasn't afraid to take it. At this moment, he aimed to uncover what would make me burn with need.

Yet, despite his gentleness, I couldn't shake off the nervousness that hummed through my veins. It was a testament to how quickly the dynamic between us had shifted from playful teasing to this—him taking complete control over me. My lower lip started to quiver, and I quickly bit down on it.

"Relax," he instructed. "Blindfolding you enhances everything you'll feel in the best of ways."

He wrapped his hand around the back of my neck, pressing his fingers gently against my throat. It was a gesture of dominance, a claim of ownership that sent a thrill coursing through me. His other arm slid under my knees, and he lifted me effortlessly off the floor before lowering me gently back onto the blankets of our makeshift bed. The softness of the fabric against my bare skin and the warmth of the nearby fireplace soothed my nerves.

His hand, the one that had been under my knees, glided up my shin to my knee, pressing down firmly before pulling my leg open. Instinctively, I reacted by snapping my legs together.

"Mm-mm," he growled. "Don't move unless I say so." He moved my leg back, opening me up to him, leaving me exposed and vulnerable.

Then came the rustling sound of him shoving his sweatpants down, the fabric sliding against his skin and hitting the floor with a soft thud. I could picture him standing there, naked and proud, his eyes roaming over my body. Even without my sight, he was larger than life, his presence filling the room. He exuded strength and control. At this moment, I had no doubt he knew exactly what he was doing.

He moved between my knees, carefully pushing my other leg to the side. For a moment, there was nothing but the sound of Christmas music playing softly in the background. The silence told me he was scrutinizing every inch of my body, laid bare before him, and the thought sent a rush of heat flooding through me. A hot flush spread from my chest to my cheeks as my heart rate kicked up.

He moved his hands slowly, tracing the curves of my waist and hips with deliberate precision. His thumbs grazed my skin, dipping into the hollows just above my hip bones, making me shiver. Then his breath was tickling my chest, his lips brushing across my ribcage. He moved down toward my belly, nipping lightly. Each touch was calculated, every press of his lips sending little jolts of heat coursing through me. His grip tightened on my hips, strong and possessive, as my body melted under him, surrendering to his touch.

Then he shifted, and his warm hands came to rest on my thighs. He let out an approving growl. "Now, that's the prettiest present I ever did see."

"Oh, my—"

"Don't speak," he commanded.

I rolled my lips in, fighting the urge to talk. I was a talker, always had been, and he knew it. He knew how hard this was for me, how much I wanted to fill the silence with words. But he also knew that I got off on this, on him being in charge, on him pushing my boundaries. And damn if it didn't send an electric current rushing over my skin and a delicious tingle straight to my clit. It was intoxicating to be the focus of his attention, as though I were truly the center of his universe.

Kol seemed intent on savoring every moment, stretching time until it became a malleable, pliant thing in his hands. His deliberate and precise way of claiming my body would leave an indelible mark on my memory. It was both exciting and a little terrifying, the thought of this confident, possessive pilot taking command of my pleasure.

His fingertips traced the sensitive skin of my inner thigh with a featherlight touch that sent fiery sparks zinging across my nerve endings, causing me to squeeze my legs together involuntarily once more. This time, his rebuke came swiftly, a harsh "No" that acted as both a warning and a reminder of who held the reins.

He was testing me—I knew it—but I didn't dare move, not because I was afraid but because ever since he'd walked up to me at the airport with that ready-to-do-battle scowl, I'd wanted to take him on, to push him to his limits, and see who would end up on top.

Just as quickly as he had breezed in between my legs, he was gone, withdrawing his touch and leaving me wanting. I lay there, practically vibrating with need and frustration, my skin overly sensitive, my pussy throbbing with every beat of my heart, aching for his touch.

And so I waited in silence for him to make the next move. It was a calculated risk, placing my trust in him, but after everything we'd shared today, this was just another step along the path we were now on together. And as uncomfortable as it was to let go, to relinquish control, something deep inside told me it was worth it to see where this journey with Mr. Captain might ultimately lead.

I heard Kol in the kitchen—the pantry door creaking open, followed by the clatter of a drawer being pulled out and shut again. My senses were on high alert, every sound magnified, every nerve ending tingling. Here I was, sprawled out on the floor, legs spread wide, feeling ridiculous. Was he really grabbing a snack? But I didn't move, didn't call out to him. I couldn't.

The vibration of the floor under my back signaled his approach. The rasp of a metal can being tugged open right in front of me made me curious. He was there, looming over me, but I still didn't move or speak.

"How is it, Stinkerbelle," he mused, "that sometimes you submit to me so completely, while at other times you're impossible to tame?"

I didn't reply. He was baiting me, trying to provoke a reaction. But I was too stubborn to relent. I wanted him too much to risk saying something stupid and causing him to walk away for the night. The idea of the yummy ways he might punish me did cross my mind, but I pushed it aside. I needed him—for him to want me when no one else did.

Kol chuckled. *Good*, I thought. I'd pleased him. Now, I just needed to wait for my reward.

It didn't take long. Kol's lips found mine in a soft, sweet kiss. He tasted of pineapple, and I licked the juice from my lips as he moved away. He remained close, crunching on a chunk of pineapple. I swallowed hard, my mouth watering, but I remained unmoving and silent.

The blankets moved, and there was a clunk on the end table as he set down the can. Then, he settled next to me, draping one leg between my thighs. His muscular thigh pressed against my center, sending a jolt of pleasure through me. His hard shaft bulged against my hip, promising more to come. He ran a hand up the side of my leg before moving over the curves of my waist and coming to rest around the swell of my breast. His large hand was just big enough to envelop it.

I couldn't stop the needy whine that escaped me. I arched into his hand, desperate for more.

"You like that, don't you?" Kol murmured. "You like being at my mercy, don't you, Stinkerbelle?"

I gave a small, helpless nod. I did like it. I liked it too much.

His thumb brushed over my nipple, a light, teasing touch that had me gasping. He circled it slowly, gently. I squirmed beneath him, trying to press closer to increase the friction. But he held me in place.

"Not so fast," he chided. "We're doing this my way, remember?"

A whimper of frustration and need escaped me. I wanted him to go faster, to give me more.

His hand moved to my other breast, giving it the same treatment. His touch was slow and deliberate, each brush of his thumb sending tingles of pleasure straight to my core. Wetness pooled between my legs. My body was begging for his touch.

"Kol," I breathed, his name a plea on my lips. "Please…"

He leaned down, brushing his lips against mine. "Please what?" he murmured, his voice a low growl. "Tell me what you want."

I hesitated, heat spreading across my cheeks again. I wasn't used to being so open. But Kol made me want to be. He made me want to bare myself to him, body and soul.

"I want you," I whispered, my voice barely audible. "I want you to touch me. To make me come."

He smiled against my lips. "Good girl," he praised. "That's what I wanted to hear."

Kol's lips found that ever-so-sensitive spot behind my ear, and he trailed kisses down my jaw before claiming my mouth with his. He entwined the fingers of his other hand in my hair, pulling me toward him. While he pressed his lips hard against mine, his tongue explored every crevice with wicked intent. The lingering taste of pineapple made my mouth water as my own juices pooled against his thigh. Of course, he felt it too, and rewarded me by sliding his thigh up and down my core.

Kol kissed me ferociously, as if it would be the last kiss he would ever experience. Our tongues tangled in a teasing battle. Letting my submissive role slip, I captured his tongue with my lips and sucked on it in a methodical rhythm that made his cock jerk next to my hip. With a grunt, he pulled back, capturing my lower lip between his teeth and slowly dragging them back as I'd done to him earlier—a pleasurable payback.

Kol kissed my cheek and then maneuvered around the bow tied under my chin, nipping and licking his way across my collarbone and down my breast, finally taking my nipple with his teeth. He tugged on it, which fired off an inferno of need that settled low in my belly. I didn't know if it was from the heat of the fireplace or the heat of his body, but suddenly I was burning with desire.

Oh, how I wanted him to give me friction where I craved him most, but I knew better than to demand it. His need for control radiated from every inch of his being, and after everything he'd done for me today, I wanted to please him more than I wanted to be satisfied.

I realized then that my fingers were so tightly entwined in the blankets that they ached. I desperately wanted to touch him, but he'd not given me permission, so I held onto the blankets for dear life as his mouth worked wonders on my taut, aching breasts.

Then, with no warning, his thigh moved away from my center and to my side, leaving me cold and still unsatisfied. His hand wandered over every contour and curve of my body and then ventured lower, gliding over my mound and coming to rest there. He held still for a moment, his hand cupping me as if he were claiming me. Then his middle finger dipped into my wet center before moving up to the little bundle of nerves that was begging for his attention. Taking his time, he caressed and flicked my clit, making my belly coil tight with tension. My walls clenched with need. Leisurely, he pushed one finger, then two, inside of me, eliciting a whimper.

"Mmm, baby, how fucking wet your needy little pussy is for me."

His movement was slow and easy at first, but as I arched toward each of his strokes, his rhythm became more fierce, sending wave after wave of pleasure through me. Just when I was on the brink of climaxing, he cruelly withdrew his fingers, not allowing me to come.

I cried out in frustration, "Please don't stop!" A chuckle rang out from deep within his chest.

I lay there, panting, my body aching and unfulfilled.

He moved away from me, the warmth of his body replaced with a cool chill from the air. The snowstorm still raged outside, the wind whistling through the night, making the shutters rattle as a blizzard of emotions swirled within me.

Kol Vinter

Chapter Fourteen

12/23 late night

I sat still and quiet next to Noelle, my gaze devouring the sight of her body lying bare before me, her legs spread open, an offering that was both a challenge and an invitation. God, she was magnificent, a wildfire against the iciness of my soul. She was feisty and playful even now, after her life had been turned upside down. This woman was all flame and fury, a tempest that could level everything in her path.

And here she was, a feast for my senses, her fiery spirit subdued for the moment, waiting for me. I'd always preferred women who were more like me—reserved, cool, and collected. But Noelle, a whirlwind of emotions and desires, had burrowed under my skin, challenging my preconceived notions of what I wanted, what I needed.

Noelle deserved a man who would put her needs first and lose himself in all she had to offer—not just in the moment, but forever. She needed a man who didn't just want to use her to fuck, but someone who would love and protect her, support all her dreams. And dammit, I wanted to be that man. Love at first sight was a ridiculous notion, but somehow this smart-mouthed woman had affected me in ways I'd never imagined.

Her frustrated whine pulled me from my thoughts, her body squirming with need as she struggled to obey my command to remain still. I'd edged her way beyond what I thought she would ever tolerate, and yet she hadn't asked me to stop. She was a paradox—a woman who could light up a room with her presence but was still willing to submit to my will.

I wanted to taste every inch of her, to map her body with my tongue and commit her to memory. She was unlike anyone I'd ever known. She was so fucking hot, but she didn't know it. Blindfolding her had allowed me to really see her, scrutinize her even. It was a level of trust I hadn't expected from someone as headstrong as Noelle, especially considering what she'd just been through with her ex.

As I sat there making her wait a moment longer, I realized I would never allow another man to have this—to witness her like this. The possessive instinct that surged within me was as surprising as it was undeniable. Tonight I was staking my claim, and whether or not she realized it, Noelle was mine.

My gaze wandered over her body again, and I wondered, half-amused, how such a petite girl could have such a big, round ass. It was firm, as though she'd done a million squats over the years. Maybe that came from growing up riding horses. I grinned, imagining the countless hours she must have spent in the saddle, her body becoming toned and strong from the demanding physicality of riding.

She'd mentioned her equestrian background in passing, speaking of it with a certain hint of fondness and sorrow. It made me curious about her, this girl who I imagined had once sat fearlessly atop a horse that cantered through challenging courses. What had her life been like? Saratoga, a community with a long history tied to horses, seemed like a place she would love to call home. Yet, she was hesitant to return to the life she'd once known here. I wanted to understand her reluctance and uncover the pieces that made her who she was. But that had to wait. For now, I was captivated by the present—by the woman before me. Tonight I was going to get to know everything about my little elf's magical body.

Noelle was doing her best to please me, even though it was so clearly against her nature to be submissive. I found it amusing how hard she was working to stay still. Her fingers looked like they were about to shred the blankets they were entwined in. There was a wildness, an unpredictability about her that kept me intrigued, that made me want to tame her—not fully, but enough to bring her the release she so desperately craved.

She was eight years younger than me, and even though she could be a smart aleck, there was also a certain maturity about her, a depth of experience most women her age didn't have. This was a trait we shared—I'd grown up a lot during my time in the Army—the result of facing life's harsh realities and coming out stronger on the other side.

Watching her squirm and frantically grip the blankets made me smile. The blindfold I had fashioned from the ribbon was serving its purpose well, keeping her anchored in the moment, heightening her other senses as she navigated the darkness I had imposed upon her. I enjoyed keeping her on edge, making her wonder about my next move, my next touch. She had practically begged me for a complete distraction, a way to escape the turmoil of her thoughts, and I was all too willing to provide it.

Tying the ribbon around her neck had been a calculated risk, a way to elicit a sense of fear to keep her off-balance and focused on me and the sensations I was eliciting from her body. Her calm acceptance of it made me wonder just how far I could push her.

Noelle huffed out an impatient breath. I could sense her frustration, her need for release, and it only fueled my desire to keep edging her until she was teetering on the brink. I wanted her to shatter into a million pieces, to forget everything except the pleasure I could give her.

I had to taste her. Her glistening pussy was aching for my attention. I moved between her legs and placed a hand on her calf. She jumped and let out a little yelp. Her mind must have been a million miles away for her not to have heard or felt me kneel before her.

A low, throaty rumble echoed in my chest. "Patience, Elle. Good things come to those who wait," I growled.

I stretched my legs out behind me, thoroughly enjoying the opportunity to study her without her watching me.

Lightly I trailed my fingers over her leg, prompting goose bumps to surface on her skin. She was fighting a smile and biting down hard on her lip, her body shaking with silent laughter. I loved how sensitive she was.

Sliding my hands under her thighs, I shoved them apart, then shifted so I could rest my forearms on her thighs, opening her further up to me. I peppered the insides of her thighs with soft kisses before darting my tongue out and flicking her clit. She jerked, gasping.

Enveloping her in the warmth of my mouth, I feasted.

Her moans were music to my ears, urging me on as I sucked and licked her sensitive nub. The tangy sweetness of her juices made my mouth water, and I savored the exquisite flavor. "God, you're so wet for me," I praised before slipping my tongue deep within her channel.

Her walls clenched as she purred, "Yes, sirrr." Beneath her hands, the blanket started to rip. She was desperate to touch me.

Pulling my mouth away, I chuckled. "It's okay to touch me," I said before returning to nibble on the tight bundle of nerves at her apex.

In a flash, she tangled her fingers in my hair, drawing me tighter to her. Two of my fingers slid into her wetness, curling in search of her most sensitive spot while I continued to tease her clit. Her hips bucked, her breathing becoming ragged as my fingers brushed against that magic button deep inside her. The combination had her writhing beneath me, her body seeking the release that I held just out of reach.

Instead of allowing her to plunge over that edge, I withdrew my fingers and gave her a quick kiss on the top of her mound. She let out a needy little whimper, followed by a growl. She understood the game I was playing full well.

Immediately, her hand moved to her pussy. I froze. Would she seize control of giving herself the release she sought? Or would she be a good girl and allow me to give her what she needed? My fingers wrapped around her hip, digging into her flesh. It was a warning she heeded. She slapped her hand to the floor with a frustrated "Ugh!" trembling with the effort it took to restrain herself.

I smiled at her frustration. It was a beautiful thing, watching her walk the fine line between control and breaking. She was a fighter, my little elf, but in this moment, she was mine to please, mine to command. And I would take my time until she was begging for release. It was intoxicating, and I wanted more. I wanted to explore every inch of her, to learn what made her tick, what made her moan. I wanted to push her to the edge and then pull her back, only to do it all over again. I wanted to hear her scream my name.

I wanted to own her, body and soul. Only then would I allow her to fall apart in my arms.

I kissed my way up her body to the space between the swells of her breasts, capturing one of her nipples with my fingers and the other with my mouth, worshiping them reverently. Savoring the moment, I licked and sucked, circling my tongue around the taut peak before gently biting down, drawing a gasp from her. Noelle arched into my touch, her body begging for more. I obliged, increasing the pressure, teasing her with the edge of my teeth before soothing the sting with my tongue. Her breath hitched, and she clutched my shoulders, holding me in place as I lavished attention on each breast.

Her reactions were intoxicating, each moan and whimper spurring me on. Her heart raced under my touch. Her nipples were hard and rosy, and I couldn't get enough of them. I licked, sucked, and bit with a tenderness that belied the fierce desire burning within me. Her body thrashed beneath me, her hips bucking in a silent plea for more.

Somehow, this woman was once again on the verge of coming. Pausing, I pushed up onto my elbows and watched as she squinched up her face and grit her teeth in frustration. Her body was a live wire, ready to spark at the slightest touch. It was a heady feeling, knowing I had that kind of power over her.

Now, I wasn't only pushing her to the edge, I was pushing myself. Fuck, there were so many ways I wanted to get to know her body. I had to get control of myself. I sat back on my heels, inhaling deeply and planning my path forward. If only I could keep it together long enough, we'd both have a chance to explode.

A look of disappointment overtook Noelle's face. She was so close yet so far from the release she craved.

Once I was in control of my own needs, I leaned over her and pulled her knees up, spreading them wide and opening her completely to me. "God, how I want your tight pussy wrapped around my cock." I ran the head of it over her clit, watching her body tense in anticipation. The way she gasped as I pressed against her entrance sent a surge of satisfaction through me.

Slowly, I pushed in, sighing at the delicious way she stretched around me as I sank deeper, inch by inch. Her soft whimpers lit me up, but it was her mouth dropping open in a breathy cry that really did it for me—wide, desperate, and full of need. I didn't stop until I was buried to the hilt, my entire weight pressing down on her.

The sensual gratification of being inside her, that tight heat wrapping around me, was almost my undoing. I clenched my teeth, reveling in the way her body reacted to me as I began to thrust. Each stroke was powerful, and I hit that perfect spot inside her with each movement. Her nails dug into the skin of my arms, but the pain only fueled me more.

There was no tenderness now, no hesitation—just raw, unfiltered pleasure. It was the kind of sex that stripped everything down to pure sensation, the kind that blocked out thought until all that was left was the moment, the storm of passion. "You feel so good, so fucking tight," I growled.

Noelle dug her heels into the floor and started meeting me stroke for stroke. She fisted my hair and dragged me down to her in a demanding kiss, her tongue sweeping into my mouth as she sought to take control.

For a moment, I let her, and our tongues tangled in a sensual battle. But then I yanked away. "No, my little elf. I'm not yours to control."

With that, I pulled out. It was one of the hardest things I'd ever done. I was so close, my balls were aching. But I needed her to understand who was in charge. I needed her to submit to me completely. And I was willing to wait, to push us both until we were ready to ignite together.

I sat back on my heels once more, my chest heaving as I struggled to regain my composure. She was so fucking beautiful. And in that moment, I knew I was in deep—deeper than I had ever been before.

Noelle's voice sliced through the fog of lust in my head, her words sharp and demanding.

"For Christ's sake, make me come already, Kol. I'm done with your fucking games. If you don't give me what I need, and I mean right now, I'm going to lose my ever-loving mind!" Her voice resonated with frustration and longing, her body tense with exasperation, and for a moment, I hesitated—a split-second of indecision before instinct took over.

Before she could say any more, I scooped her up and flipped her over onto my knee. My palm connected with her flesh with a sharp crack that echoed off the walls. She yelped.

"Let me go, you big oaf! You're all show and no go," she spat, writhing in my lap. For that, I smacked her three more times. My hand stung from the impact.

Though her struggles were futile, she didn't stop trying to break free. "You've got a sassy mouth that deserves a spanking and an ass that begs for it," I threatened in a low rumble that betrayed the depth of my arousal.

She jerked against my splayed-out hand that was holding her in place. This earned her a couple more smacks. As I held her, I could feel the fight draining out of her, replaced by a different kind of tension.

"It's not about what you want," I said. "It's about learning to trust someone to give you what you need." With that, she finally surrendered beneath my hand, and fuck, it was exhilarating. Trust was a two-way street, and in that moment, I was asking for a lot—more than I had any right to ask for. Her submission meant everything to me.

I lowered my knee, allowing her to slide off and onto the floor. Without giving her a chance to catch her breath, I gripped her hips and maneuvered her in front of me. Then, using my knee, I knocked her thighs apart and shoved them forward, leaving her ass in the air. I ran my hand up her spine, pressing her shoulders down, and she responded by arching her back and twisting her fingers in the blankets beneath us.

In one fell swoop, I thrust my throbbing cock into her tight little pussy. I slowly inhaled, trying to regain some semblance of control, the ecstasy of being inside her almost too much to bear. I took a moment to explore her body, my hands roaming over her curves, teasing her nipples.

She was perfect—a fiery, passionate woman who challenged me at every turn. I kissed her shoulder, nipping at her skin as I moved along her neck. Then, reaching around, I untied the bow under her chin, leaving the half-knot in place as a reminder of the possibilities that lay ahead.

"Relax. Trust me, I'm here to make you forget your name, remember?" I teased. The muscles of her back relaxed just enough to let me know that her interest was piqued.

With the ribbon ends still in my hand, I began to move inside her, setting a slow, deliberate pace. Immediately, she responded to me, her body arching to meet each thrust. My free hand glided over her curves and found the bundle of nerves at the apex of her thighs, my fingers tracing circles in time with the rhythm of my cock. A satisfied, soft sigh escaped her lips as she gave herself over to the sensation. This was definitely working for her. Her walls pulsed around my shaft.

"Oh, yes," she whined, her voice trembling. She was close— so close—and the knowledge that I was the one taking her there filled me with satisfaction. But I wasn't ready to let her fall over the edge just yet.

I raised myself up, gripping her hips as I increased the pace, my own need for release growing with each stroke. Tension coiled inside me, a tight spring that was moments away from snapping. It was time to test her limits, to push her to the brink and see if she would trust me enough to follow me over.

Taking one end of the ribbon in each hand, I gently tightened it around her throat. Her response was immediate, her body tensing.

"Touch yourself, and when I tell you to come...you will."

She hesitated for only a moment before her hand moved to where we were joined, and she began working her clit.

"Yes, baby. That's it. That's my good girl," I praised. My words seemed to spur her on.

The tension in my lower back began to zing. I pulled against the ribbons like sexy reins. I was aware the instant she could no longer breathe, which started an internal clock ticking in my mind. She didn't panic. She was brave, this one. The longer it went on, the tighter her pussy clenched down on my cock and the more frantically her fingers moved. My balls drew up—my climax knocking on the door. She was there too.

Releasing the ribbons, I demanded, "Come, Noelle." And she did.

After heaving in a breath of air, she cried out my name. The sound was a sweet melody that triggered my own release. Wave after wave of pleasure crashed over me, my body shuddering as I emptied myself inside her. For several long moments, we remained locked together, our bodies moving in sync as we rode out the aftershocks of our shared climax.

Finally, when the intensity of the moment had passed, I wrapped my arm around her and she collapsed into my hold as I withdrew. I lowered us both to the floor and pulled her against me. She curled up tight to me, her body trembling slightly as the adrenaline wore off. I reached up and untied the ribbon, letting it fall away as I pressed a tender kiss to her temple.

She turned her face to me, blinking as her eyes adjusted to the light. "That was amazing, Mr. Captain," she whispered. The firelight cast a warm golden glow over her glistening skin, making her look like a goddess—my perfect goddess.

Her hand came up and gently cupped my cheek, her thumb brushing across my skin in a soft, soothing motion. She drew me in for a chaste kiss—a sweet, simple gesture that held more meaning than any words ever could. That moment sealed my fate. Noelle had claimed a piece of my soul, and I belonged to her—irrevocably, undeniably, for now and always.

I pulled the thick quilt over us, tucking it around her shoulders as she snuggled into me. Her eyes were already fluttering closed, and she let out a soft sigh, relaxing into me. Her heartbeat slowed, matching the steady rhythm of my own. The storm outside raged on, but inside we were wrapped up together in the peaceful afterglow of our passion. Tenderly, I kissed the top of her head, inhaling the sweet scent of her hair. She murmured something incoherent, a small smile playing on her lips as she drifted off to sleep.

Contentment washed over me—something I hadn't experienced in a long time. I let my eyes close and allowed her soft breaths to lull me into a peaceful sleep.

Chapter Fifteen

12/24 morning

I awoke cocooned in warmth, gradually realizing my body was curled around a solid form... Oh my God, a man! And not just any man, *Mr. Captain*. I froze, my eyes flying open as I tried to place where I was; a few too many glasses of wine muddled my mind. A smirk tugged at my lips. Who needed a heater when you had a human furnace in bed with you? I hadn't slept that soundly in years, and it was all thanks to the man next to me. My nose was practically frozen—the fire was barely giving off any heat now—but my body was toasty warm under the blanket.

The room was dim, lit by the dying embers in the fireplace and the soft morning light filtering in through the blinds. Everything had an almost surreal quality to it—a stillness I wanted to hold onto before my world kicked back into motion.

I was caught in the haze between dreaming and waking, reluctant to fully surface. Then reality hit—hard. I was naked, wrapped around Kol like a koala clinging to a big, burly tree. Not wanting to wake him, but too curious to resist, I lifted the quilt to sneak a peek. Good Lord, the man was a masterpiece. My eyes studied the lines of his body. He was a Greek statue come to life, all sharp angles and smooth planes. I allowed myself a moment of shameless appreciation, my gaze tracing the tattoos on his chest and arms and lingering on the defined ridges of his abs. His chest rose and fell in a steady rhythm, the tantalizing *V-cut* of his hips pointing the way to his impressive morning wood.

There, in all its glory, was his morning erection, standing at attention like a soldier ready for duty. I chuckled softly. No wonder I was sore in places I hadn't even known could ache. Kol was... Well-endowed would be an understatement. He was fine as fuck, and I felt a twinge of insecurity. Here I was, probably looking like something the cat dragged in, with my hair a wild, tangled mess after he'd rocked my world. God only knew what my face looked like. He'd put me through the wringer—or perhaps more accurately, I'd launched myself into a bottle of wine, and my inhibitions had flown right out the window. In return, he'd edged me halfway to death, blindfolded, no less.

We'd drunk a lot last night, and I remembered Kol telling me about how he was some sort of wine expert—I couldn't remember what word he'd used for it though. My mind sputtered through bits of last night's haze. It had been intensely frustrating, but I'd had the best sex of my life. The man had pushed me outside of my comfort zone, and it had been well worth it. I would never be able to look at his lips again without a molten river of fire pooling between my thighs.

No man had never made love to me like that—as if he were savoring every part of me. It was something a woman could only dream of.

I knew he didn't love me; we'd just met. But the way he'd taken his time...touched me possessively...it was like he owned me, and I'd never imagined I'd love surrendering so much.

How could a man like Kol be interested in someone like me, someone whose life was so discombobulated? How had no one scooped him up and married him yet? How was he still available? He was every woman's ideal man—strong yet gentle, dominant yet considerate. I had so many questions.

My reveries slowly dissipated as the real world began to creep in. Oh shit, the memory of how I'd laid there sprawled out in front of him without a modicum of modesty flashed back. A tidal wave of embarrassment crashed over me, washing away the euphoria from the night before. I'd just had sex with a complete stranger—a man I'd known for less than twenty-four hours! Granted, he was the most attractive man I'd ever met, and we had spent hours stuck together because of the snowstorm, but that was no excuse. My mind reeled. Had I really been that desperate? I was the cringeworthy cliché of every romance novel ever written: Some gorgeous man shows up out of nowhere, saves you from your troubles—and then *bang*! He's taking advantage of your vulnerability while you're too tipsy to resist. Seriously, what had I been thinking?

I mentally smacked myself, feeling like the world's biggest sleazebag. I'd let him have his way with me! I mean, sure, he was a walking, talking fantasy, but that didn't give me the right to jump him like some sort of sex-starved animal. My cheeks flushed as memories filtered through my mind like an old film reel. Each frame replayed a piece of what we'd done: the wine, the fire, the heated kisses, his commanding hands exploring my body, my own uninhibited responses, and the mind-blowing sex. Oh God, the best sex. My body ached in all the right places, a testament to just how thorough Kol had been. I was amazingly satisfied and utterly mortified all at once. What had I done?

My mind raced as I silently accused him of taking advantage of me. He'd plied me with wine, for heaven's sake! Okay, so I'd willingly partaken. But still—he could've at least tried to resist my charms. The man was a walking temptation, and now, here I was running down Guilt Trip Lane. Mr. Wine Connoisseur had to have known how it would affect me! There was no other explanation for how I'd lost all sense of reason and handed him the reins to take control of me.

Ready to get out of my own head and on with the day, I pulled away from Kol's sleeping form, a chill creeping over my skin. I grabbed the blanket and wrapped it around myself, leaving him exposed to the cool morning air. It served him right for being so damn irresistible.

Despite my inner turmoil, though, I couldn't deny the satisfaction that still hummed through my veins. I'd been thoroughly and completely ravished, and a part of me—a very big part—wanted to do it all over again.

But first, I needed to regain some semblance of dignity. I extended my leg and gave him a gentle nudge with my toe. "Hey," I said, trying to sound stern, "wake up."

Kol stirred, and his eyes opened slowly, revealing those rich chocolate depths laced with glimmers of gold that were impossible to look away from. He blinked sleepily at me, a slow, lazy smile spreading across his face. "Good morning, beautiful," he said, his voice husky with sleep.

I scowled at him, trying to ignore how utterly fuckable he looked with his hair all mussed and a smirk on his face that sent a zing straight between my legs.

"Don't you *good morning* me," I retorted. "You look way too cute and innocent for someone who just ravaged a perfect stranger."

He chuckled as he scrutinized me. "After last night, you know there's nothing innocent about me." His gaze drifted down to his very hard dick. "And I'm ready to fuck you again, if you're up for it." He reached out, trying to pull me down to him.

I dodged his grasp, my heart pounding. "Oh no, you don't," I said, backing away. "You took advantage of me, Mr. Captain. You got me drunk and had your wicked way with me."

He arched a brow and then frowned. "Is that how you remember it? Because I distinctly recall *you* being the aggressor."

I gasped, feigning outrage and wrapping the blanket tighter around myself. "Me? An aggressor? Please, you plied me with wine and used your worldly charm to seduce me. I was vulnerable, and you took advantage."

He sat up, scooting back to lean against the edge of the sofa. "You practically threw yourself at me, Noelle. And I was more than happy to catch you."

"I was merely being friendly," I lied. "You're the one who turned it into an...an...aerial maneuver."

Kol burst out laughing. "An aerial maneuver? That's a new one. Okay, Top Gun, should I call you Maverick?"

I rolled my eyes and shook my head. "You're impossible. I can't believe I let you talk me into—"

"Into what?" he growled as he moved closer to me, reaching for my face. "Noelle, you were the one straddling my lap, your hot pussy dripping for me. I was just the lucky bastard who got to fuck you senseless. But if I'm a regret—"

Preventing him from completing that thought, I pressed my finger against his lips. "Maybe sometimes a girl wants to be taken advantage of," I whispered, dropping my chin and blinking up at him through my lashes.

Kol's hand slipped to the back of my neck, his fingers tangling in my hair. He pulled me toward him, forcing me to look him straight in those golden-brown eyes. "I would never take advantage of a woman," he said without blinking. "But I'd fuck the attitude right out of her."

My breath hitched, and a throb of desire shot between my legs. I should be outraged, should pull away and assert my independence, but all I could think about was how much I wanted him to follow through on his threat. God, this man was going to be the death of me. I opened my mouth to respond, but he cut me off, pulling me into a fierce kiss. I melted into him, all thoughts of protest forgotten as his tongue slid against mine, igniting a fire.

When he finally pulled away, I was breathless and dizzy with need. He smirked, his grip on my hair tightening just enough to make my heart race faster. "Now, are you going to keep arguing, or are you going to let me fuck you again?"

I bit my lip, a smile tugging at the corners of my mouth. "Well, when you put it that way..."

Letting the blanket fall around my waist, I took advantage of Kol's momentary distraction and launched myself at him, tackling him back onto the blankets. He grunted in surprise, his arms automatically wrapping around me as he tried to regain control. But I was quicker, straddling his waist as I pinned his hands above his head.

"What's the matter, Mr. Captain?" I teased, leaning down to nip at his bottom lip. "Can't handle a little turbulence?"

"I can handle anything you throw at me, Stinkerbelle," he grunted. He grabbed my forearms. In a swift motion, he flipped us over, pinning me beneath him. I squealed, trying to buck him off, but the man was a solid wall of muscle.

We tussled and tangled, sliding and bumping against each other as we each tried to gain the upper hand. He was stronger than me, but I was faster, and I used my smaller size to my advantage. As we wrestled, our laughter filled the room. His hands were everywhere—tickling, teasing, pinning me down. I retaliated by squirming and wriggling—trying every trick I knew to end up on top. But Kol was a formidable opponent—his movements swift and precise as befitted a man with military training. I'd never stood a chance against him.

He caught my wrists, pinning them above my head with one hand. His other hand trailed down my side, and he dug his fingers into my ribs, finding every ticklish spot. I thrashed and giggled, trying to free myself, but he held firm, his body pressing me into the pallet of blankets beneath us.

"Say uncle," he commanded in a low rumble.

"Never," I said between laughs, trying to knee him in the side. He dodged my attempt, sliding his hips between my legs and pressing his cock against my core. I sucked in a breath, heat flooding through me at the contact.

He leaned down, brushing his lips against mine in a teasing kiss. "Liar," he whispered.

His laughter faded, replaced by a hungry gaze. Then, with a pounce, he captured my lips in a savage kiss. My body arched up to meet his, my struggle forgotten as desire took over.

His hard shaft slid up and down along my core, giving me the delicious friction I craved. I moaned into his mouth, my hips moving in sync with his. The head of his cock rubbed against my clit with each slow thrust, and my aching need to be filled grew.

The fire's heat was long gone, but our bodies were blazing. Our breaths came out in visible clouds, hot and ragged in the chilly air. Kol released my wrists and trailed his fingers down my body, stopping at my breast to cup it. As his thumb circled my nipple, I moaned, the sensation sending a jolt of pleasure straight to my clit.

Noelle Nichols

Chapter Sixteen

12/24 morning

I shivered, the cold seeping into my bones now that the heat of our passion had faded. "This room is freezing," Kol said, rubbing my arm. He pushed up slightly on his elbows.

"Noo, I don't want you to leave," I whined. "I love the way you fill me, the way you keep me warm."

He gave me a tender, sweet smile that made my heart ache. "I'm not going anywhere, Noelle," he promised. "But we do need to get going, build up the fire, find out what's happened now that the snowstorm has passed, and eat something."

As if on cue, his stomach growled loudly, a reminder that we'd worked up quite an appetite. I laughed.

He stamped a kiss on my forehead before pulling out of me. "I'm going to rekindle the fire, and then we can see what we can scrounge up for breakfast."

Unabashedly I stared at him as he moved to stand next to me, his muscles flexing and contracting with each movement. This man was a sight to behold, and I marveled at how far we'd come in such a short amount of time. We'd gone from strangers to lovers, and although it was too soon to tell where this would lead, I knew one thing for certain—I was falling for my captain, and I was falling hard.

The warmth of his body lingered on my skin as I sat up and spotted his open suitcase behind me on the sofa. I reached for the T-shirt lying on top and pulled it on. It was way too big, but the soft fabric and the scent of him made it perfect.

Kol's stomach growled again, louder this time.

"Hungry much?" I teased.

He raised a brow, smirking in that way that drove me insane. "Can't help it. All that cardio worked up an appetite," he said, pulling on a pair of sweatpants and a crewneck sweatshirt.

"Cardio? Is that what you're calling it now?" I shot back. I rose to my feet, wincing when my ankle protested at the sudden movement. His brows tightened, but I waved off his concerned look. "I'm fine. It's just a little tender."

He narrowed his eyes slightly. "You're not fine if you're in pain...well, that is, except for the kind only I can deliver." He winked, raking his gaze up and down my body.

Trying to steer the conversation back to our current circumstances, I said, "The power's still out."

"How long do you think it'll take before it's restored?" he asked.

I shrugged. "Hard to say, but Saratogians are experts at dealing with snow. They get buried every year and somehow manage to dig out quickly. So, probably not too much longer."

I took a couple of cautious steps toward the kitchen.

Kol tilted his head slightly, the corners of his mouth tightening as he studied me. "Sit down," he commanded, wrapping his arm around my waist and guiding me to sit in the armchair by the sofa. "I don't want you to overdo it." He leaned down and gave me a quick kiss before pulling away. "I'll be right back."

He disappeared upstairs. I spotted his bomber jacket hanging on the back of the chair and slipped it on. The smell of leather and Kol wrapping around me was divine. The jacket was way too big and a lot heavier than I'd expected, but it was exactly what I needed to stay warm.

A few minutes later, Kol returned with a compression bandage and some thick fuzzy socks. His eyes roamed over me, slow and possessive, as he took in the sight of me in his jacket. "You look incredibly sexy in that," he growled, leaning down and cupping my cheek, brushing his thumb over my lower lip. "But let's take care of that ankle. I rummaged around one of the bathrooms and found this. It should give your ankle the support it needs."

He kneeled before me and wrapped the bandage around my ankle gently. It was a sweet, caring gesture. "Thank you," I said as butterflies fluttered in my tummy. There was more to this man than met the eye.

He handed me the socks, and I propped my foot up on the edge of the seat, inadvertently flashing him. In response, he grunted and leaned in just a bit. My knee seemed to have a will of its own as it fell open. He yanked my foot down, pressing my knees together. I couldn't help but giggle at his annoyance.

"That will have to wait for now," he ordered.

With that, he stood and moved to the fireplace, placing some wood on the remaining embers. He added a little more kindling and poked at it, making it spark.

I slipped the socks on and headed for the kitchen but then decided to take a quick detour to the quaint little powder room just off the hallway, quickly taking care of my business and ignoring my disheveled reflection in the mirror. The bandage's support was just what my ankle needed—I could walk without any pain now, ready for the rest of the day.

"Come on, let's fix something to eat. The fire will be fine!" I shouted over my shoulder as I entered the kitchen. "You're not the only one who's hungry."

When he joined me, we searched through the freezer and pantry, finding a bag of frozen blueberries and a box of pancake mix. Kol grabbed a pan from the cabinet and set it on the gas stove. The blue flame flickered right to life when he turned the knob—thank God for appliances that didn't rely on electricity.

I mixed up the batter, adding water since we had no milk. Kol stood behind me, his arms caging me in as he watched. "You're doing it wrong," he teased, his breath warm on my neck.

I elbowed him playfully. "Oh, really? And I suppose you're the pancake expert?"

He chuckled, taking the bowl from me. "As a matter of fact, I am."

Reaching for one of the eggs, he cracked it into the bowl. Taking the spoon, he barely mixed the ingredients. "Now we need to let the batter rest while I warm up the little bag of blueberries. I used to make pancakes for my sisters all the time."

He shoved the bag halfway into his pants, covering it with his shirt.

"Yikes, that's one way to do it," I said with a laugh.

While we waited, he put the teakettle on to heat. Once the water came to a boil, he teased, "There goes Stinkerbelle." He laughed at his own joke as I glared at him. He then filled a coffee filter with grounds, tied it closed with roasting string, and added it to the water to steep. He called it cowboy coffee. I didn't care what he called it; I was desperate for some caffeine and a couple of headache tablets after all the wine we'd drunk. After a while, he proclaimed that the berries were thawed and the batter rested.

He lightly buttered the hot skillet before pouring in some batter and sprinkling a handful of berries on top.

I leaned against the counter, watching him. "So, you're a man of many talents, huh?"

He flipped the pancake with a flourish. "You have no idea."

As the pancakes cooked, Kol grabbed his phone to put on some Christmas music, and soon the festive tunes filled the kitchen. He sang along, his voice surprisingly good. I laughed, joining in as he made a stack of blueberry pancakes. It felt...domestic. Comfortable. Like we'd done this a thousand times before.

Midway through the second song, Kol pulled me into a dance, wrapping his arms around my waist. He leaned in close, his breath warm against my ear, whispering a string of dirty sweet nothings that made my cheeks flush with embarrassment and excitement. Each naughty promise he made sent a thrill through me. His words were a tantalizing preview of what I hoped was to come. Kol could make even the simplest things seem electric, and here in this freezing house, with the aroma of fresh pancakes wafting through the air and his arms locked around me, he made me feel like the only woman in the world.

After a few minutes, he spun me around and let go. Then he poured us each a steaming-hot cup of coffee, and we sat down to eat, the stack of pancakes piled on a plate between us. We drizzled syrup over them and dug in.

Eagerly I took a bite of the pancake, the blueberries bursting in my mouth, and sighed in pleasure. "So, what's your plan for the day?" I tried to keep my tone casual, but my heart was pounding in my chest as I waited for his response. I didn't want him to leave, but I also didn't want to seem desperate. Despite the coziness and the fabulous sex we'd had, I was still plagued by something he'd said last night.

His words replayed in my mind: "*I'll help you in the morning with whatever you need to get sorted before I get out of here.*"

Kol looked up from his plate, his mouth twisting into a devilish grin. "Well, I was thinking about making a quick exit. You know, before you start singing Christmas songs again."

I rolled my eyes, fighting a smile. "Ha ha, very funny. But seriously, are you taking off after breakfast? You seemed pretty eager to *get out of here* last night."

He leaned back in his chair. "Well, I should be heading out soon. But if some blondie elf needed me to stay, I suppose I could make that happen."

My stomach fluttered, but I tried to play it cool. "I'm sure you have Christmas plans with your family. Big meal, presents, all that jazz."

Kol's expression softened, and he shook his head. "Actually, I don't have any plans this year. As a new and very junior captain, I was scheduled to work a three-day trip over Christmas, but thanks to a certain snowstorm, my entire trip was canceled."

This news sparked a little hope that he'd stay with me. I hated Christmas Eve and really didn't want to spend it alone, here, of all places. "Oh, so you're saying you're free for the holidays?"

He shrugged, pinching his lips together, fighting a grin. "Yes, but if you don't want me here, I can take off. My Bronco could probably handle the snow apocalypse."

I snorted, trying to hide my eagerness for him to stay. "Oh, sure, because driving through two feet of snow is totally sane. Your Bronco might be tough, but it's no match for a Saratoga snowstorm. But then again, if Holly is right, your big red sleigh probably could fly you out of here. I'm sure Mr. Claus needs lots of help tonight."

His eyes crinkled at the corners as he studied me. "Is that a challenge, Noelle?"

"Maybe it is. But seriously, you're welcome to stay. I mean, if you want to. You really shouldn't drive in this kind of snow and ice. Besides, I'm sure there are ways we can stay warm and keep ourselves entertained without the power on."

"Well, there's always more of what we did last night," he said, giving me a sideways glance. "I mean, it was quite effective at keeping us warm."

Heat rose to my cheeks. "Yeah, but we can't spend all day doing that...can we?"

"Oh, you'd be surprised how creative I can get when it comes to staying warm."

"Is that so?" I said, giving him a mock-serious look. "I'll have to hold you to that then."

"I might just enjoy spending more time with you," he said, running his fingers across his lips and nodding.

"Well, in that case, I have a proposition for you."

He raised his chin, squinting in curiosity. "Oh, really? And what might that be?"

I leaned forward, toying with a bite of pancake on my plate. "I propose we adventure out into the snow apocalypse and walk into town. See if anyone else is out and about. It is Christmas Eve, after all."

He considered this for a moment. Then he nodded, a slow smile spreading across his face. "All right, Stinkerbelle. Not exactly what I had in mind, but I'll play along. You pick what we do during the daylight hours, and I'll pick what we do once night falls. Is that a deal?"

I bit my lip, excited at the thought of spending more time with him. "Deal."

"Good. But don't say I took advantage of you when the sun goes down."

Anticipation raced through me. "I'm sure you're not that demanding and we'll get a little sleep."

He chuckled, shaking his head. "No, not demanding at all. But I warn you, I may ruin you for any future men...and as for sleep, I'm not making you any promises."

He didn't know it, but he had already ruined me for other men. No man I'd ever been with had come close to making my body light up like he had. He was better than any fantasy, bringing an edge of danger with him into the bed. The mere thought of it had me growing wet. I wasn't a naturally submissive person, but if it meant him introducing me to a new world of possibilities, I was all in.

"Ruin me, hmm," I said. "That's some bravado you have there."

He reached over and took my hand, glancing down at my plate... Well, this was embarrassing. The bite of pancake I'd been spinning around on my plate was now only a small pile of purple mush. I set my fork down and took a deep breath.

That earned me another of his deep belly laughs. "Let's go see what Saratoga has to offer on Christmas Eve." He beamed excitedly at me.

I nodded, cutting off another bite from the unharmed pancakes on my plate, not able to look up at him just yet.

As we finished our breakfast, contentment washed over me. Despite the power outage, despite the snowstorm, despite everything, I was happy. Happy to be here, spending Christmas Eve with Kol.

Chapter Seventeen

12/24 afternoon

Noelle's gaze drifted around the old kitchen, and she frowned slightly. "I've got to have a shower. I mean, after traveling and all the...um, sexy time, I just have to get clean. I don't even care how cold it is. Professional athletes take ice baths all the time and survive, right?!" she declared, her nose scrunching up in an adorable way that made me want to kiss her again.

"Mmm, I like the *just-fucked* look on you. Means I did my job well and you enjoyed yourself."

"Oh my Lord, only you would think that me looking like a troll earned you fuckery points. All the same, I still really need to clean up, but it feels so weird using my Aunt Mary's personal things. I feel like such a visitor in her home."

I sat back in the chair. "Well, it all belongs to you now. Try not to overthink it. After all, it's just stuff. She doesn't need it anymore."

"At least while I'm stuck here in Saratoga," she muttered under her breath.

Surely, she'd change her mind about keeping this place. I wanted to convince her to stay, but bottom line, it was up to her.

I pushed back from the table, the legs of the chair scraping against the floor, and an errant idea formed in my mind. "I'm going to get a shower and use all the hot water!" I shouted, taking off in a sprint toward the stairs.

"What? No you're not!" I heard her chair clatter to the floor, followed by the sound of her feet pounding against the wooden steps as she chased after me. We raced up the stairs and down the hallway, the old planks creaking beneath us.

We burst into the bathroom, laughing and breathing hard.

The black-and-white tiles, claw-foot tub, and ornate cast-iron fixtures spoke of a bygone era. "This place must not have been updated since nineteen twenty," Noelle said, still panting. "It's so cute though. You know this house would make the perfect bed-and-breakfast."

It was good to hear her speaking of future possibilities for the house. But I didn't give her any more time to daydream. My sweatpants and shirt hit the floor in record time, and I turned on the water, stepping into the shower while the water was still ice-cold. Noelle, not one to shy away from a challenge, hurriedly shrugged off my jacket and undressed—revealing that glorious body of hers. Then she unwrapped her ankle and joined me under the spray.

She squealed as the cold water pelted her and tried to jump out, but I grabbed her, wrapping my arms around her and forcing her under the icy stream. We wrestled and laughed, our bodies slipping against each other, the friction igniting a fire that no amount of cold water could extinguish.

When the water was warm, I took her face in my hands and kissed her with an all-consuming hunger. Her lips parted, welcoming my tongue eagerly.

Forcing myself to release her, I reached for the soap and lathered my hands before running them over her curves. I washed her with a reverence that belied our previous teasing, my fingers exploring every curve and dip. She let out an appreciative moan as I began paying special attention to her breasts, her nipples pebbling under my touch while the water streamed over them.

"You're insatiable, Mr. Captain."

"And you're perfect," I murmured, my hands continuing to caress every inch of her. I'd never been with a woman I couldn't keep my hands off of, and Noelle was driving me crazy.

"You're going to make me think you only want me for my body," she sassed.

"Damn right," I growled. "But I also like your smart mouth."

She bit her lower lip, looking up at me through those long lashes. "Well, then...maybe you should find a better use for it."

Challenge accepted. I captured her lips in a kiss, pouring every ounce of my desire into it, but that wasn't enough for Noelle; she was a wildfire—uncontainable. She broke away, her mouth blazing a trail of heat down my torso, leaving a wake of tingling skin. I loved watching her focus on giving me the pleasure I craved. My breath hitched as she descended, her intentions clear and her destination unmistakable. Her lips charted a course straight to my cock, and when she arrived, the memory of last night shot through my mind. The way she'd taken me—it had been so fucking hot. My shaft twitched as she slid her tongue along it. She cupped my balls, opened her mouth wide, and glided down my cock, taking me to the back of her throat.

Damn, this woman gave the best head. She eagerly went to town on my dick. Almost immediately, I was right there. Jerking out of her to prevent things from ending too soon, I spun her around and pressed her against the tiled wall. She gasped as the cool tile met her skin. I nudged her legs apart with my knee, my hand traveling down to find her slick and ready for me.

"Kol," she breathed wantonly.

"Hold on, baby," I warned, positioning myself at her entrance. With one swift thrust, I was inside her, the tight, wet heat of her pussy enveloping me completely.

She cried out, her fingers scrabbling against the tiles as I set a punishing rhythm. I couldn't get enough of her—the feel of her body, the sounds she made, the way she moved against me. It felt so fucking good.

Soon I was breathing hard, and I thought I was going to lose my mind. I could fuck her for a lifetime and never get enough.

"Kol," she whispered, her legs trembling.

"I've got you, Elle," I assured her. I pulled out and whirled her around. Reaching down, I grabbed the backs of her thighs and lifted her up. She eagerly wrapped her legs around my waist, digging her heels into my back. Her slick pussy clenched around my cock as I continued to drive into her. She moaned, sinking her fingers into my shoulders as I moved inside her. The water streamed over us, steam rising around us as our bodies slid together. Her moans urged me on, driving me to pound into her, hard and deep, over and over again.

Soon my orgasm was building, a fire running through my veins, pooling in my balls. Determined to wait for her to come, I reached between us, finding her clit with my thumb and rubbing circles. She clenched around me, her body shaking as she shattered, her cries echoing off the bathroom walls.

She was absolutely perfect.

With one last thrust, I came harder than I ever had before. My vision blurred, my body grew rigid, and I followed her over the edge, my release barreling through me.

I rested my forehead on the wall behind her. We stayed like that for a moment, panting and spent, the warm water cascading over us.

After catching our breath, we had fun helping each other wash up. It was so easy to relax and be playful with Noelle—something I hadn't experienced with a woman since my early days in the Army. It wasn't until we stepped out of the shower that we realized how cold the room was. Noelle shivered, her teeth chattering as she reached for a towel. I wrapped one around my waist, watching her as she dried herself off with quick, efficient movements. I handed her another towel, and she wrapped it around herself before sitting on the little vanity chair. I picked up the compression bandage and helped her wrap her ankle back up.

The cold air motivated us to grab our things and rush back to the living room, which was relatively warm again from the wood I'd added to the fire earlier. We quickly scrounged through our bags and threw on some clean clothes. Noelle was still cold, so she threw on my jacket. Seeing her in it did something to my heart. I never wanted her to wear another man's clothes. It made me possessive of her in a way I'd never felt about any other woman. Maybe my buddy McAllister was right: finding the right woman to snuggle up with at night was worth the risk.

"Your hair," I said, eyeing the damp curls. "We can't leave the house until it's dry. You'll catch a cold."

"Okay, *Mom*," she teased, moving to sit as close to the fireplace as she dared, running her fingers through her hair.

While she sat there before the crackling fire, I took the opportunity to go outside and collect an armful of wood. I returned and stacked it neatly along the hearth to dry out. The cold air from outside clung to me, but the sight of Noelle, warm and glowing in the firelight, chased it away.

As I watched her, I wondered how I was ever supposed to walk away from her after the snow cleared. The thought alone was enough to make my chest tighten.

But that was a worry for another day. Who knew how long this storm would have us trapped in Saratoga? For now, I had a fierce, feisty woman to keep warm, and I was going to enjoy every moment of it.

She turned her gaze to me, twisting a tendril of hair around her finger. "You know, I never thought I'd say this, but I'm actually glad the flight got canceled."

I grinned, leaning against the mantel. "Me too, Noelle. Me too."

We spent the next hour by the fire, waiting for Noelle's hair to fully dry, chitchatting about random stuff. Boy, could the girl talk. There was never an awkward silence. Once her hair had dried, I suggested we explore the house a little and find a proper bedroom for the night. "Let's take our stuff upstairs," I said, standing and offering her my hand. "My guess is, they'll have the power restored sometime today."

I grabbed our luggage. She found her tote and my flight bag, and we started up the staircase. At the top, she paused outside her aunt Mary's old bedroom, looking uncomfortable. "Not this one," she said firmly. "I can't sleep in here. It feels...wrong. Creepy even. Like I'm intruding." She shuddered, stepping back from the door. "Sleeping in a dead person's room? No thanks."

I nodded, understanding. "Fair enough. Let's pick a different one."

We ended up choosing one of the other bedrooms down the hallway. It wasn't quite as large as some of the others, but it still had its own en suite bathroom, and the bed looked comfortable. Noelle set her tote and my bag on the dresser, heaving a sigh.

"This feels much better."

I dropped our suitcases on the bed while she moved to the opposite side of the room. "Hate to say it," she said with a grin, "but I really don't want to take this jacket off. It's too cozy."

"Well, I wouldn't mind seeing you in nothing *but* my coat." I smirked. "All the time."

"Yeah, yeah, yeah. Do all pilots have a one-track mind?" she asked, though there was a flicker in her eyes that told me she liked the idea. "I should probably add some layers if we're going to walk all the way over to Broadway in the snow. I wonder what all my aunt might have stored in here? I could use a decent pair of boots."

I laughed. "Yeah, those pretty spiky ones won't cut in this kind of weather."

Noelle wandered over to the closet and opened it. "Looks like she stored her winter clothes in this one. I'll just have to pretend like I'm borrowing something from Amanda. That way it won't feel so weird." She rummaged through, pulling out a few things. "Hey, check this out," she said, holding up a thick sweater, some gloves, and a couple of woolen scarves. "We can use some of this stuff to stay warm outside."

She continued to search the closet with an enthusiasm that surprised me. Soon she turned with a triumphant grin spread across her face, holding up two beanies—one a navy blue, the other a light gray. "Look what I found!" she exclaimed, tossing the navy one at me. "Now, we won't freeze our ears off out there."

I caught the hat. "Isn't this a little too...*cute* for me?"

"Nope," she said firmly. "They're practical. And adorable."

I rolled my eyes. "What else did you find in your treasure hunt?"

She turned back to the closet and pulled out a pair of boots. "Oh my God, these Hunter tall wellies are amazing and just my size!"

That made me laugh. "So you're trading your fancy, spiky heels for chunky lug-soled boots?"

Noelle shot me a mock glare. "Those Louboutins were perfect for the trip until the snow apocalypse wrecked my life." She slipped the boots on, giving me a defiant look. "For your information, I pick the appropriate shoes for the occasion. Those were perfect for the airport. But these"—she gestured out the window at the snow-covered landscape—"are perfect for today. I'm not about to break my other ankle just to look cute."

"The snow apocalypse seems to have wrecked your fashion plans, huh?" I teased.

She took off my jacket and tugged the sweater she'd found over her other top. Then she shrugged on her pretty red coat and pulled on the gray beanie. At least she'd be easy to spot against all the white outside.

"Something like that," she said. "Now come on, let's go outside and see what we're dealing with. And don't forget to put your hat on."

I pulled on my jacket, and we headed back downstairs and out the front door. The snow was deeper than I'd expected, easily two feet, with drifts even higher where the wind had blown it against the house. Noelle started down the porch steps, insisting she didn't need help, but I wasn't having it. I wrapped an arm around her waist, ignoring her protests.

"I don't want you taking another nosedive," I said, guiding her carefully.

She huffed but didn't pull away. "Fine, fine. But only because I don't want to face-plant into the snow again."

We made our way across the sidewalk, the snow and ice crunching under our boots. The driveway was a solid blanket of white, so we trudged slowly across it, down to the street, which was barely visible beneath the snow.

The neighborhood came to life when we reached Caroline Street. Kids bundled in brightly colored snow gear played in front yards. Adults were out shoveling driveways, and a few brave souls navigated the roads on cross-country skis. I took Noelle's hand, and we turned toward Broadway, taking off in earnest.

Her eyes widened as she took it all in. "It's like a winter wonderland out here." She laughed, kicking at the snow. "You never see this in Atlanta. I've missed it."

I smiled, squeezing her hand. "It is perfect for Christmas Eve. And it's even better with you." Oh God, this girl had me being all sappy like some die-hard romantic.

She looked up at me, her cheeks flushed from the cold, her eyes sparkling. "You're just saying that because I'm the only one here to keep you warm."

"Ha! Maybe. But it's still true."

As we were passing a large parking lot, a barrage of snowballs pelted us.

"Ambush!" Noelle shrieked, ducking behind me for cover. I scanned the area, spotting some kids hiding behind snow-covered cars and bushes. They had turned the parking lot into a battleground.

"Oh, it's on now," I growled, dragging Noelle with me as I dashed for safety behind a car. "Quick! Take cover!" Several more snowballs sailed our way.

While we crouched behind the car, I quickly formed some snowballs and launched them back at the kids.

"Kol, what are you doing?" she asked. "They're just little kids."

"We're under attack," I said, packing more snow into a ball. "We have to defend ourselves. And trust me, some of those minions have a good arm on them."

She rolled her eyes but started making her own snowball. "Fine. But I warn you, I'm terrible at this."

I grinned. "That's okay. I've got enough skill for both of us."

We started launching snowballs at the kids. Their giggles rang out as they scattered. Noelle's throws were wild, most of them missing the kids by a mile. She wasn't wrong about being terrible at this. I'd never seen anyone with such bad aim.

"Nice try," I teased as one of her snowballs fell apart mid-air.

"Shut up!" She laughed, throwing another pathetic snowball, which landed only a couple of yards away from us.

I showed off, packing tight ones and hurling them with precision at our tiny attackers. The kids tried to surround us, but with tactical efficiency, I pulled Noelle out from behind the car, and we took cover behind the corner of a building.

"That's cheating!" a kid yelled as another of my snowballs hit one of them squarely in the chest.

"We're just using superior strategy!" I called back.

"You're pretty good at this," Noelle said, packing another snowball.

I winked at her. "Military training. It comes in handy."

She snorted. "I bet they didn't teach you how to dodge snowballs thrown by eight-year-olds."

"You'd be surprised. There's a lot of crossover between snowball fights and combat tactics."

She threw her snowball, which sailed wide, missing the kids completely. When they jeered playfully, she groaned, stomping her foot. "This is ridiculous. I can't even hit a stationary target." Then she laughed so hard she nearly fell over. Her next attempt hit me square in the back of the head instead.

I turned.

"Oh, no!" She gasped dramatically, tossing one straight in my face. "Friendly fire!"

I narrowed my eyes. "You're gonna pay for that."

Before she could react, I grabbed a handful of snow and shoved it right into her face. She squealed, flailing her arms and grabbing my jacket as she went down, taking me with her. We tumbled into the snowbank next to the building and rolled down an embankment.

When we finally came to a stop, laughing like idiots, we found ourselves face-to-face, with me on top. Our breaths mingled in white puffs between us before I closed the gap and kissed her thoroughly. The world around us faded away, the kids' laughter and the distant hum of the city disappearing until all that was left was the two of us, lost in each other.

Suddenly, a chorus of "Ewww!" broke through our little bubble. We pulled apart to see the kids staring at us, their faces scrunched up in disgust.

"Gross!" one of them shouted, and they all took off running and laughing.

Noelle buried her face in my chest. "Well, that's one way to end a snowball fight."

I grinned, wrapping my arms around her. "Looks like we won."

"Yeah," she murmured against my mouth. "We definitely won."

Chapter Eighteen

12/24 afternoon

We climbed out of the snowbank, brushed off the cold powder clinging to our clothes, and resumed walking toward Broadway. The streets were bustling with people bundled up in winter gear, families and couples who were out and about enjoying the Christmas festivities.

"Looks like the whole town came out to play," I said.

"It's always like this around Christmas. Saratoga knows how to celebrate."

We crossed Broadway and found ourselves at a local market. "Look, the power's back on here," I said. "Maybe they'll get your aunt's house up and running before we get back."

Out front stood the city's Christmas tree, towering and beautifully decorated with lights, tinsel, and oversized ornaments. Nearby stood Santa's Cottage, outside of which was a long line of kids. They were all waiting to get pictures taken with Old St. Nick himself.

The streets were alive with a festive energy that was impossible to ignore. Lights twinkled from every surface, and the air was filled with the scents of pine and peppermint. We leisurely strolled down Broadway, hand in hand.

Noelle tugged me toward a small shop nestled between two larger buildings. "Let's go in here," she said, her voice bubbling with enthusiasm.

Inside the shop was a treasure trove of holiday items. Everywhere we looked, there were ornaments, trinkets, and knickknacks. Noelle's eyes lit up when she spotted a tree covered in decorations. She rushed to it, her fingers brushing over some of the ornaments.

"Check these out. These handmade crochet ornaments are adorable," she gushed, holding up a small delicate wreath. "Look at the detail."

I picked up a snowflake, examining the intricate pattern. "They're impressive. You should get one."

She shook her head, putting the wreath back. "Nah, I don't really celebrate Christmas anymore. And Aunt Mary's tree is already overflowing with ornaments."

"Suit yourself," I said with a shrug, making a mental note to come back later.

We continued browsing the shop, moving on to a display of nutcrackers. "That one looks like me," I said, pointing to a nutcracker dressed in a navy blue uniform.

She laughed, picking it up. "It does! You should get it. A little memento of our snowed-in adventure."

I took it from her, examining it. "Maybe some other time. There are a million shops in this area. Let's see what else there is." I set the little guy on the counter, and we meandered toward the door.

After leaving the shop, we found ourselves outside a local toy store that looked like it had been plucked straight from a child's dream. The window displays were filled with toys of all kinds—trains, dolls, action figures.

"Want to go in?" I asked.

Her face lit up. "Absolutely!"

Going inside was like stepping back in time. The shelves were lined with toys from every era, and kids were running, playing, and shouting everywhere.

Noelle beelined for the section with horse figurines and playsets. "Oh my gosh, look at these. They were my favorites growing up," she said, picking up a stable set. "I had this exact one. I loved it so much."

"You were a total horse girl, huh?"

She nodded enthusiastically. "Oh yeah. I had every horse toy imaginable. And I loved hanging out in the barn with my dad. He taught me everything about horses."

I wandered over to the military toys, picking up a G.I. Joe. "I was more into these. My dad got me a whole set for my birthday one year. I played with them nonstop."

Noelle came over, wrapping her arms around my waist. "That's cute. I can just imagine little Kol, running around with his G.I. Joes, saving the world."

I laughed, putting the figure back. "Something like that."

We moved on to a case filled with Breyer horses. "Oh wow! Look at these!" she shouted, pointing out each breed. "That's a Morgan. And that's a quarter horse. Oh, and that's a thoroughbred. Isn't she gorgeous?"

Impressed by her knowledge and charmed by her enthusiasm, I nodded. "They're all beautiful. Just like you."

She blushed, turning to me. "You're laying it on thick today, aren't you?"

I grinned, leaning in to kiss her. "Just stating the facts, ma'am."

After looking around for a few more minutes, we left the toy store, walking hand in hand, and made our way down the street. Noelle was recognized by several people she knew—friends from school and old neighbors.

"Noelle! It's been ages!" one woman exclaimed as she hugged her tightly.

"Oh, hi, it's so good to see you!" Noelle responded warmly.

"And who's this?" the lady asked with an inquisitive smile.

"Oh...um...Mrs. Norwood, this is Kol. Kol, this is Mrs. Norwood, my freshman biology teacher," Noelle stammered slightly.

"Nice to meet you, ma'am," I said, reaching out to shake her hand. The woman cut Noelle a side glance, beaming brightly.

"Nice to meet you as well, Kol. Will you two lovebirds be staying in town long?"

"Oh, no. No," Noelle said. "It's not like that. He's just a... Good Samaritan who helped me get home when my flight got canceled yesterday."

I found her embarrassed response funny. Bending down close to her, I brushed a kiss over her cheek and whispered in her ear, "Just a Good Samaritan?"

Her cheeks turned an even brighter shade of red, and Mrs. Norwood giggled.

"Well, it's good to see you back in town, Noelle. Don't be a stranger. Enjoy your visit...both of you," the woman said, looking between us.

"Yes, ma'am," we said in unison.

As we walked away, I tugged Noelle close. "You're adorable when you're flustered; you know that?"

She elbowed me. "Shut up. I can't help it. I'm not used to...this."

"This?" I asked, raising an eyebrow.

She gestured between us. "You know, being with someone. In public, here in Saratoga."

I pulled her into a hug. "Well, get used to it. Because I plan on being with you in public a lot more."

She looked up at me. "Yeah?"

I nodded. "Yeah."

We continued our walk, soon reaching a candy store. The sweet scents of chocolate and other confections wafted out into the street, luring us inside. At the front of the store, kids screamed for their favorite candies, their faces pressed against the glass cases. Noelle and I perused the aisles, filling a bag with an assortment of holiday treats.

When we arrived at the counter, I added a box of chocolate fudge to our haul. And as we stepped out of the store, I leaned over, whispering in her ear, "You know, I don't think I'll ever be able to eat fudge again without thinking about last night."

She coyly looked up at me and gave a little shrug but didn't say anything.

Next door was a coffee shop. "Let's stop and get something hot to drink with our candy," I suggested, steering us toward the entrance.

The coffee shop hummed with noise—animated conversation, merry laughter, and the hiss of steaming milk. We ordered, and I waited for our coffees while Noelle found a table.

The coffees were made quickly, and a few minutes later I was sliding into a booth across from her. She wrapped her hands around her peppermint latte and brought it up to her nose.

"This is the smell of Christmas. Mmm, so good."

I took a careful sip of mine.

"Caramel brûlée? Really? That's the drink of choice for a guy like you?" she teased, brows bouncing.

I shrugged. "It's good. You should try branching out sometime. Not everyone needs a peppermint explosion just because it's the holidays."

She relaxed back in the booth, studying me. "Hmm, I thought you liked black coffee. Strong, no-nonsense."

"Well, I do like my coffee black. But sometimes, a man needs a little sweetness in his life." Letting the double meaning sink in, I held her gaze.

"Is that so?"

I nodded, taking a sip of my latte. "Absolutely."

For a while we sipped our drinks, surrounded by the cozy chaos of Christmas Eve. I broke out the candy we'd bought, taking a bite of the fudge. "This is good, but not nearly as good as your aunt's fudge. Do you think she left the recipe somewhere?"

"I'm sure she did, but the challenge will be finding it among all the—who knows how many—other recipes she has. As you can tell by her home, she was quite the pack rat," Noelle said, staring out the window at the people passing by.

I stretched my legs under the table, catching her ankle and giving it a gentle nudge.

"So," I asked, "were you one of those kids who couldn't wait for Christmas morning? Or were you more of a *wait by the fire and pretend to be patient* type?"

She laughed, her foot tapping mine playfully. "Oh, I was the worst. Up at four in the morning, ripping into presents like it was a race. My poor parents had to stay up practically all night just to sneak the presents under the tree and be ready when I came flying down the stairs. I think all they got most years was a nap on the sofa."

I smiled, enjoying the mental picture. "I can see you doing that. I was more of the *wait until everyone else was done opening their gifts so they had to sit and watch me open mine* kind of kid. Drove my younger siblings crazy."

Noelle snorted, shaking her head. "Of course you did that. Always calm, always in control."

Her attention drifted to the window again. "Christmas was always my favorite time of year when I was a kid," she said, her expression turning a bit melancholy. "Everything was just so magical, you know?"

I followed her gaze. "Yeah, I get that. There's something about the snow and the lights that makes everything feel...pure. Like a fresh start." Then, reaching across the table, I took her hand. "I'm glad you're having fun today."

She squeezed my hand, turning to give me a soft smile. "Me too."

All at once, an idea struck me. I needed to make a quick move without raising suspicion.

"I'll be right back," I said, standing abruptly.

"Bathroom?" Noelle asked, eyeing me over the rim of her cup.

I nodded, playing it cool. "Yeah, that's it. I don't see a restroom here, so I'll walk over to the market we just passed. I won't be long."

I stepped outside and headed back to the Christmas shop, the cold biting through my coat as I jogged. The tiny bell above the door jingled as I rushed in and scanned for the tree. The ornament Noelle had loved—a delicate crocheted wreath—was still there. I grabbed it, paid quickly, and tucked the little box into my coat pocket before racing back to the coffee shop.

As I approached, I caught sight of Noelle standing on the sidewalk, her back to me. She was facing an older woman who was walking toward her, gesturing animatedly. I slowed down, not wanting to interrupt.

The lady was as round as she was short, dressed in a vibrant purple coat with fur trim. Her white hair stood out starkly against the colorful outfit. I paused, positioning myself to the side and slipping into the background so I could see their faces as I listened in.

"Noelle, darling, it's been *so* long!" the woman said, her voice carrying strongly over the sounds of the street.

Noelle laughed, hugging the woman. "Mrs. Dottie! It's good to see you. It's been ages."

Mrs. Dottie stepped back, holding Noelle at arm's length, her smile wide. "Oh, and look at you! Still as beautiful as ever. My, my, it's so wonderful to have you back in town. Especially today of all days! I can't believe it's been exactly four years already. I still remember your parents like it was yesterday."

I froze, the hair on the back of my neck standing up. Four years? Parents?

Noelle's smile faded, her body tensing. "Yes, today...it has been four years," she said softly.

Mrs. Dottie clucked her tongue. "Such a shame, dear. Such a shame. They were taken too soon, too soon indeed. I think of them often, especially at this time of year. It's just so sad. Such a tragedy."

I moved closer, my instincts kicking in. At this point, Noelle was frozen like a deer caught in the headlights. Something was very wrong, but before I could cut in, Mrs. Dottie yammered on.

"And now, with your aunt Mary gone too..." Mrs. Dottie shook her head. "Death is such a cruel finality, isn't it? I miss them all so much."

Noelle's breath hitched, and she clenched her hands at her sides. I stepped up behind her, wrapping an arm around her waist. She leaned into me slightly, trembling.

Mrs. Dottie appeared to notice neither my arrival nor Noelle's distress. "It's such a shame you weren't here when it happened," she went on. "Maybe if you'd stayed closer to home, they wouldn't have felt the need to travel so far to see you."

I stiffened, anger rising in me. Who was this woman to say such things?

Noelle's breaths were coming faster now, her body shaking even more. I tightened my hold on her, trying to offer some comfort.

"It must be hard to celebrate Christmas after what happened," Mrs. Dottie continued. "I don't even know how you manage to be here at all, sweetheart. But you're strong, I suppose. Stronger than I could be if I had lost my parents so young. Oh, they were such good people. Gone much too soon." This woman's voice was really grating on my nerves. "I guess you're lucky they saw you succeed before they passed, right? At least you've got that."

She reached out and patted Noelle on the cheek. "I'm sure work helps though. Keeps you busy, right? Keeps you from thinking too much. Even so, this must be unbearable for you."

Noelle remained speechless, breathing fast and heavy. She wasn't even blinking, her eyes unfocused, and I could tell she was spiraling.

"They're all in a better place now though," Mrs. Dottie said with a somber nod. "Watching over you, I'm sure. They wouldn't want you to dwell on the past, especially not at Christmas. It's time to move on, isn't it? Time to enjoy the holidays again."

Noelle's shoulders hunched as if she was physically shrinking under the weight of Mrs. Dottie's words. I tightened my grip on her waist. I couldn't take it anymore. I opened my mouth to tell Mrs. Dottie to shut the fuck up, but Noelle suddenly pushed away from me and bolted across the street, weaving through people like a woman possessed, her blonde curls bouncing behind her.

"Noelle!" I called after her, but she didn't stop. Without another glance at Mrs. Dottie, I took off after Noelle. She was fast, cutting through alleys, her pace frantic. But I didn't try to stop her. I let her run, let her burn through whatever had just been unleashed inside her.

I followed at a safe distance, keeping her in my line of sight.

She ran along the fringes of Broadway until she came to Lincoln Avenue, where she took a left. I kept up, my heart pounding—not from the exertion but from the look on her face before she had taken off. The sheer panic, the overwhelming grief.

I didn't know what had happened to her parents, but I was familiar with that kind of pain, the kind that made you want to run until you couldn't feel anything anymore.

So I remained close, letting her do what she needed to do, ready to catch her when she fell.

Chapter Nineteen

12/24 night

Noelle sprinted down the street, and I raced after her, dread twisting in my chest with every frantic step. She was a storm of emotions. This wasn't just a run—it was an escape. She was trying to outrun something far more profound than the old woman's cruel words.

She took a sharp right into St. Peter's Cemetery, the snow crunching under her boots. I hesitated at the entrance, watching her fight her way across the slippery snow- and ice-covered ground toward a specific gravesite. The cemetery was eerily quiet; the silence broken only by the harsh sound of her labored breathing.

I kept my distance but stayed close enough to hear her anguished whispers. She stumbled forward, stopping in front of a large black headstone that was barely visible beneath the thick layer of snow.

Her body trembled, her chest heaving as she took quick, shuddering breaths. Right now, her grief was raw and bleeding, a wound that refused to heal. She flung out her arm, shoving the snow from the top of the headstone in a single, desperate motion.

"Why did you leave me?!" she screamed, her voice echoing through the silent cemetery. "Why did you drive in that damn storm?"

I stood frozen, every muscle in my body tensing as I watched her unravel. Her pain was palpable, a physical force that hit me like a punch to the gut. I could feel it—every ounce of her agony—as if it were my own.

She clawed at the snow in front of the headstone, revealing the engraved names of her parents.

"You didn't have to come! I didn't need you to come!" Noelle's voice wavered with sorrow. "If I hadn't been working, if I had just come home..."

I wanted to go to her, wrap her in my arms and tell her it wasn't her fault. But she needed this, needed to let it all out. So I stayed rooted to the spot, watching as she continued to swipe the snow away, her movements frenzied and desperate.

"You left me all alone. For what? For fucking Christmas?" Her hands shot out to her sides, fingers splayed and arms flailing wildly.

"Everyone always says such stupid things," she spat out. "Like Mrs. Dottie—saying you're in a better place or that it's God's plan. It doesn't help! It just hurts more!"

She gripped the edge of the headstone, falling to her knees in the snow. Her sobs were heart-wrenching, tearing through me like shards of glass.

"It's all my fault you died!" she screamed, pounding her fist against her chest. "Why did you leave me all alone? Why is my life such a disaster? Why does no one love me?"

Her other hand slid down the face of the headstone, gliding over their names. "Why should I get to live when you don't? I don't deserve to be here."

Her questions were a litany of pain, a desperate plea for answers that would never come. Letting her head droop, she beat her fists on the ground while her tears melted the snow beneath her. "I can't do this! Why...why?"

She screamed again and again, pouring out years of pent-up grief and anger. I moved closer but stopped just short of touching distance. This moment belonged to Noelle and her parents. My heart broke for her—she'd been carrying this weight alone for too long.

All I could do was stand there, a silent sentinel in the face of her storm. All I could do was watch as she wept, her tears a river of grief that flowed from the deepest parts of her soul. All I could do was be here for her, a steady presence in the midst of her chaos.

As much as it hurt to watch, I knew this was a necessary step for her healing—a step that seemed long overdue—so I waited.

Eventually her screams faded to sobs.

She started to shake uncontrollably. I couldn't stand by and watch her suffer any longer. I needed to hold her, to let her know she wasn't alone.

But as soon as I reached out to touch her shoulder, she whirled around, her eyes wild. "Don't," she hissed. "Don't touch me."

I froze, my hand hovering in the air between us. Her eyes flashed with unfiltered agony—it was tearing her apart. And I resolved, in that moment, that I would do anything to take her pain away—anything to make her whole again.

"I'm not leaving you here," I said firmly. "We need to get you home."

"No! You should just leave me like everyone else does. I'm no good for you," she barked.

Her words cut me like a knife, but I stood my ground. "I'm not everyone else."

"You had your easy fuck. Now leave. Get in your shiny red Bronco and get the hell out of here."

Her words were meant to hurt, to push me away. I'd seen it before, in the eyes of soldiers who'd lost too much. But I wasn't going to leave her, not like this.

"Noelle, you need to come home and get warmed up. It's freezing out here."

"This isn't your issue!" she yelled, pounding her fists against the snow-covered ground. "Go be with your perfect family, because hanging around with me will only bring you bad luck."

"I'm not leaving you. Not now, not ever."

"Just go away, Kol! Leave me alone!" she shouted, but there was a crack in her voice this time—a crack that told me she didn't really want me to leave. I stepped closer.

She looked up at me, her eyes wild with grief and anger. "Why? Why do you even care? I'm a mess, Kol. A complete fucking mess. You should walk away. No, you should *run* far away from me."

Bending down toward her, I said simply, "You matter to me. And I'm not running anywhere."

I took a deep breath, bracing myself for what I had to do next. Before she could react, I scooped her up, throwing her over my shoulder like a sack of potatoes. She yelped, pounding her fists against my back and kicking her legs wildly.

"What the hell are you doing? Put me down!" she yelled against my back. "I hate you! I fucking hate you!"

I tightened my grip. "No you don't. You can say you hate me all you want. You're angry and hurt, but you don't hate me, and I'm not letting you go."

Although she continued to squirm and fight, I held on, my long strides eating up the distance as I hiked back toward the house. Her screams filled the air, and her fists pummeled my back, but I didn't falter. She needed this—needed to fight, to rage against the pain.

"You can't just carry me off like this!" she shouted. "Do you think you can just swoop in and save me? You think you can fix this?"

"I can, and I am," I replied bluntly.

Within a few minutes, her struggles were starting to weaken, exhaustion setting in. In silence, I kept going—walking down the street, trudging up the driveway, and climbing the porch steps.

I opened the door with my free hand and stepped inside. The house was warm and toasty—the power was back on. Without hesitation, I marched us straight upstairs and kicked open the bathroom door. I set Noelle down on the vanity. Her silence said it all—she was completely drained, both physically and emotionally.

"Stay put," I commanded.

I went over to the claw-foot tub and turned on the faucet. Soon the hot water began steaming up the room. I tested the temperature, ensuring it was nice and hot, but not scalding, before returning to her.

She sat there, her eyes red and puffy, her cheeks streaked with tears. She looked broken, shattered into a million pieces.

"You're not leaving me, Kol?" she whispered, her voice barely audible.

I met her gaze. "No, Noelle. I'm not leaving you."

Kol
Vinter

Chapter Twenty

12/24 night

While Noelle sat silently on the vanity, staring ahead vacantly, I stripped off my clothes. The steam from the bath now filled the room, creating a warm bubble that was far removed from the cold, harsh world outside. I turned to Noelle, who was now slumped over, practically curled up into a ball in her exhaustion, and gently lifted her down from the vanity. I carefully undressed her, treating her as though she were something fragile, in need of protection. She didn't resist but let me take over.

Once she was undressed, I lifted her again, cradling her against my chest as I stepped into the tub. She gasped slightly when the hot water made contact with her skin. I lowered us both into the tub, positioning her so that she was lying back against my chest, then wrapped my arms around her.

We sat there for a long while, neither of us speaking, just breathing. The only sound was the occasional drip from the faucet. The heat of the water seeped into our bones, melting away the chill from outside. Her heart beat strongly against my skin while her chest rose and fell steadily, the tension in her body slowly ebbing away.

"I'm sorry, Noelle," I murmured, pressing my lips to the top of her head. "I didn't know about your parents. If I had, I wouldn't have been so insensitive earlier when we drove up here or asked so much about keeping your aunt's house. I had no idea what you've been through."

She didn't respond right away, but there was a slight shift in her posture—a softening. I tightened my arms around her, holding her closer.

"You're one of the strongest people I've ever known," I continued. "You've managed to live on your own, working at a high-stress job for these last four years. You didn't let your grief ruin your future. That takes incredible strength."

She shook her head slightly, her blonde curls brushing against my chest. "I'm not strong, Kol," she whispered. "I'm just...broken."

"No, you're not," I insisted. "You're brave. You took a chance on your dream job, and no matter what happened because of that lying cheat, Blake, you're amazing. You'll find another job. Don't worry about staying if living here isn't what you want. Even though things didn't work out the way you planned, you're still standing. You're still fighting. That's strength."

She was silent for a moment, her fingers tracing patterns in the water. "Thank you, Kol—for being there for me. I'd probably still be at the cemetery if you hadn't dragged me home."

I gave her a squeeze. "You don't have to thank me for that."

"No," she insisted softly. "I do." She took a deep breath before continuing. "I'm sorry for all the stupid, angry comments I made earlier too. I have a crazy mouth when I lose my cool."

I chuckled, pressing a kiss to her temple. "Yeah, well...you could slay a man with that sharp tongue of yours."

Again, Noelle inhaled slowly, her body trembling slightly against mine. "There's more, Kol. The situation with the house... it's not as simple as whether or not I want to keep it."

I waited, giving her the space to speak, to share her truth.

"Remember how I told you there was a clause in Aunt Mary's will? Well...it's a doozy." She paused for a moment. "In order to keep the house, I have to move back to Saratoga and live here for the next year. If I don't, everything goes to the church."

That ultimatum was definitely a surprise.

"There's more, Kol. Aunt Mary didn't just leave me her house. She left me the home and farm I grew up on. The place where my parents...where they..."

She didn't finish the sentence. My heart ached for her. This wasn't just about inheriting property; this was about reclaiming pieces of herself she'd thought were lost forever.

"Shh, it's okay," I murmured, rocking her gently in my arms. "You don't have to say it. I understand."

As I held her, I made a silent vow. I would be there for her, no matter what. I would help her through this, help her find her strength, her courage. I would be her rock, her safe haven, her home, because she deserved it. She deserved to be loved, to be cherished, to be protected. And I would be the one to give her that. No matter what it took, no matter what it cost me, I would be there for her. Always.

"I don't know what all I said or what you heard at the gravesite, but my parents' deaths are my fault." She said this as though it were a matter of fact.

Her words jarred me. "Noelle, that's not true. It's not your fault. You can't blame yourself for what happened."

She sniffled, wiping her nose with the back of her hand. "You don't understand. I'd only been working at the Martindale Agency for six months, and it was a whirlwind of chaos with all the holiday and year-end campaigns. I was the most junior ad specialist and didn't have a choice whether I stayed and worked. It was just part of the job."

"That doesn't make it your fault, Noelle. You were doing your job."

She took a shaky breath. "I didn't know my parents would decide to surprise me by driving down for Christmas. But they did... There was a big snowstorm rolling in—just like this one—when they set out. Evidently, a tractor-trailer jackknifed just in front of them. It was bad... The police told me they died instantly, but that piece of information didn't make me feel any better."

"I'm so sorry. I can't imagine how hard that must have been for you."

"I don't really remember much after the police called me. My boss was super nice, and between her and Amanda, I managed to make it home to Saratoga on Christmas Day. I can't really explain it, but the next thing I remember is getting on a flight to Atlanta on January fourth. My parents had been buried, and my Aunt Mary had received my parents' entire estate. I never even thought to contest it. I think a part of me was glad I wouldn't have to go live there without them. It was easier just to put one foot in front of the other and focus on work. I shoved away my past and my memories and only let myself think about the future, about getting the promotion...and the next promotion."

"You did what you had to do to survive. There's no shame in that."

She sighed, drumming her fingers on the side of the tub for a few seconds before continuing with her story. "I never went back. Never visited. It was like that part of my life didn't exist as long as I never thought about it. Then, when my aunt passed away a few weeks ago, I was in the middle of the biggest project of my career, so I rushed to Saratoga and left without stopping to think."

She shook her head slightly, a bitter laugh escaping her lips. "I was angry with Aunt Mary too. Soon after my parents died, she sold all our horses, and I thought she'd sold my parents' farm too. I never reached out to her, assuming the worst about her."

Noelle buried her face in her hands. "Kol, she never sold the place. She kept it for me. For when I worked through my grief. And the horses are only down the way at a neighboring farm."

Her breath hitched from her sobs, and I hugged her tightly, offering what little comfort I could.

"Shh... It's okay," I murmured against her hair.

She sniffed. "She left me the farm... Then, today, meeting people I knew and seeing everything, it all came back. And then...and then, with Mrs. Dottie, the dam just broke." Her sobs grew louder as she turned her body and buried her face in my chest.

"I've been so wrong about everything, absolutely everything," she choked out. "Wrong about pursuing a meaningless career, wrong about trusting a narcissist like Blake, wrong about the people who matter...wrong about everything. You probably think I'm the dumbest, shallowest person on earth."

I took her chin between my fingers and tilted her face, forcing her to look at me. "Noelle, I don't think that. You've been through hell. You're neither dumb nor shallow. You're human. You're one incredible woman who has faced unimaginable loss while moving forward despite how difficult things got."

She looked down, her cheeks flushed with embarrassment. "I'm so sorry that I'm so emotional and dramatic. Please forgive me."

I pulled her chin back toward me, saying firmly, "There's nothing to forgive. You've been carrying this pain for too long. It's time to let it go."

She shook her head, tears welling up in her eyes again. "I can't believe I'm crying like this. I'm such a mess."

I brushed a tear from her cheek, my thumb tracing its path. "You're not a mess. You're hurting. And it's okay to hurt. It's okay to cry. It's okay to feel all of this."

She took a deep, shuddering breath. "I just...I don't know what to do. I don't know how to fix this."

"You don't have to fix anything right now. You just have to feel it. Let it out. Let yourself grieve."

She nodded, her tears flowing freely now. "I miss them so much. I miss my parents so, so much."

I rocked her gently in my arms. "I know, sweetheart. I know."

My fingers brushed her skin in soothing patterns.

"You'd think after all this time it wouldn't bother me so much."

"No, that's not so. I don't think you'll ever stop missing them, but time will help you manage your emotions better. There will always be triggers that will make the pain resurface," I insisted. "When that woman outside the coffee shop started going on and on... God, I wanted to rip her throat out. What an insensitive hag."

Noelle shook her head slightly. "She didn't mean any harm. It's just her way." She heaved a sigh. "Mrs. Dottie used to babysit me when I was little. Hell, she even babysat my mom when she was a kid. She's the same age as Aunt Mary, who was ten years older than my mom."

"So your aunt and your mom were close?"

"No, not really. They had a strained relationship, but they loved each other. And I know Aunt Mary loved me too."

"All families are complicated."

She turned slightly to look up at me. "Well, your family doesn't sound complicated."

"Oh, trust me, it is. Big Catholic family, remember? Being the oldest son in a large family comes with its own set of complications—especially when you've *lapsed*, as you so politely put it. Plus, you haven't met them yet."

A hint of a smile played on her lips. "Yet?" she echoed.

I grinned, imagining the chaos that would ensue when I brought Noelle home. "When I take you to family dinner, you'll be the first girl since high school. My momma will lose her mind. She'll be all over you."

Her cheeks turned a delightful shade of pink, and for the first time since we'd arrived back at the house, her natural enthusiasm flickered back into life.

"You must think I'm a total nutjob after the stunt I pulled in the cemetery," she whispered.

"Absolutely not. I understand the tragedy of death and the process of grief as well as anyone."

She looked at me, her eyes filled with questions. I took a deep breath, preparing to delve into a part of my past I rarely talked about.

"Afghanistan changed me—changed everything about how I see the world," I began. "I saw things…things that no one should ever have to see. The Taliban treats women like property. They beat them, stone them, sell them like cattle. I saw a woman stoned to death because she was *accused* of adultery. I saw a girl, no older than twelve, sold to a man old enough to be her grandfather."

Noelle watched me closely, waiting for me to continue.

"I saw so much death and destruction over there...so many innocent lives lost." My voice cracked slightly as memories surfaced—memories I'd tried so hard to forget.

"One day, I was flying a mission to take out a high-value target—a Taliban leader responsible for countless atrocities." My throat tightened as images from that day replayed vividly in my mind.

"I had him in my sights and had just launched a missile," I said, every word stabbing me in the chest like a knife. "And then, out of nowhere, this car came barreling into view—a mother and her two children inside."

I paused, struggling to keep my voice steady.

"They drove right into the path of the missile I'd just launched. I watched as the car exploded, their bodies tossed like rag dolls. The devastation unfolded in my viewfinder, and I was helpless—unable to do anything but watch them die."

Noelle's eyes widened in horror.

The familiar ache in my chest returned, the guilt that never truly went away. "That day, a piece of me died. It made me doubt everything—my faith, human nature... It all seemed so incongruous to the hell I was surrounded by. For the first time, I understood the true cost of war. The innocence lost, the lives shattered. So believe me when I say I understand your feelings of both anger and sorrow."

Noelle's eyes were brimming with tears once more. She reached up, cupping my cheek in her hand, her thumb brushing away a tear I hadn't even realized had fallen. She leaned in, pressing her lips softly against my cheek.

"I'm so sorry, Kol," she whispered. "I'm so sorry you had to go through that."

I closed my eyes, savoring the warmth of her touch, the softness of her lips.

I was falling for her—falling hard and fast, like a skydiver without a parachute. But I didn't care. I wanted to fall, to lose myself in her, to let her heal the broken parts of me. Healing wasn't just about leaning on someone else; it was about confronting the pain head-on, something I still struggled with. Noelle had been bottling up her pain, just like I had—pushing it down instead of facing it. But burying this kind of trauma only made it fester and grow.

"Have you ever talked to someone about your parents? Like a therapist?" I asked.

She stiffened in my arms, her fingers pausing their idle tracing patterns. "No," she admitted, her voice barely above a whisper. "I couldn't... I didn't want to talk about it. It was easier to just... not think about it. You know?"

I nodded, understanding exactly how she felt.

A bitter laugh escaped her lips. "Talking to anyone about my parents' deaths just made everything worse. I thought focusing on work was the best way to move forward. It was the perfect distraction. I could lose myself in campaigns and deadlines and pretend nothing had happened."

A pang of sympathy went through me; I knew all too well the danger of using work as a coping mechanism. "And now?" I asked, kissing her temple again.

"Now, I don't know. Being back here, seeing everyone, it's like...it's like everything is rushing back, and I can't stop it."

"You can't run from it forever. Trust me, I've tried."

She raised her face, her dark blue eyes searching mine. "What about you? Have you worked with a therapist?"

I hesitated. This was a topic I usually avoided. But she deserved the truth. "In the military, we go through psych evals. It's mandatory. But I was careful not to get stuck in that trap."

"Trap?" she asked.

"Yeah, in the military, especially for pilots, getting labeled with PTSD or any mental health issue can get you grounded. So you learn to tell the doctors what they want to hear."

Her brow furrowed, a frown forming on her lips. "But why would they not let you fly if you sought help? Why is getting mental health care a bad thing?"

I sighed, running a hand through my hair. "It's complicated. For pilots, mental health is...it's a tricky subject. We can't just admit to having issues, not without risking our careers."

"But that's ridiculous. If you're struggling, you should be able to get help. That doesn't seem fair."

"It's not fair, but it's the reality of the situation. The FAA has strict regulations about it. If they think you're unstable or unfit to fly, you're grounded. No medical, no job. And very likely the end of your career. Trust me, they don't take kindly to pilots with mental health issues."

"So, what do you do? Just...deal with it on your own?"

I shook my head. "Not exactly. I have a group of buddies who are in the same boat as me, so we support each other. Some of them are pilots like me and can't get official help, but others can and have. We talk and work through stuff together. We share what we've learned from those who can get help and apply it to ourselves as best we can."

She bit her lip, looking thoughtful. "So...just talking helps?"

"Yeah, it does. It doesn't fix everything overnight, but it helps to know you're not alone in your struggles. It's not the same as seeing a therapist, but it's something. Over time, I've worked through a lot of the guilt."

"Guilt? What do you have to feel guilty about?"

I hesitated, but she had opened up to me, so I owed her the same honesty. "Survivor's guilt. Seeing things, doing things... that change you. Knowing you made it out but others didn't."

"And what about now? Do you still struggle with it?"

I shook my head. "Not like I used to. I've come to terms with a lot of it. And I'm lucky. I have a big family, people who love and support me. That makes a difference too."

She was silent for a moment. "I wish I had that. I wish I had someone who loved me like that, someone who would be there for me no matter what."

I tightened my arms around her, a fierce protectiveness rising within me. "You do. You have me."

She regarded me carefully. "But for how long? What happens when you decide I'm too much drama, too much baggage? What happens when you decide you don't want to deal with my shit anymore?"

I cupped her face in my hands, forcing her to look at me. "I'm not going anywhere."

She shook her head. "You can't promise that. You can't promise you won't leave me too."

She was right. I couldn't promise her forever, not yet. But I could promise her now. "I'm here now, Noelle."

"Okay," she whispered.

We both had our demons that haunted us. And if we wanted to build something real, something lasting, we'd have to face them together.

I just hoped we were strong enough to do it. Noelle deserved that—deserved to be happy, to be loved. And maybe I did too.

Noelle shivered.

"I think it's time to get out of this tub," I said with a chuckle, ruffling the ends of her wet hair. "The water's turning into a mini ice rink. I don't need you turning into a Noelle-sicle on me."

She groaned, resting her head on my chest. "Ugh, you're right. My fingers are all pruned up. But, hey, at least the house is warmer now."

I stood and pulled her up with me, water cascading off us. She rolled her eyes but smiled. We climbed out, and I handed her a towel. She whipped the towel around her and tucked the corner in so that it looked like a dress.

I smirked. "You know, you even make a towel look like designer clothes."

She laughed, shaking her head. "Please, I look like a drowned rat."

"If that's what drowned rats look like, I've been severely misinformed."

She wrinkled her nose at me and rummaged through her tote, pulling out a small bag of toiletries and placing it on the vanity before darting into the closet. I tugged on a pair of jeans and slid on a sweatshirt, then ran a comb through my hair.

Noelle returned sporting dark red flannel pajamas with with a snowflake and reindeer pattern, her face lighting up with mock-pride.

"Check these out," she said, walking toward me and turning slowly with her arms held out. "Adorable, right?"

I rolled my lips in, trying to suppress a laugh. "Adorable doesn't even begin to cover it. I guess you're going for *granny festive* tonight?"

She gave me a playful nudge with her elbow. "Hey, don't knock them until you've tried them. They're cozy. I spotted them in the closet earlier. I think my aunt must have just bought them, because the tags were still on."

"Whatever you say, but just so you know, if you start jingling when you walk, we're gonna have to have a talk."

"Jingle?!" She blinked a few times, almost looking offended. "These are classy reindeer PJs, thank you very much. And they most definitely do not jingle."

"Okay, I take it back. Those might be the best pajamas I've ever seen."

"Damn right they are," she said, flipping her hair back dramatically. She bent over, searched under the counter, and straightened up triumphantly with a blow-dryer in hand. "Yes! Now we're talking."

I walked over and wrapped my arms around her waist from behind. She leaned back into me, and I buried my face in her damp hair, kissing her neck.

"I'm going to run out and grab us some food for dinner," I murmured against her ear.

She turned her head slightly. "You're not trying to escape my reindeer pajamas, are you?"

I chuckled, giving her a gentle squeeze. "Nope, I promise the reindeer are safe from me, at least for now. But I figure you're going to need something warm and comforting to eat. Pizza? Chinese?"

She tilted her head in thought, the blow-dryer still clutched in her hand. "Mmm, pizza sounds good. But I'm craving something with extra cheese. Make it happen, Mr. Captain."

I kissed her temple and released her. "You got it. Extra cheese, coming right up."

She smiled, turning back to the mirror and plugging in the blow-dryer as I headed out.

Chapter Twenty-One

12/24 late night

Once my hair was dry, I splashed cold water on my face, trying to erase the evidence of hours spent crying. Grabbing a towel, I patted my skin dry and glanced at my reflection in the mirror. My eyes were still a bit puffy, but the redness had faded. I dabbed on some concealer, swiped mascara over my lashes, and ran a brush through my curls. There, that was better.

My breakdown in the cemetery had been cathartic, like lancing a wound that had festered for too long. I'd never let myself go like that in front of anyone—not even Amanda, and especially not Blake. He would have just scoffed and told me to get over it. But Kol...Kol had stood there calmly, letting me rail and cry and blame myself. And then he'd shared his own pain, his own guilt.

I leaned against the bathroom counter, remembering the warmth in his eyes, the understanding. No man had ever been that emotionally available to me. It was shocking really. When I'd first met Kol, he had struck me as anything but compassionate. The way he'd set me straight at the airport had made me think he would be cold or dismissive—like Blake always was. But he had turned out to be the opposite of all my assumptions in every way that mattered. His thoughtfulness and kindness didn't align with my preconceptions about Army Night Stalkers or airline pilots, and he surprised me at every turn.

I let out a small laugh. Misjudging Mr. Captain had been easy when he was calling me out for being an obnoxious brat at the airport. My cheeks burned as I thought about how rude I'd been. Yet, Kol hadn't held it against me; instead, he'd offered me a ride.

My thoughts drifted to last night, to that other side of him— the dominant, possessive one. It sent a shudder down my spine and made heat pool in my belly. That side had commanded and teased and pushed me to the edge of pleasure. I'd never experienced anything like it. It was delicious, intoxicating. And I wanted more.

I took a deep breath, steeling myself for what came next. I didn't know what this thing between Kol and me was, but I knew I wanted to explore it. I wanted to see where it could go. And that meant putting myself out there. It meant taking a risk.

After finishing up in the bathroom, I made my way downstairs. While waiting for Kol, I danced around the kitchen and gathered a few ingredients for a special treat, humming along to the Christmas tunes playing from my phone. I was glad my ankle was only a little sore now.

I glanced at the clock, excited for him to return with the pizza. I hadn't baked in ages, but these cookies were my jam—

yummy and always a hit. Plus, they were pink, which made them even better.

Christmas Eve would be special for the first time in a long time. I was grateful for Kol's help. Without him, I would have never made it to Holly Winters's office or discovered the truth about everything that had happened after my parents' deaths. Kol had been my rock, carrying me into the house when I'd twisted my ankle and then again after I broke down in the cemetery. He was my guardian angel, like in...what was that old movie? Oh yeah, *It's a Wonderful Life*.

I stirred the dough one last time and started dropping spoonfuls onto the baking sheet. Chocolate cherry chip cookies were my secret weapon. They were easy to make and always perfect. They didn't even require an electric mixer—just mix, drop, and bake.

I popped them into the oven and set about cleaning up the kitchen, which we'd left a mess after dashing off this morning.

When the timer dinged, I grabbed the oven mitts, pulling out a tray of perfectly pink cookies with golden edges. I set them down to cool, resisting the urge to shove one of them straight into my mouth. Kol would be back any minute, and I wanted him to try this unique twist on the classic chocolate chip cookie.

As if on cue, the front door creaked open, and Kol's deep voice echoed through the house. "Noelle? Where you at?"

"In the kitchen!" I called out, wiping my hands on a festive towel.

Kol stepped in, carrying two large pizzas and a bag of drinks. Snowflakes dusted his hair like powdered sugar on brownies.

"Got dinner," he announced, setting the pizza boxes on one counter and the drinks on the other. He scanned the room, his eyes lingering on the tray of cookies. "Mmm, what's that tasty smell?"

I grinned, leaning against the counter. "Cookies. The best you've ever had. You said your favorite was chocolate chip, but these take it a step beyond."

He raised an eyebrow at the sight of them. "Whoa, whoa, whoa. Those are pink!"

I laughed, rolling my eyes. "You're not wrong. Pink is my favorite color. So I waved my magic wand, and poof, they were pink. Try one."

Kol eyed the cookies skeptically.

"Oh, don't be a baby," I teased. "They're pink because they're chocolate cherry chip cookies. When I saw the cake mix in the pantry, I knew I had to make them."

His brow furrowed. "Wait, what? Did you make cake or cookies? I'm so confused."

I chuckled, shaking my head. "I made cookies from cake mix. Now, take a bite."

Kol wrinkled his nose, looking adorably uncertain. "I don't think so."

"Come on," I coaxed, picking up a cookie straight from the pan and waving it in front of him. "You said you love chocolate chip. These are even better. Don't be a Scrooge."

He sighed, giving in. "Fine, fine. But if I die from pink cookie poisoning, it's on you."

I zoomed the cookie toward his mouth like an airplane landing on a runway. With an exaggerated sigh, Kol took a big bite. His eyes widened as he chewed.

"Well?" I asked expectantly.

He grabbed the cookie from my hand and popped the rest of it into his mouth all at once. Then he reached for another. "These are...amazing."

I grinned triumphantly. "Told you so! Are they better than those you bragged about on our drive up here?"

He moved closer, kissing me softly. His lips tasted like chocolate and cherries, and I melted into him. "They're even better than my momma's," he murmured against my mouth. "But don't ever tell her I said that."

Laughing, I wrapped my arms around his neck. "Your secret's safe with me." I stole a quick kiss, my heart suddenly light and carefree. I didn't know why his praise meant so much to me, but it did, and a smile spread across my face. For the first time in forever, I was truly happy—here, in this sweet moment with Kol.

I pulled back, still smiling, and moved to the counter. "Okay, okay, as much as I'd love to keep kissing you, I need to get these cookies onto a plate so I can get the next batch in the oven." I grabbed the spatula, humming softly as I carefully transferred the warm cookies from the pan.

For some reason, I felt like I was floating, like I'd downed a bottle of champagne and the bubbles were fizzing through my veins. I turned to Kol and tried to put this into words.

"You want to know what's really odd? After everything today—after what happened in the cemetery and all the tears—I shouldn't feel this...happy. Should I?"

He propped himself against the counter next to me. "It's not that you shouldn't feel happy. It's that you've let go of something you've been holding onto for a long time. All that pain—it's been sitting there, dragging you down. You finally let yourself feel all of it. You've had all that hurt, all that anger buried deep inside, eating away at you. And today at the gravesite, and with me in the tub, you finally let it out. You let yourself feel everything you've been avoiding. And that release—it's powerful."

I frowned, scooping more cookie dough onto the pan. "But it feels weird, as though I shouldn't be this...okay after what happened. Like I'm betraying them."

Kol stepped closer and placed a hand on my back. "It's not weird, Noelle. It's normal. Suppressed grief starts to control you, even when you don't realize it. But now that you've let it go—even just a little—it's like your mind and body can finally breathe. That's the euphoria. Subconsciously, you probably thought letting it go would mean losing a part of your parents. But that's not what's happening." He squeezed my arm gently. "What you're feeling right now, that lightness, that happiness—it's because you're finally allowing yourself to move forward."

I bit my lip, turned, and opened the oven to put the last batch of cookies in. "So, this is normal? Feeling happy after all of that?"

"Completely normal. Trust me, I've been through it. It doesn't mean you've forgotten or stopped caring—it just means you're allowing yourself to feel joy again."

I let his words sink in, glancing toward the living room and catching sight of the decorations. An idea struck me. "I haven't really celebrated Christmas Eve in years. But tonight, I want to."

"What do you have in mind?"

"I was thinking...what if we made a big picnic right there in the living room by the fire? We've got pizza—one with extra cheese—cookies, and if you can find some more of that wine...it would be lovely! We could relax and enjoy tonight...and maybe each other as well," I added with a playful wink.

His grin widened, and he pulled me into a hug. "A Christmas Eve picnic by the fire with a gorgeous blonde? Now, that sounds perfect." He kissed my forehead softly, then turned toward the fridge. "And as for the wine...I think there might be just enough to make this celebration happen."

While I set to work grabbing plates and napkins for our impromptu indoor picnic by our cozy fireplace, Kol synced his Christmas playlist to the little speaker he'd found. Soon the soft strains of "Have Yourself a Merry Little Christmas" filled the room. He headed to the fireplace, tossing on a few logs and stoking the embers until the flames danced and crackled, then disappeared back into the kitchen.

I set the plates down by the fire, opened the pizza boxes—one with the works and one with extra cheese, spinach, and tomatoes—and placed a few cookies on a plate nearby. Kol returned with two glasses of wine and a bottle tucked under his arm. He handed me a well-filled glass before settling down beside me on the blanket.

"To new beginnings," he said, clinking his glass against mine.

I took a sip, wondering if he was hoping for a new beginning with *me* as much as I was with him. "To new beginnings."

We dug into the pizza, the cheese stretching deliciously between slices. I laughed when he took a bite and a string of cheese clung to his chin.

"You've got a little something..." I teased, showing him the cheese on my finger.

He grinned, capturing my hand and licking it off my finger. A shiver ran down my spine all the way to my toes.

"Delicious," he murmured, his eyes locked onto mine.

I swallowed, my face heating. "You really do make the best fires," I said, scooting to sit closer to him. The flames flickered, highlighting the gold flecks in his eyes. "That's awfully romantic for a Night Stalker."

Kol chuckled, settling back on his elbow and giving me a crooked grin. "Romantic, huh? Didn't know firebuilding could score me points."

I nudged him with my shoulder. "Oh, it does. And don't even get me started on how cozy this whole picnic is." I gestured at the crackling fire and the blanket beneath us. "You've got this whole vibe down."

His smile grew. "What can I say? I'm a man of many talents."

"You sure are." I sighed, wishing I could lose myself in him again.

He moved his face to within inches of mine, his gaze dropping to my lips. "Well, if the fire's that good, maybe we should see if we can make things a little hotter in here."

My pulse quickened. I eased closer, brushing a kiss across his cheek, teasing him with just enough contact to keep him guessing. "I could use a little warming up," I whispered, my lips grazing his ear.

He wrapped an arm around my waist, pulling me closer until our faces were almost touching. "You keep talking like that, and we might burn the house down," he said in a rough way that made my stomach flip.

Biting my lip, I ran my hand over his chest, feeling the muscles beneath his shirt. "I think we can handle a little heat," I said, trailing my fingers down to rest on his thigh.

He captured my mouth with his, kissing me softly at first, then quickly deepened the kiss.

He pulled away slightly, just enough to break the kiss, and his expression made my heart leap. His usual cocky grin was gone, replaced with something new, something vulnerable. For the first time, I saw him without his defenses—and the way he looked at me stole my breath. He was mine, completely, and the realization both thrilled and terrified me.

He brushed a lock of my hair behind my ear, his fingers lingering on my cheek, then trailed kisses from my temple down to my jaw, each one deliberate. When his lips met mine again, it was unlike anything I'd experienced before—soft yet intense, filled with an emotion I couldn't quite place but didn't want to let go of. It was tentative and sweet, as if he was trying to show me all the love in the world. He was pouring everything into this kiss. It was tender, almost reverent, a promise of things to come.

He cradled my face in his hands, his thumbs stroking my cheeks. Taking his time, he explored my mouth, savoring the moment with gentle affection. It was the kind of kiss I'd only ever read about in books or seen in movies, the kind that made your knees weak and your heart race. And it was happening to me, with Kol.

He eased back, his eyes searching mine briefly before he reached for the hem of my flannel pajama top. I lifted my arms, allowing him to remove it, leaving me bare to him.

"You're perfect," he murmured, his gaze sweeping over me. "Every inch of you."

The sudden chill of the room caused goose bumps to rise on my skin, but the heat in Kol's gaze was enough to warm me from the inside out. He leaned forward, pressing gentle kisses along my collarbones. His lips traveled downward, over the swells of my breasts, lingering at the valley between them as he lay me down on the blanket. Then his fingers began tracing the curves of my sides. He took his time, worshipping my body with a tenderness that made me feel adored.

"You're so beautiful, Noelle," he whispered against my skin. "And you're all mine."

Arching into his touch, I tangled my fingers in his hair, needing something to ground me. This differed from the aggressive, passionate sex we'd had before—this Kol was all about giving, about showing me how much he cherished me.

I gasped when he lowered his head, taking one of my sensitive peaks into his mouth. For a few delicious, fervent moments, he lavished attention on it, swirling his tongue around the tight bud before turning his attention to the other.

Too soon, Kol broke away long enough to remove his shirt, revealing his broad chest and defined muscles. My fingers itched to touch him, to trace the lines of his tattoos, but he was already moving, his hands sliding down to the waistband of my pajama bottoms.

He hooked his fingers under the fabric, wiggling them down my hips. He took a moment to appreciate the sight of me, his gaze roaming over my body with a hunger that made it clear how much he craved me.

Quickly, he removed his own pants, revealing the evidence of his arousal. But instead of rushing to take things further, he positioned his face between my thighs, his breath hot against my skin. His tongue started tracing a path up my inner thigh, making me shiver with anticipation.

When he finally reached my center, he didn't waste any time. He lapped at my flesh, his tongue delving into my folds with a skill that left me breathless. His tongue flicked out, tracing slow circles around my clit before dipping lower to taste all of me. He was relentless in his pursuit of my gratification, his mouth working tirelessly to bring me to the brink.

His fingers joined in, sliding inside me while his tongue continued its ravenous torment of my clit. He used just enough pressure—just enough teeth. An orgasm was building within me, a slow burn that grew more intense with each passing second.

"Kol," I gasped, my fingers twisting in his hair. "Please..."

He looked up at me, his eyes dark with desire. "What do you need, baby?"

"You," I breathed. "I need you."

He smiled a slow, sexy smile that made my heart flutter. Then he lowered his head. His tongue circled my clit, and his fingers moved faster, pushing me closer to the edge. My raging need built, coiling tight in my belly, ready to explode.

And then, just when I thought I couldn't take any more, his finger curled in a way that left stars dancing behind my closed eyelids. He'd found that sweet spot within me, and I shattered, my body convulsing as the most intense orgasm of my life ripped through me.

He didn't stop, not even as I came down from my high. He continued to lick and suck and tease, drawing out every last drop of pleasure until I was a boneless, sated mess beneath him.

When he finally pulled away, his lips were glistening with my release. I reached for him, pulling him up to lie beside me. Wrapping my arms around him, I pressed a kiss to his lips and tasted myself on his tongue. It was intimate and erotic, and it made me want him all over again.

Kol positioned himself between my thighs and hovered above me. I reached up, tracing the lines of his tattoos with my fingertips.

He gave me a smile then, one that set my heart ablaze, its heat spreading through my chest and down to my core. At that moment, I was acutely aware of just how perfect he was—not just physically, with his chiseled features and strong, muscular body, but in his heart. He had been so patient, taking care of me when I was at my worst.

We had only just met, but it felt like I had known him forever. My heart was his, completely and irrevocably, in a way I had never imagined possible. And when he looked at me, with that knowing glint in his eyes, I wondered if he felt it too—this magnetic pull that defied logic and time.

I watched, entranced, as he took his cock in his hand, stroking it a few times before running it along my folds, paying particular attention to my clit. The sensation ignited a spark, another orgasm already coiling in my core, ready to explode at his command.

With a tenderness that belied his size, he inched his way inside me, his eyes never leaving mine. My walls clenched around him; the fit was so deliciously tight. He lowered himself to his elbows, his body pressing against mine as he began to move.

"You're so beautiful, Noelle," he murmured, leaning down to capture my lips with his.

His kiss was tender, but there was a hunger beneath it that rivaled my own. I wrapped my arms around his neck, pulling him closer, needing more of him.

Each of his thrusts was slow and deep, stroking against my bundle of nerves, giving me the friction that would send me over the edge. Our lips melded together as he swallowed my moans.

I dug my heels into the floor and met each of his thrusts with my own, urging him on. Our bodies moved in perfect harmony, the rhythm building with each passing moment. He was close; I could see it in the tension of his jaw, the way his muscles strained. I could also sense he was holding back, refusing to let himself go until I did. The knowledge that he was so attuned to my pleasure that he was willing to sacrifice his own for mine unleashed an inferno of need that tore through me, consuming every last bit of restraint I had.

"Kol," I gasped, squeezing his shoulders hard. "I'm so close..."

He looked down at me, his eyes filled with an affection I'd never known. "Come for me, baby," he murmured. "Let me feel you come."

With all my might, I clamped down on his shaft. And with his one last thrust, my climax hit, waves of ecstasy crashing over me. Kol's control shattered, and he tumbled over the edge with me, his body shuddering as he found his release.

He collapsed on top of me, his weight a comfort rather than a burden. His fingers tangled in my hair as he nuzzled into my neck, pressing tender kisses against my heated skin.

"You're incredible, Noelle," he whispered, his breath warm against my body. "I can't get enough of you. I never want to let you go." His words were soft, a murmur of praise that filled my heart to the brim.

In a split second, it all made sense: he was just as addicted to me as I was to him. It was there in the way he held me, in the way he touched me, in the way he looked at me like I was the only woman in the world. And although the word *love* lingered on the tip of my tongue, it was too soon to speak it aloud. Instead, I showed him with my touches, with my kisses, with the way I melted into him, surrendering myself completely.

My eyes fluttered closed as exhaustion swept over me. I was beyond emotionally and physically spent; my body was limp as his strong arms held me.

He pulled out of me slowly, and a soft sigh escaped my lips at the loss of contact. But before I could mourn the separation, he lifted me into his arms, cradling me against his chest like I weighed nothing at all.

The world blurred around the edges while he carried me up the stairs, the soft glow of the Christmas lights casting a kaleidoscope of colors on the walls. I hazily registered the coolness of sheets against my skin as he laid me down on the bed, tucking me in.

"Sleep, my firecracker," he whispered, kissing my forehead. "I've got you."

And with that promise hanging in the air, I let the darkness swallow me whole, slipping into the warm, comforting embrace of sleep, secure knowing that Kol would be there when I woke up.

Noelle Nichols

Chapter Twenty-Two

12/25 Christmas late morning

The bright sunlight streaming through the window dragged me back to consciousness but made it nearly impossible for me to open my eyelids. Memories from last night drifted through my mind—Kol's touch, the way he had worshiped every inch of me—and I wanted to stay wrapped up in the warm cocoon of satisfaction. Waking up slowly, I stretched like a lazy cat under the covers. My muscles were deliciously sore. The ache reminded me of how thoroughly he had taken his time, leaving me spent, blissful, and drifting off to an unworried sleep.

My mind started to clear as I came fully awake, and the chill at my back told me Kol wasn't there. Stretching an arm out confirmed it—just empty space and cold sheets. I cracked open an eye and scanned the room. There were no lights on in the bathroom, and the house was completely quiet...maybe a little too quiet. No signs of him anywhere. He was probably downstairs, waiting for me to wake up.

I sat up, the events of the day before replaying in my mind. He hadn't pitied me, hadn't offered any of the hollow sympathy I'd gotten used to receiving from others. No, Kol had seen me—all of me—and still looked at me like I was everything he'd ever wanted. Like I was his beginning, his end, and everything in between. It was heady, knowing I had that kind of effect on him. And coming from a man like Kol, someone as guarded as he was? That made it all the more potent.

Eager to find him, I rolled out of bed. Christmas Day with my very own Captain Santa? Yes, please! Maybe we'd take his *big red sleigh*, as Mrs. Winters had so aptly called his Bronco, out for some adventuring. The thought made me grin as I headed to the bathroom.

I cleaned up quickly, brushing my teeth and washing my face before putting on some black leggings and an oversized red sweater that was just long enough to cover my booty. Casual but cute. I pulled a brush through my hair, letting the curls settle in their usual wild state before tying half of it up with a red bow. The ends of the ribbon draped down along the back of my hair, adding just the right touch of festive cheer.

After applying a little makeup, I was ready to find Kol. I was surprised he hadn't come up when he'd heard me stirring.

I rushed downstairs, the wooden planks creaking under my feet, anticipation bubbling up inside me. Kol was probably in the living room or kitchen.

But he wasn't there, and all the lights were off in the living room. The usual warmth from the fireplace was absent. Something wasn't right.

"Kol?" I called out, my voice echoing through the silent house. No response. I darted into the kitchen, expecting for him to be there, leaning against the counter, coffee in hand. But it was empty and silent save for the ticking of the vintage cat clock, its tail swinging with each second. It wasn't just empty; it was clean—spotless. The pizza boxes from last night were gone, the plate of cookies I'd made had vanished, and the countertops sparkled like they'd just been scrubbed. It looked as though no one had touched a single thing since we'd arrived.

A niggle of unease wormed its way into my stomach. Had he left?

I moved to the back door, peeking out into the yard, half-expecting to see him gathering wood. But there was no sign of him; the snow was undisturbed. No footprints, no Kol.

The knot of worry tightened in my stomach. Maybe he'd gone to get breakfast. Yeah, that had to be it. He had gone to grab us something to eat and would be returning any minute, and I'd laugh about how silly I'd been, worrying over nothing.

I rushed back into the living room, flipping on the lights. My breath hitched. The room was too neat, too perfect. The blankets we'd used for our makeshift bed were gone, the sofa cushions were back in place, and the Christmas afghan lay draped over the back of the couch.

I blinked and stared at the tree, my gaze narrowing on the velvet ribbon Kol had used to blindfold me. It was back on the tree, wrapped perfectly around the branches, as though it had never left.

This didn't make sense. Not one bit.

I spun around, my eyes landing on the fireplace. It was clean—no fire, no ashes, just wood stacked neatly on the hearth. It was like we'd never been here at all.

This was too weird, too fucking creepy.

Had I dreamed the last two days? The laughter, the tears, Kol's presence? It couldn't have all been in my head. But as I stood there, looking around at this room that had been scrubbed of all evidence, uncertainty began to stir. My feet moved of their own accord, and I started pacing, rubbing my temples, trying to find some solid ground. My body ached in places that screamed of last night's reality. It hadn't been a dream. Kol had been here.

But where the hell was he now?

Bolting back to the kitchen, I snatched my phone from the counter. I had to call him and figure out what was happening. But as I stared at the screen, my heart sank. I didn't have his number. We'd been together almost every minute since the airport—no need for texts or calls. I tossed the phone back onto the counter.

Think, Noelle, think. There had to be a note, something that would explain all this. I rummaged through the kitchen, opening drawers and cabinets, searching for something—anything—that might tell me where he'd gone. Nothing. Not a single clue.

My mind raced, my thoughts spiraling out of control. Had I said something? Maybe he'd changed his mind about me, about us. Maybe he'd decided I wasn't worth the hassle. But that didn't make sense. He'd been so sweet, so loving. He was the most understanding guy I'd ever met, like fate had sent him to me to help restore my faith that life was worth living. He'd held me while I cried, for fuck's sake. He wouldn't just leave, not without saying something.

I took a deep breath, trying to calm myself. And then it hit me—was his luggage still here? We'd taken our bags upstairs to the bedroom. I flew up the stairs and down the hallway, my heart pounding in my chest. *Please, please, please.* I chanted a silent mantra. *Please let his bag be there.*

I flung open the door and scanned the room. Everything was as I'd left it—the bed unmade, the curtains drawn. I rushed to the closet, my heart in my throat. And then I saw it. My bag, sitting there all alone. His was gone.

I stumbled back, shock coursing through my veins. He'd left. Kol had left without a trace, without a note, without the decency to say goodbye. I sank onto the edge of the bed, my body shaking with disbelief. This couldn't be happening, not like this.

Tears pricked my eyes. I had let him in, let him see me, all of me. And he'd left, just like everyone else, just like Blake, just like my parents.

But I refused to allow a single teardrop to fall. I'd cried more yesterday than I had in the last four years. I was done. I'd been such a fool, such a fucking idiot. I'd thought he was different, thought he cared. But he was just like the rest of them. And now I was alone again. Alone in this big, empty house, with nothing but the ghosts of my past to keep me company.

I sat on the edge of the bed, reality sinking in. Kol was gone. My body shook, filled with a toxic swirl of hurt and anger. I hugged my arms around myself, trying to ward off the chill that had nothing to do with the temperature.

I shouldn't have been surprised. After my meltdown at the cemetery yesterday, who wouldn't have run? I'd probably scared the hell out of him. Hell, I scared myself sometimes. At some point last night, he must have come to his senses and decided I wasn't worth it. I'd been a hot mess of ugly tears.

I glanced around the room, my gaze landing on the rumpled sheets and the indent on his pillow. What had last night been about then? Had he just felt sorry for me? The tenderness in his eyes, the softness in his touch—it must have been pity. That had to be it. It had been nothing more than a sympathy fuck. God, how embarrassing. I squeezed my eyes shut, cringing at the thought. Why else would a guy like Kol waste his time with someone like me?

Men like him had options. They had their pick of the litter, and I was just a broken, jobless loser. I should've seen this coming. Everyone left eventually. They always did. The minute they realized I was too much, they slipped away. Kol had just done it in the middle of the night while I slept like a fool, thinking he'd still be here in the morning.

Anger surged through me, hot and fierce. I clenched my fists, digging my nails into my palms. I wasn't a loser. I wasn't some weak, pathetic thing to be pitied. I was Noelle fucking Nichols, and I was done apologizing for who I was. If I was too much—too loud, too fiery—well, they could go find less. No one got to set limits on me or dictate my volume. I wasn't born to be some quiet little thing, biting my tongue and playing office politics like a good little girl. I was a goddamn wild mustang, not some show pony. Why the hell was I letting anyone make me feel otherwise?

I had to get out of here, go back to Atlanta and figure out what to do with the rest of my life. The idea of being stuck here, in the midst of all these ghosts and empty promises, made my skin crawl. But Atlanta wasn't much better. All I had there was an empty apartment and no job. And I'd be back at the starting line of my career.

Well, not everything there sucked. Amanda was there. The only sunlight in Atlanta was Amanda. She was the one person who had stuck around all these years. She was loud like me. Fun like me. A sister from another mother, a kindred spirit who was trying to find a good guy who didn't just want to fuck around.

Amanda. I needed to talk to Amanda. She'd know what to do, how to fix this mess I'd made of my life. I could call her, maybe. God, how would I even explain all of this? *Hey, so after I quit my job, I gave my heart to a guy after two days, and he bailed on Christmas Morning. How's your holiday going?* This whole Kol situation was insane. She'd think I'd lost my mind. And the clause—God, the clause. I couldn't even think about that right now.

I was stuck, trapped in this goddamn limbo, and I hated it.

I snatched my phone from the nightstand, scrolling to Amanda's number. My thumb hovered over the call button. No, I couldn't do this to her. Not today. It was Christmas, for fuck's sake. She'd be with her family and friends. I couldn't dump this on her, not now.

I had to deal with this myself, figure out what I wanted and where the hell I belonged.

For a few minutes, I sat on the bed, staring at my phone as if it might suddenly light up with an explanation from Kol. But I was only greeted by silence and a blank screen of course. He no more had my number than I had his.

How had I read him so wrong? The way he'd held me last night, the way he'd touched me—none of that had screamed, "*I'm leaving in the middle of the night without a word.*" In fact, he had promised he wasn't going anywhere. What kind of guy said that and then ghosted?

I glanced around the room again, and a hollow feeling settled in my stomach. Huffing an angry breath, I swiped open my phone, going straight to the airline app. If Kol had left, then I sure as hell wasn't sticking around to mope.

Scrolling through flights, I found one leaving Albany for Atlanta in a few hours—only one. I booked it without thinking twice, but then it hit me—I didn't have a rental car, and there was no way I could get one in Saratoga on Christmas Morning.

Then I remembered my aunt's old car parked outside under the carport. Surely, the keys were somewhere in the house.

Technically, the house—and everything on the premises—was mine now, right? I had signed the papers. Borrowing it wasn't wrong. I'd return it. Eventually.

"Right," I muttered, grabbing my suitcase from the closet. "Big-girl panties on. Compartmentalize. Lock it all up tight and move." I tossed my clothes haphazardly into the bag, zipped it shut, and slung my tote over my shoulder. The suitcase thudded against the floor as I dragged it across the hallway, down the stairs, and to the front door. I left it there while I went to hunt for the car keys.

The kitchen seemed like the most logical place to start. It was where I always left my keys. I scanned the countertops. Nothing. I moved on to the drawers, yanking them open one by one, searching through piles of old papers, takeout menus, and spare batteries. Still nothing. The hooks by the door? Nope. I bent down, rummaging through the junk drawer under the microwave, tossing aside rubber bands and random screws. Panic started to rise, a tight knot forming in my chest. I didn't have time for this. I needed to get to the airport.

Frantically, I rushed upstairs, taking the steps two at a time. Maybe she kept the keys in her bedroom. I hesitated at the door, a pang of guilt hitting me. It felt wrong, invading her space like this. But I shook it off. This was my house now, right? And I was just borrowing the car. I'd leave it at the airport and deal with it later.

I pushed open the door, the hinges creaking softly. The room was neat. The bed was made, and a faint scent of lavender lingered in the air. I started with the nightstand, then moved to the dresser, careful not to disturb anything too much. But again, there were no keys.

I stood in the middle of the room, hands on my hips, trying to think. Where the hell would she keep them? Closing my eyes,

I pictured Aunt Mary. She was practical, no-nonsense. She wouldn't leave them just anywhere. She'd put them somewhere safe, somewhere she wouldn't forget.

My eyes snapped open. Of course. I remembered seeing a little dish on the table by the back door, the closest door to the carport. I'd breezed right past it several times.

I rushed back downstairs. There they were, sitting in the dish—a heart-shaped keychain with a horse on it that matched the house keys. Relief flooded through me as I snatched them up. Now, where had I put the other keys? Good grief. I was so scattered. Ah, yes, my tote.

I headed back through the living room. As I walked by one of the bookshelves, something caught my eye—a small picture frame nestled among the books. I hesitated, then reached out, lifting it from the shelf. I froze when I saw the photo. It was me, maybe six years old, sandwiched between my parents at the racetrack here in town.

We were smiling. My dad's arm was wrapped around my shoulders, his ball cap pulled low, shielding his eyes from the summer sun. Mom leaned in close. Her face was lit up in the way it always used to when she was at her happiest. And I stood between them with a bright pink stuffed horse, beaming like I'd just won the lottery. That day had been perfect.

I ran my thumb gently over their faces, my chest aching. There was something brutal about this beautiful photo. All those years of happiness, and yet here I was, alone.

I should leave. I needed to leave. Start fresh in Atlanta. Get as far away from all of this as I could. But then again, maybe I shouldn't run. Maybe there was something here worth staying for—something that could give me more than the empty hustle Atlanta ever could. This was my past, my history. The good, the bad, all of it intertwined, inseparable. And I was standing at a crossroads, torn between running away and facing it head-on. There was something profound about returning to your roots, like a tree reaching deep into the earth, drawing strength from the past to grow tall and strong. It could be the best thing for me, a chance to rebuild. This was a place where I didn't have to be perfect, where people remembered the girl I'd been before life tore me apart. It could be a chance to start over—not somewhere new, but where it all began.

I sighed, setting the frame gently back on the shelf, my fingers brushing against something cool and metallic. Curious, I picked the object up, turning it over in my hand. It was a shiny silver dollar. The date on it made me pause. My birth year. A strange coincidence. I turned it over, running my thumb along its smooth edges. "Huh. What are the odds?" I muttered.

There was no telling what else might be hidden in this house, old treasures buried under years of dust. But as I held the coin, an idea struck me. What if I let fate decide? Flip a coin. Why not? It wasn't like my choices had been all that stellar lately. Maybe there was a higher power, something that would guide the outcome of the coin. I could use a little divine intervention right about now.

Biting my lip, I considered it. Heads, I would stay in my hometown. Tails for a new start anywhere but here. Let the universe figure out what I was supposed to do.

I closed my eyes for a second. Then, opening them, I flipped the coin hard and watched it. Time seemed to slow as it spun upward, catching the light that was streaming in through the window. It rotated, again and again, the sun glinting off the silver. I stood there, transfixed, my heart in my throat. This was it—the moment that would decide my future.

The shiny silver dollar spun in the air, rotating slowly at the very peak of its flight. It caught the sun in a burst of brightness that made me squint.

The front door banged open, the noise jarring me out of my trance. I jumped, letting out a startled yelp as the coin clattered onto the floor with a metallic ring. My heart raced, and I whipped around.

Kol stood silhouetted in the doorway, his broad frame backlit by the morning sun, looking like something straight out of a dream...or a nightmare.

Chapter Twenty-Three

12/25 Christmas midday

Kol walked in and nearly tripped over my suitcase, dropping a couple of bags by the door. Time seemed to freeze as we stood there. I blinked in stunned silence, my eyes darting between him and the coin on the floor. He broke the silence first.

"What's with the suitcase?" he asked gruffly, a tight line forming between his brows. "Are you leaving? Just going to walk out without a word?"

His words snapped me back to real time. I slammed my fists onto my hips as anger bubbled to the surface. "Walk out without a word? Are you serious right now?" My voice rose with each syllable. "That's hilarious, coming from you. You left! No note, no nothing. Cleaned up, took everything—including your damn toothbrush—and just disappeared! You didn't even wake me up! You're the jerk here, not me. How dare you waltz in here and try to accuse me of something? I got your message loud and clear. Just get out and stay out."

Kol shook his head as if he was trying to back up and restart. He marched toward me, kicking the door shut with his boot. "What the hell are you talking about?"

His eyes flashed with anger, and the space between us shrank to nothing.

He was close—too close—his nostrils flaring, his jaw tight. I looked him up and down, noticing details that didn't add up. His face was cleanly shaven, his hair perfectly tousled. He wore a dark-colored flannel shirt rolled up to the elbows, a pair of jeans, and hiking boots—nothing I recalled him having in his suitcase.

Kol gripped my shoulders, giving me a shake. "You really do have some serious trust issues." His voice was rough, like gravel under a truck tire, but his eyes held a softness that contradicted his tone.

I was confused, my mind spinning like a top. "You left," I repeated. "I woke up, and you were gone. Everything was gone. What was I supposed to think?"

A muscle twitched in his cheek. "I went to get supplies. We needed food; I figured you'd want something more than just pancakes."

He heaved a sigh that seemed to come from the depths of him. "Since I joined the Army, I've always woken up at the ass-crack of dawn. You were out cold, sleeping peacefully— beautifully tranquil, I might add. So, I busied myself cleaning up, which didn't take long. Then it hit me that there was something important I needed to do. Plus, I needed fresh clothes. I figured I had plenty of time to run home and grab a few things. Rotterdam's not that far away, and based on those contented little snores you were making, I figured you wouldn't even notice I was gone."

I bristled, heat rising to my cheeks. "I do not snore!"

He chuckled. "Oh, you do, and it's adorable. You talk in your sleep too."

Mortified, I spun around, breaking away from his hold on me. "No! You're just saying that to throw me off. No one has ever mentioned it. Don't try to change the subject. You left. I knew you would... Everyone else has."

He didn't miss a beat; he wrapped his arms around me from behind, splaying one hand across my stomach and resting the other on my hip. With his chin resting atop my head, he rocked us gently. "No, sweetheart. You've got it all wrong. I'm not going anywhere. I always keep my promises."

I sighed, the fight draining out of me. "I thought you'd left. No goodbye...just *gone,* as if you'd never existed. It's awful when someone you care about disappears."

He squeezed me tighter and softly kissed my cheek. "I'm not leaving, Noelle. How about I make us breakfast, and then we can talk about where we go from here?" He released me and returned to the bags he'd dropped by the door. "Brought a few things from home since all the stores are closed today."

I bent down, picking up the coin from where it had fallen earlier, studying it. Heads. I bit my lip, my mind whirring. Maybe there *was* a higher power, something guiding all this chaos.

"Whatcha got there?" Kol asked, glancing over his shoulder as he passed me on his way to the kitchen.

"It's just a coin I found. Nothing really."

I followed him, setting the coin on the kitchen table and tracing my fingers over it contemplatively.

Kol started unloading the bags, setting eggs, bacon, ham, some veggies, a loaf of bread, orange juice, and several more items onto the counter. He caught me watching him and winked. "We've got to keep our strength up. Who knows what the day will bring?"

Crossing my arms over my chest, I smiled softly. Maybe the coin had been a sign. Maybe Kol was right—maybe I did have it all wrong. Maybe, for once, someone was here to stay.

I made my way over to the counter next to him, ready to pitch in with breakfast. "You can chop those if you want," he said, gesturing to the veggies he'd brought. After washing his hands, he cracked a few eggs into a bowl, whisking them with a quick flick of his wrist. "I'm glad you're not some vegan," he said, tossing a handful of diced ham into the pan. "No way a *meat-asaurus* like me could last for long with a woman like that."

I nudged him with my elbow, grinning as I slid the cutting board with the bell peppers and tomatoes I'd just cut up closer to him. "*Meat-asaurus?* Is that even a word?" I snorted. "And don't worry, I won't make you eat tofu. That stuff is gross."

He chuckled, sprinkling the veggies into the pan alongside the ham. "*Meat-asaurus* is definitely in my vocabulary. Besides, you can't deny that bacon makes everything better."

I rolled my eyes and laughed. "Well, I can't argue with that logic." The sizzle of bacon filled the kitchen, making my stomach rumble. While he worked, I canceled the flight I'd just booked.

When everything was ready, I laid a couple of plates on the counter, watching as Kol expertly folded the omelet with the spatula, cut it in half, and flipped the pieces onto the plates like a pro.

"Not bad, Mr. Captain," I teased, grabbing some salt and pepper.

"You learn to cook when you spend half your life in the middle of nowhere," he replied, shooting me a playful wink as he pushed a plate toward me. "But seriously, no tofu. Ever."

Laughing, I shook my head and moved to the table to set my plate down. Then I grabbed some utensils and poured a couple of glasses of juice. Everything about this felt easy—like we'd been doing it for years instead of days.

But underneath that ease, something twisted in my stomach, gnawing at me.

When we sat down to eat, Kol dived into his omelet without hesitation. I took a bite, savoring the flavors, but my mind was elsewhere. Was he going to stick around? Or was this just another fleeting moment in a life full of them? I'd given him my heart, and while he seemed to be offering his in return, the morning's confusion had shaken me more than I wanted to admit.

Kol paused mid-bite, watching me push my food around the plate. "What's going on in that mind of yours, Noelle?"

I set my fork down, staring at the table before finally meeting his eyes. "Please don't break my heart. There's not much of it left."

Slowly, he placed his fork on his plate, then leaned forward, elbows on the table, and studied me. He reached a hand across the table, covering mine. His thumb traced circles on my skin, the rough calluses sending goose bumps up my arm. "I'm not here to hurt you. You've been through so much already. But you don't have to carry everything by yourself anymore. I'm here to help with the load." His eyes held mine, the golden flecks in his irises catching the light. "You deserve someone who's going to be straight with you, always. And that's what I'm offering. I know words are easy, but I'm not just about words. I'll prove it to you. I'm not going anywhere. I'm not going to rush you. But I want you to know I'm here for the long haul—no matter how long it takes for you to believe that."

My breath hitched. Without thinking, I stood up and moved behind him, wrapping my arms around his shoulders and resting my hands on his chest. I bent down, kissing his cheek softly, lingering there for just a second.

Kol turned to gently cup my cheek in his hand, and then he pulled me in for a sweet kiss.

I melted into it.

When I broke away, I caressed the edge of his jaw with my fingertips before letting my hands fall to my sides. I slipped back into my chair, my heart lighter than it had been all morning. Kol studied me for a moment, and then we both returned to our omelets.

After a few more bites, he cleared his throat. "By the way, the roads are looking much better now. Between the sun and the city's cleanup, there's no problem getting out. And barely anyone's out since it's Christmas Morning."

I took a sip of juice, a playful grin creeping onto my face. "Oh, so you're saying we should take your big red sleigh out for a flight?"

Kol chuckled, shaking his head as he wiped his mouth with a napkin. "If that's what Miss Claus wants, we'll fire it up. No reindeer required. Maybe I'll even let you fly it this time."

"Ooo, you trust me that much?"

"It's a chance I'm willing to take," he teased, rising from the table and placing his dish in the sink.

"I'll clean up the kitchen if you build me a fire," I said. "I don't think I'll ever be able to look at that fireplace without thinking about..."

Memories of his hands on my body skittered through my mind.

Kol's eyes darkened with desire. "Trust me, I'll never forget how the firelight flickered over your...skin." He cleared his throat and blinked away the hunger in his eyes. "I'd be happy to build you a fire. I'm an expert, remember?"

Before he got to work, I called out after him, "Why'd you clean the firebox up so well this morning? It was spotless."

271

Kol glanced over his shoulder. "It's all about maintenance. You've got to take good care of a fireplace. Keeping the ashes out makes it burn cleaner and safer. A clean firebox means a hotter fire. And who doesn't want that? Plus, if you don't do it, it's a mess. And I'm not a fan of messes." He winked before heading to the living room, and I started cleaning up.

Soon the scent of burning wood filled the air. I'd forever associate that smell with...us. I was wiping down the counters and putting away the last dishes when Kol's voice boomed from the living room. "Noelle, get in here!"

His boyish excitement had me curious. Drying my hands on a towel, I hurried into the living room.

My breath caught. The Christmas tree sparkled, lights shimmering on every branch. Aunt Mary's beloved figurines were all lit up, their little mechanical parts whirring and clicking as they moved—tiny little dancers spinning. The sight of it all was stunning. It was like walking into a winter wonderland.

I wandered through the room, taking it all in, brushing my fingers against the tree's boughs. It was perfect. My heart swelled. Stopping before the tree, I gazed up at the angel perched on top. She was old, her paint chipped and her wings slightly askew, but she was perfect.

"Thank you, Aunt Mary," I whispered, a lump forming in my throat. This was the Christmas I hadn't known I needed.

Kol stood by the fireplace. "I have a surprise for you," he said, a half smirk playing on his lips.

I turned and walked over to him, lifting my brow. "You didn't have to get me anything. I didn't—"

Before I could finish, Kol leaned in, silencing me with a kiss. It was sweet and gentle, enough to make my words disappear. When he pulled back, he held out a long, slender box. It was old, the velvet worn and the edges frayed.

"Go ahead, open it," he said.

I hesitated for a moment, then slowly untied the ribbon and opened the lid. Nestled inside was the most stunning necklace I'd ever seen—a diamond halo pendant. Its brilliant center stone and the surrounding intricate details glinted in the soft light of the room. It was clearly old, the setting ornate and full of history. And it was breathtaking.

"Kol, I—I can't accept this," I stuttered, overwhelmed. "It's too much."

Before I could protest further, he gently took the necklace from the box, spun me around, and fastened it behind my neck. He wrapped his arms around me from behind, pulling me into a tight embrace. I relaxed back into him, reveling in the warmth of his body.

"This necklace was my grandma's," he said quietly, his lips brushing the top of my head. "She gave it to me before she passed away. Originally, it was given to her by her mother when she was a young woman. She told me it was a gift of strength, a symbol of resilience and beauty."

He paused, his thumbs tracing circles on my shoulders. I turned to face him, my hand instinctively reaching up to touch the pendant as his words sank in.

"My great-grandmother kept it close to her heart through many trials and tribulations—World War One, the Depression. She gave the necklace to my grandma because she, too, had to face tragic circumstances. Losing her husband in World War Two and facing polio," he continued, keeping his gaze steady on me. "It was their reminder that, no matter how hard life got, they were tough. She told me to give it to a special girl one day—a girl who sparkled even during the worst of times."

A tear rolled down my cheek, and Kol brushed it away with his thumb.

"I've met no one more deserving of this necklace than you," he whispered. "Not even my little sisters. You're strong, Noelle, even though you don't realize it. It was meant for you. No matter what happens between us, you will always have a reminder of how strong you are and that you are a precious gem. You should never doubt that you were meant to be born. I don't know what your future holds, but I do know you're special and that there's an important purpose for you."

Speechless, I stared at him, my heart filled to bursting. This was more than I could have ever imagined.

I threw my arms around him, burying my face in his chest. "Thank you, thank you so much. For this, for everything. You have no idea what this means to me," I murmured, the words muffled against his chest. "Thank you for giving me the best gift ever." I sniffed. Inhaling deeply, I looked up at him. "Not the necklace, but the belief that life is worth living."

Kol held me tight, resting his chin on top of my head. "You don't have to thank me. I'm just giving you what you deserve."

At that moment, a sense of peace seeped into my bones. Whatever the future held, I knew I could face it. With Kol by my side, I was unstoppable.

Noelle Nichols

Chapter Twenty-Four

12/25 Christmas midday through 12/28

Out of nowhere, a toy train ran off its track and veered toward the kitchen, its little wheels spinning furiously, drawing Kol's attention.

"Damn thing's got a mind of its own," he said, releasing me and chasing after it. I stood there, staring down at the necklace, still reeling from its history and meaning. As I traced my fingers over the delicate pendant, I promised myself I'd never take it off and that, someday, I'd find just the right girl to pass it on to.

Walking over to Kol, I watched as he tinkered with the train, his large hands surprisingly nimble as he worked. He crouched by the tree, trying to get the stubborn toy to cooperate and stay on the track. His patience was admirable, but I had something bigger on my mind.

"Kol, will you take me home?"

He froze, his hands going still. Slowly, he rose to his feet and wrapped his strong arms around me. After a moment, he took my face between his hands and brushed his thumbs gently against my cheeks. Tenderly, he kissed my forehead. "I'd be happy to make that journey with you, sweetheart."

It didn't take long for us to bundle up and head out. We remained silent for a while as we drove to the farm, listening to the hum of the engine and the songs on the radio.

"You know," I said, breaking the silence, "I've been going over it in my head—the reasons to stay in Atlanta and the reasons to move back here."

Kol glanced at me, his eyes reflecting the lights from the dashboard. "And?"

"And it's not as straightforward as it seems." I sighed. "I doubt there are any marketing executive jobs remotely similar to my old one here. But I'm not even sure that's what I want to do anymore. It all seems so...superficial."

Kol nodded, his thumb tapping a rhythm on the wheel. "Life has a way of changing our priorities."

"Exactly," I agreed. "The hardest part would be leaving Amanda. She's been my rock. I don't want to hurt her."

"She'll understand. True friends want what's best for you, no matter where you are. And from what you've told me about Amanda, she doesn't seem like the type to let a little distance get in the way."

I stared out the window, watching the trees blur past.

"And then there's the fact that I'd be alone here," I pointed out. "But then again, my life would be turned upside down regardless of whether I stay or go."

Kol reached over, finding my hand and squeezing it. "You wouldn't be alone, Noelle. You'd have me."

I smiled at him. "The best thing about coming home would be keeping the farm and Aunt Mary's house. Especially right now, when I'm jobless and unsure about what I want to do with the rest of my life."

Kol's thumb traced circles on the back of my hand. "It's a good place to figure things out. It'd be a fresh start."

"To most people, this would be an easy decision, a no-brainer," I said, "but for me, being here without my parents... it might be more than I'm capable of emotionally. Everything reminds me of them. It's not that I want to forget them; it's that I want the memories to stop being painful."

Kol's grip on my hand tightened. "I understand. The mind has a way of shutting itself off to memories that are too painful to cope with."

"I can't believe it's already been four years since they died. I thought I had it handled because I just... I didn't let myself think about them as gone. It was easier to pretend we hadn't seen each other in a long time. I know that sounds crazy, but since I never went back to the farm after the funeral, it still wasn't real in my mind."

Kol's eyes were filled with understanding. "It's not crazy. And, hey, I just want you to know it means a lot to me that you asked me to go with you. I hope it will help you find closure."

I smiled, appreciating the steady calm he always seemed to offer. "I feel bad for taking up so much of your time. You probably need to get back to your life, your job..."

He chuckled. "I already got in touch with my chief pilot and took off a couple of days. Work'll be there when I get back."

That stopped me in my tracks. "You...you took time off? For me?"

He glanced over, a half smile curving his lips. "Right now, you're what matters."

Stunned, I stared at him. I couldn't believe he'd made me such a priority.

After a few more minutes, we had arrived in Greenfield and the truck was maneuvering up the long gravel driveway, the tires crunching along and kicking up slush and small stones. As the house came into view, Kol let out a low whistle. "This is not what I was expecting."

I grinned, my eyes fixed on the white farmhouse with its wraparound porch. "It's just a typical middle-class farmhouse. Nothing fancy."

"It's not just the house, Noelle. It's the property." He scanned the sprawling land, taking in the big red barn, the riding arena with its weathered fencing, the paddocks still covered in snow, and the trails snaking off into the woods beyond. "How big is this place?"

"About forty acres, I think."

"That's big enough for a lot of horses," he replied, shielding his eyes from the sun as he looked around.

He put the truck in park, and I started to hop out.

"Wait! I have another present," he said, reaching into the pocket of his jacket. "It's just a little something I picked up for you."

I paused, one foot on the ground, caught off guard. "Kol, no...you shouldn't have." I climbed back into the seat. "You've already given me such a beautiful gift today." My fingers brushed over the pendant. "I didn't get you anything. Now I feel terrible."

Kol just shook his head, that easy smile playing on his lips. "It's nothing big, I promise. Just a little something. I'd stuck it in my pocket, and with everything that happened with Mrs. Dottie, I almost forgot about it." He fished around in his coat pocket before finally pulling out a small bundle wrapped in tissue paper and handing it to me.

I peeled back the tissue, revealing a crocheted wreath ornament—the one I'd pointed out in the store yesterday. It was simple yet beautiful. "Kol..." I whispered, the words sticking in my throat. "You went back and got it? When?"

"Of course I did. You remember...when I left the coffee shop," he said, tilting his head and straightening up. "It was obvious how much you loved it when you saw it. Your face always shows exactly what you're thinking. You said you didn't want it, but..."

"I do! I love it," I said in a rush. "It's a little piece of art... not plastic and shiny. It's something someone took their time to make with their hands. Like the ones my momma made for gifts." I swallowed hard, running my fingers over the soft, tiny stitches. "Thank you."

Kol's smile softened. "It's just a little thing, but it can be the start of new memories...happy ones. I loved watching your face light up when you saw it." He shrugged.

I nodded, unable to trust my voice to speak without cracking. Instead, I reached up and looped the little wreath over the Bronco's rearview mirror, adjusting it until it hung just right. The soft lacy yarn stood out against the rugged interior. "It looks so good there," I said, finding my voice again. "The red and green go perfectly with your big red sleigh."

Kol laughed.

I glanced out at the barn and then back at him. "Thank you, Kol. Really." My fingers brushed over the little wreath again. This guy just kept blowing me away. How had I gotten so lucky for him to fall into my life?

He reached over, his hand finding mine, squeezing gently. "Come on," he said, nodding toward the barn. "Let's go in."

As we got out, the crisp winter air bit at my nose. Kol's boots scuffed on the gravel as we walked toward the stables. After shoving open the barn door, the smell hit me first—that warm, earthy scent of horses and old leather. Memories flooded back, good ones I'd pushed aside for too long.

Inside, dust motes danced in the shafts of sunlight filtering in through the windows. I spotted an old grooming brush on the shelf and picked it up. Holding it to my nose, I inhaled the distinct aromas of horses and sweat. It transported me back to summers spent mucking stalls and riding until the sun went down. God, it smelled good.

"This is where I spent most of my childhood. I used to spend hours in here," I said, twirling the brush in my hand. "I loved the smell of the hay, the sound of the horses shuffling in their stalls, the leather of the bridles in my hands."

Kol rested his shoulder on one of the stalls, watching me as I moved around the space. He didn't say much, remaining quiet but attentive, as though everything I said mattered.

"I'll never forget the first time I cantered," I continued, unable to hold back my enthusiasm. "The freedom of it, the way the horse's muscles moved beneath me as we covered so much ground together."

"Tell me more," Kol said, his voice low and rumbly.

I laughed, bubbling over with memories. "The first time a horse took off with me, I was maybe twelve. My dad had told me what to do—pull his nose all the way over to my boot. It's hard for a horse to go very fast with their neck bent over. So, I did that, and eventually, he slowed down. Still, I was terrified."

Kol raised an eyebrow. "Sounds dangerous."

"Oh, it was. But you learn fast with horses. They can spook at anything. One day, I was riding Vixen at a walk from the barn to a paddock, and something must have stung her. She jumped into the air, twisted, and bolted. I was lucky to have my wits about me and do an emergency dismount, because she freaked the fuck out and didn't stop until she was across the back field, covered in sweat and foam."

"Jesus, Noelle." Kol's eyes widened, but I just grinned.

"It's a miracle my reins didn't trip her up. Thankfully, she didn't get hurt. It just goes to show you that even the best of horses can spook." I moved to the tack room, running my hands over the leather saddles and bridles. "I loved it all though. The smells, the feel of the leathers, the thrill of jumping..."

Kol followed me. "So you like jumping horses a lot, huh?"

"Oh, yeah." I turned to him, excited by all the memories. "My first jump was over a little cross rail when I was just around six years old. I loved the exhilaration of a horse lifting off the ground. As the jumps got higher, the feeling of the horse leaping up and over the fences was magic. It was like flying."

He reached out, tucking a strand of hair behind my ear. "You light up when you talk about this."

My face heated, and I leaned into his touch. I hadn't allowed myself to think about this place in so long, but now it all came rushing back—the trail rides with my family, the competitions, and how the barn always smelled.

"I can't believe how much I miss it," I admitted softly. "It was a family affair, you know? We all worked together to take the best care of our horses. It was our life."

Hand in hand, we walked out of the barn. The sun was bright in the sky, casting a golden glow over the fields.

"When I went off to college, my parents would send me pictures of all the horses' antics. Like the time my dad's horse, Dasher, learned to unlatch the paddock gate and showed up on the back porch eating Mom's sunflowers."

Kol chuckled—a deep, warm sound that made my heart flutter. "Which was your favorite horse?"

"Vixen, she was my heart horse," I said without hesitation. "She was small for a warmblood, only fourteen and a half hands, but perfect for a ten-year-old learning how to do a three-foot course. She was this beautiful bay with a coat that shined like a new penny."

I led him to the first paddock, my hands animating my stories. "Vixen was very well trained when we got her at thirteen years old, and boy, did she know her job. She trained me. If I didn't ask her properly for a turn or a distance, she'd let me know the hard way."

Kol rested a foot on the fence, his eyes never leaving me. "She sounds like a Catholic school teacher."

"She was the princess in the barn and a bossy mare that would put the biggest, baddest gelding in his place. Everyone knew Vixen had a wide bubble for her personal space and to never cross the line or they'd get bitten or kicked." I laughed. "She was amazing; she made me a good rider. I can't tell you how many ribbons I earned on that horse. God, I miss her."

Kol reached out, pulling me close. "I love the way you talk about all your horses. Maybe you could teach me to ride one day. I've never been on a horse."

"I'd like that." I bet he'd like it too.

We strolled toward the house. As we got nearer, I became nervous, my palms growing clammy and my steps slowing. Kol looked at me questioningly. After a moment, he asked, "Do you want to go inside the house?"

I hesitated, looking at the farmhouse. Kol must have sensed my apprehension because he squeezed my hand. "We can take it slow; there's no rush."

Taking a deep breath, I steeled myself for the wave of memories that were sure to come. "Yeah. Let's do it."

At the top of the porch steps, I inhaled slowly a couple of times, the cold air stinging my lungs. "I think it's time," I whispered. Kol's eyes softened. "I'm so grateful Aunt Mary didn't sell the place," I added, trying to keep my voice steady.

We stood there, the wind whipping around us, as I fumbled with the keys Mrs. Winters had given me. My fingers trembled slightly while I tried to find the right one. Kol stood patiently beside me, his breath misting in the cold air.

After trying a couple of keys, I finally found the correct one. It turned in the lock with a satisfying click. I pushed the door open, and we stepped inside. The scent hit me first—a mix of dust, disuse, and my mother's perfume. It was overwhelming, a sensory overload that made my heart ache.

The farmhouse had been restored around thirty years ago, modernized in some ways, but it still held onto its old charm. Wide wooden planks lined the floor, stretching into the living room, and exposed beams crossed the ceiling. The place hadn't changed. No one had touched it since my parents passed. Dust coated everything like a fine film, and I swore I saw something dart across the floor—a mouse, maybe. I swallowed hard. This was home, but it was also so much more than that.

Then I spotted it. The artificial Christmas tree, bedraggled and worn, stood slumped in the corner of the living room. Gifts, still wrapped, sat underneath it. My breath hitched as memories slammed into me, one after another—Christmases filled with music, the warmth of my parents' hugs, the smell of cinnamon rolls and fresh pine from the real trees we used to have before they replaced them with this plastic thing when I'd gone off to college. I hadn't expected the wave of grief to crash into me so hard, but there it was, suffocating and overwhelming.

Kol's hand was on my back—a warm, steady pressure. "Take your time," he soothed.

I nodded, unable to speak. The room swam before me. I could almost see my mom in the kitchen and hear my dad's laughter echoing through the house. Their absence pressed down on me, a physical force that made breathing hard.

This was my childhood, my past, my pain. And it was all wrapped up in this house.

I took a step forward, and Kol stayed right by my side. We moved through the room slowly, each step stirring difficult memories. There was the fireplace where we'd hung our stockings, the couch where we'd watched countless movies, the dining table where we'd shared so many meals.

But it was the Christmas tree that drew me in. The gifts were covered in dust, their wrapping paper faded. I knelt, my fingers tracing the edges of the boxes. Each one was a time capsule, a piece of the past frozen in place.

My eyes filled with tears, and I blinked them back, my vision blurring. Kol crouched beside me, resting his hand on my shoulder. He didn't say anything; he just stayed there, silently supporting me.

I picked up one gift, a small box wrapped in shiny red paper. My name was written on the tag in my dad's handwriting. A sob caught in my throat, and I clutched the box to my chest, the edges digging into my skin.

It was too much. I couldn't go any further. Not today.

I dropped the box and fled.

The next few days passed by in a blur, Kol staying with me at Aunt Mary's house.

The day after Christmas, we barely made it through the front door before it became too overwhelming for me, and we had to leave. Later that evening, though, we returned, spending a few quiet hours wandering through the house. Kol patiently let me take my time as I poked around, fretting over everything that needed to be done. I couldn't help but worry aloud about whether I was ready to take it all on. The following day, I spent hours exploring, sitting in my old bedroom, thumbing through dusty photo albums or sorting through boxes of forgotten things, carefully working to figure out what I should keep and what should go.

Kol was there every step of the way. He never rushed me, never pushed me to do more than I was ready for.

Eventually, I was able to go back to the gifts under the tree. I unwrapped each one carefully, as if they were the most precious things on the planet. Because they were. They were pieces of my past, pieces of my parents.

One of the gifts was a horseshoe, painted gold with a red ribbon tied through it. Attached was a note from my dad, telling me the history of how horseshoes bring luck. He wrote about how the legend started and how people believed that the seventh son of a seventh son, who was a blacksmith, could make horseshoes that brought good fortune. How you had to keep the ends pointing upward to keep the luck from spilling out, and how sailors used to nail them to the masts of their ships for protection. He said it was a reminder that, even when times were hard, luck would always be found if you believed in it. At the bottom of the note, he said this was one of Vixen's old shoes, and that he'd chosen to paint it for me as a keepsake, a reminder of how much luck I'd brought him, being his daughter.

As I read his words, I could almost hear his voice and see his smile. This gift was bittersweet, a painful reminder of what I'd lost, but it was also a comfort, a connection to the past. I clutched the horseshoe to my heart. I'd cherish this, always.

These days had brought Kol and I even closer. He shared pieces of his past with me—his darkest memories, the ones he carried deep inside—including the guilt, the anger, and the unresolved pain from his time in Afghanistan. I didn't judge him for any of it, just as he didn't judge me for my grief and the way I had tried to shut it all away. We were scarred in different ways, but we accepted each other for who we were. We were flawed but also stronger because of everything we'd been through. We were two people with both shadows and light inside of us, learning to live with both.

In that house, we didn't just find closure. We found each other.

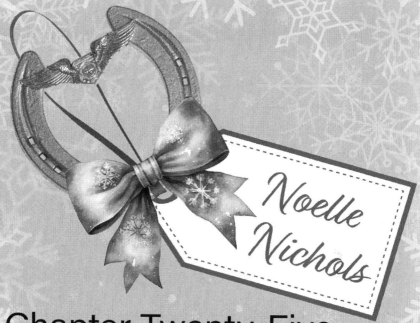

Chapter Twenty-Five

12/31 New Year's Eve

The aromas of garlic and rosemary wafted through the kitchen, mingling with the warm, homey scents of everything else I'd prepared. I hummed along to songs on my holiday playlist as I gave the prime rib one last check. It had been resting under foil for the last twenty minutes, and the smell alone was enough to make my mouth water. The butcher hadn't let me down—this was the best cut of meat I'd ever seen, and I'd done everything right to make sure it was just the way Kol liked it. I'd seared it to a beautiful, caramel brown, then slow-roasted it at a low temperature to keep it rare and juicy.

It had been three days since Kol left on his latest scheduled trip, leaving me alone for the first time since we'd met. At first, it had felt strange to be on my own again, but those days had given me the space I needed to figure out what I really wanted to do with my life. Today he was returning. His flight had landed forty-five minutes ago, which meant he'd be walking through that door any second

As I moved around the kitchen, my mind kept wandering to everything I'd dreamed up and the plans I'd made. Mrs. Winters had been such a big help guiding me through all the logistics and making sure everything would work. What I'd be endeavoring to do was something big—something my parents and my aunt would have been proud of. My inheritance had opened up a new world of possibilities, giving me the means to do something truly significant, something that would make all the loss worthwhile.

I glanced at the clock, my stomach fluttering with excitement and nerves. I couldn't wait to see Kol's face when he saw the spread I'd prepared. It was our first New Year's Eve together, and I wanted it to be perfect.

The table was set with candles and the fancy napkins I'd found in the dining room hutch, the ones with a silver monogram that matched the silverware. I'd even dug out one of Aunt Mary's old tablecloths, the white one with embroidered holly around the edges. It was festive and elegant, the perfect backdrop for the feast I'd prepared.

As soon as the front door clicked open, I rushed through the living room, unable to contain my excitement. Kol stepped inside with a bottle of champagne in one hand, his suitcase and flight bag in the other. A massive bouquet of red roses was tucked under his arm. His eyes met mine, and a slow grin spread across his face.

"Welcome home!" I squealed, launching myself at him. He let go of the luggage handle, and I threw my arms around his neck, kissing him like we'd been apart for years instead of days. He tasted like peppermint, and I couldn't get enough.

Kol chuckled against my lips, wrapping his free arm around my waist. "Well, that's quite the welcome. What's the incredible smell?" he asked, pulling back to look at me.

I beamed up at him, taking the roses and burying my nose in their soft petals. "I have a New Year's Eve surprise for you," I said, grabbing his hand and tugging him toward the kitchen.

He dropped his bags at the foot of the stairs, his eyebrows rising as he walked into the kitchen. Inhaling deeply, he looked around in curiosity.

The au gratin potatoes were ready to come out of the oven, and the asparagus was steaming in its dish. A decadent chocolate cake that I knew would be Kol's undoing sat on the table, its frosting glistening in the light of the candles I'd arranged in the center. I dramatically whisked the foil off the prime rib, revealing the perfectly seared meat underneath. Kol's eyes widened, his lips parting in awe. "Is that...?"

"Prime rib," I confirmed. "Rare, just the way you like it."

"You're spoiling me," he said, shaking his head, his eyes widening in appreciation. "I can't believe you did all this for me."

I nodded, biting my lip. "I wanted to surprise you. Welcome you home properly."

Kol stepped closer, cupping my cheek with his hand. "No one's ever done anything like this for me before," he said as he kissed me softly, his lips lingering on mine. "Thank you, sweetheart."

I blushed, turning away to hide my smile. He always called me sweetheart when I'd made him happy and Stinkerbelle when I'd annoyed him. "Well, don't just stand there," I said, placing the roses in a vase and filling it with water. "Wash up and help me plate our steaks. They won't carve themselves."

Kol laughed, rolling up his sleeves and stepping up to the counter. After he washed his hands, he took the carving knife and got to work.

"I'm the luckiest man alive. I get to come home to a woman who not only looks hot as hell but also cooks my favorite food. Hmm, maybe I'll have to reward you later," he said, winking at me.

I laughed at his praise and his not-so-subtle promise as I removed the potatoes from the oven. While I was scooping some out onto each plate, I replied, "I know how to feed my fellow meat-asaurus."

"Seriously, Noelle, this is amazing." He set the plates on the table, his eyes roaming over everything again. "You really outdid yourself." He kissed me on the cheek, and I melted into the easy warmth of his affection.

Kol popped the champagne, and I squealed in surprise when the cork bounced off the kitchen wall with a loud pop. After pouring each of us a glass, he set the bottle on the table, flashing me a grin.

"This table is so...romantic. Are you planning on seducing me later or something?"

I pursed my lips, swirling the champagne in my glass. "Oh, this isn't the only surprise I've got for you tonight," I teased, giving him a playful wink.

He wagged his brows. "Oh, really? Well, now I can't wait to see what else you've got up your sleeve." The corners of his mouth twitched into a half-smirk.

We sat down to dinner, and he started telling me about his trip.

"It's good to be home for New Year's Eve. You wouldn't believe the crap we dealt with this trip. The weather was all over the place. From below freezing up in Canada to snowstorms up and down the East Coast."

He took his first bite of the meat and paused mid-chew, letting out a low groan. "Damn, Noelle," he muttered. "This is so good. Better than any restaurant. How did you make it so...perfect?"

I smirked, shrugging like it was no big deal. "Just a little prime rib magic, that's all."

We dug into the meal and continued to chitchat about all that he'd been doing while he was gone. We both wolfed down our food, neither of us having eaten a proper meal since he'd left. After we finished the main course, I cleared our plates and brought over a couple of dessert plates while he poured us the last of the champagne. I served the cake, slicing us each a big ole piece. As soon as Kol took a bite, his eyes rolled back in his head, eliciting a pleased smile from me. When he was finished, he wiped the corners of his mouth with his napkin and sat back.

"This cake...it was delicious. You nailed it. And it pairs surprisingly well with prime rib. Reminds me of that chocolate and peanut butter fudge we had with the wine I found on our first night here."

I laughed. "Yeah, well, who knew? I'm starting to think chocolate goes with anything."

Kol huffed, shaking his head. "I still can't believe you trusted me to blindfold you that night. I mean, a strange guy you just met at the airport? You've got some guts, woman."

I threw my head back and laughed. "You're the one who told me you'd been vetted and verified more times than I could imagine. *'I served as a Night Stalker in the Army, and pilots go through FBI background checks,'* remember? You made it sound like I was safer with you than with a Secret Service agent."

Kol put his elbows on the table, frowning. "Yeah, but still. I could have been blowing smoke up your skirt and been the biggest perv you've ever met. Trust but verify, right?" Then his voice dropped a notch, turning serious. "Not that it matters now.

You're mine. No man better lay a finger on you if he wants to keep his hand attached to his arm."

I scrunched up my nose. "Ew! I could have gone my whole life without that mental picture. Gross!"

Kol grunted. "Just don't forget it," he said, his tone half-joking, half-dead serious.

Together, we cleared the table. I nudged him. "How about I do the dishes and finish putting everything away while you go upstairs and change into something warm? I've got another surprise or two waiting for you."

Without waiting for a response from me, he gave me a mocking salute, grabbed his bags, and went up the stairs, taking them two at a time. A little while later, he was back, fresh from a quick shower, dressed in jeans and a flannel shirt.

I was already at the front door, wearing my coat and jingling his keys in my hand.

He shrugged on his coat. "Where are we headed?"

I grinned, tossing him the keys. "The farm."

Kol's brow furrowed in surprise. But he didn't question me, just followed me out of the house, climbed into the driver's seat, and started the engine. As we pulled out of the driveway, flurries started falling. I fidgeted in my seat; I couldn't wait to tell him about everything.

It was late when we arrived at the farm, and the headlights cast long shadows across the barn. Instead of heading to the house, I led him to the barn. Once we'd tugged open the door, I flipped on a couple of lights. He stayed close behind me as I guided him toward one of the stalls. When I slid its door open, his eyes widened, and he let out a low whistle.

"Well, well, well. Look what we have here," he said, taking it all in.

I had turned the stall into a cozy love nest. There was a small table with a battery-powered lantern, a bottle of wine, two glasses, and a few layers of fresh hay stacked high, covered in old quilts and pillows. It was perfect for a romantic barn rendezvous.

Kol turned to me, a smirk playing on his lips. "It's eighteen degrees outside. How exactly do you plan on us staying warm in here, Stinkerbelle?"

I pointed up. "That's an infrared barn heater," I said, nodding at the glowing red light overhead. "And there's a giant heating pad under the blankets. Are you worried you won't be able to make me hot tonight?"

He scooped me up in a big bear hug, spinning me around. "I love dating a barn girl. And don't you worry; I can always bring the heat." He set me back on my feet.

"You have no idea what barn girls are capable of," I teased.

"Apparently not." His eyes swept over the barn aisle. "I see you've been hard at work cleaning." I was pleased he'd noticed how much better it looked since the last time he was here. I'd cleaned and organized all the tack, swept away all the cobwebs, and even mucked the stalls and brushed out the floors. "This place looks good."

I shrugged, trying to play it off. "I have to admit, I've hardly sat still since you left."

His eyes lit on a crop hanging by a bridle on the wall. He picked it up, examining it. "Whoa, what's this thing doing in a barn?" he asked with a smirk.

I burst out laughing, snatching the crop from him and swatting him on the butt. "It's not a sex toy, you dork. It's a horse crop. For motivating horses to behave. It's for the rider, not the stud."

I popped him again, harder this time.

"Fuck, that hurts!" he yelped, chasing me around the barn. I darted through the wash bay, then in and out of the tack room, giggling like a maniac. I tried to escape, but Kol was faster. He cornered me by the feed bins, overpowering me with ease. Grabbing the crop from my hand, he teasingly held it out of my reach. I squealed, making a break for the door, but he wasn't far behind.

In one swift move, he threw me up over his shoulder like he'd done before. I would never get used to him being able to do that so easily. I kicked and wiggled, but it was no use.

"By now, you should know you're not going anywhere," he growled. "I've got size, speed, and experience on my side. And when I want something, I get it. And right now, I want you."

He whacked me on the butt with the crop, and I yelped. A peal of giggles bubbled out of me. He brought me back to the stall, tossing me onto the makeshift bed.

Kol kicked off his boots and plopped down, stretching across me for the bottle of wine. But before he could pour us a glass, he spotted the envelope propped against the bottle. His eyes flicked to mine, and I gave him a small, nervous smile.

"Open it," I whispered, my heart racing.

Kol's fingers worked at the envelope's edge, tugging it open. He pulled out the papers, frowning in interest as he flipped through them. "What's all this?" he asked, glancing up at me with a mix of curiosity and concern.

I leaned in, my pulse racing with impatience. "Do you remember the silver dollar I found on Christmas Day?" I asked.

Kol nodded, his eyes scanning the documents. "Yeah, you left it on the kitchen table."

I bit my lip, folding my legs underneath me. "Well, as you know, after you left that morning, I freaked out. I thought you were gone for good, and I didn't know what to do with my life. I was going back and forth about whether to return to Atlanta or stay here."

Kol returned his attention to me. "And?"

"And then I found a picture of me with my parents from when I was little, and right next to it was the coin. It felt like a sign. I had this wild idea to let fate decide what I should do next, so I flipped it. Heads, I'd stay in Saratoga. Tails, I'd go back to Atlanta. But just as the coin hit the highest point in the air, you came storming through the door, in full-on 'Mr. Captain' mode."

He chuckled at that, shaking his head, but the corners of his eyes crinkled and his lips tensed as he looked down at the papers.

I nudged him gently. "Go ahead; read them."

He pulled the last page closer, squinting at the detailed map. "Wait, is this a map of the farm? What does this mean?"

I laughed, swatting his arm. "No, silly! You were supposed to start with the first page."

He flipped back to the first page and started reading through quietly. When the realization hit, he shot me a wide, boyish grin that sent warmth radiating through me.

"You're staying?" he asked, his voice cracking slightly.

I nodded. "I'm staying in Saratoga!"

Before I could react, Kol pulled me into a tight hug, settling me on his lap. "I wanted you to stay so badly, but I didn't want to pressure you. It had to be the right decision for you."

He leaned in, his lips capturing mine, and the world around us blurred. His kiss was hungry, passionate, and soon his hands moved from my face to my curves, pulling me closer. His erection grew hard under my leg, his body responding to mine with a white heat.

I pulled back just enough to catch my breath, giving him a playful shove. "There's more, Mr. Captain, so keep it in your pants long enough to finish reading the papers."

He groaned, letting me slip from his lap, though not without swatting my behind. I shook my head, taking the papers from him and smoothing out the wrinkles.

"I worked with Mrs. Winters to set up a nonprofit organization."

Kol's eyebrows shot up. "A nonprofit?"

I held up one of the papers and read aloud. "Mission Statement for Shepherds of Joy Equestrian Center—Healing Through Horses: At Shepherds of Joy Equestrian Center, we are dedicated to helping individuals navigate grief and mental health challenges using the healing power of horses. Our nonprofit provides a compassionate space where people can connect with, care for, and ride horses, fostering emotional healing, resilience, and hope in the face of loss. Through this unique bond, we empower individuals to find strength, peace, and renewal."

Kol's expression shifted from surprise to pride as he processed the words. "Noelle, that's...that's huge."

We sat there for a while, savoring the moment. I beamed as Kol scanned the map again, tracing the edge with his thumb. He seemed stunned, blown away by it all. Before he could say anything, I continued.

"There's more," I said, barely able to contain my excitement. "I wanted to do something in memory of my parents, so I'm naming the nonprofit after them—*Shepherds* for my dad, and *Joy* for my mom. I want this place to be more than just a farm. I want it to be a healing center. For people like us, who are recovering from trauma, dealing with grief, and vets who are coping with PTSD. It all came together so quickly in my head—and with Mrs. Winters's guidance—as though it was meant to be."

Kol stared at me. "You're really serious about this, aren't you?"

I nodded, a grin spreading across my face. "As a heart attack. I want to turn this place into something special, a sanctuary for people who need it most. And it doesn't stop with the farm. I'm going to turn Aunt Mary's house into a Victorian bed and breakfast—Mary O'Malley's Evergreen Inn. A cozy getaway for guests, connected to the healing center. People can come here, find peace through the horses, the land, and the house."

Kol let out a low whistle, shaking his head in disbelief. "That's...mind-blowing. You've really thought this through."

"You know, once I flipped that coin, it was like the floodgates opened. The ideas just poured in. And Mrs. Winters has been amazing, offering to do all the legal work pro bono and giving me tons of ideas too. There's a lot to do, but I'm ready."

Kol drew me into a hug, pressing his lips to my forehead. "If anyone can pull this off, it's you, sweetheart."

I relaxed into his embrace and fell silent for a moment, staring at the papers. Excitement and insecurity were buzzing inside me, but there was something else I had to say. Something bigger.

I took a deep breath and hesitated, trying to choose my words wisely.

Kol's hand came to rest on my back, his fingers grazing the fabric of my sweater. "What are you thinking about?"

Shaking off the self-doubt, I turned to face him fully. "Kol, I want you to be a part of my life. Forever."

The corners of his mouth rose. "Are you asking me to marry you?"

I rolled my eyes. "Call it whatever you want, as long as it's forever."

He cupped my face in his hands, his fingers tracing the line of my jaw. "I like the sound of forever with you, Noelle."

Without another word, I wrapped my arms around his neck and pulled him in for a hard, hungry kiss. He responded immediately, flipping me over onto the hay and blankets, pressing his body into mine.

We lost ourselves in each other. His hands roamed my body, igniting a fire within me that only he could quell. I arched into his touch, a moan escaping my lips as he trailed kisses down my neck.

"You're mine," he growled, gripping my hips possessively. "Forever."

He slipped his fingers beneath the hem of my sweater and traced my curves, dragging the fabric up my arms and over my head, revealing the pretty red lace bra I had chosen just for tonight. Between the way he looked at me and the cool air, goose bumps spread across my skin, and my nipples pebbled in anticipation.

"Fuck, you're gorgeous," he murmured, teasingly biting one of my nipples over my bra. "But this can't stay."

Kol leaned in, his lips trailing a path along my collarbone, his teeth grazing the sensitive skin of my neck. At the same time, he reached behind me, deftly unhooking my bra with a practiced ease that made me laugh.

"What's so funny?" he asked, sounding offended.

I shrugged. "I just didn't expect you to be so...efficient. But then again, being good at everything you do is your MO."

He grunted, tossing my bra aside. "Sweetheart, when it comes to getting you naked, I don't mess around."

He cupped my breasts with his hands, brushing his thumbs over my nipples. I gasped, my head falling back as pleasure coursed through me. Heat was building between my legs, a throbbing ache that only Kol could satisfy.

I went for the placket of his shirt, my fingers fumbling with the buttons. I was desperate to feel his skin against mine. With a groan of frustration, I yanked at the fabric, sending buttons flying in all directions.

"Impatient, are we?"

"You have no idea," I breathed, my heart pounding. It had been a long three days without having his hands on me.

Kol's chest was a masterpiece of hard planes, detailed tattoos, and defined muscles, and I couldn't resist running my hands over every inch of him.

His fingers slid under the waistband of my leggings, and he roughly tugged them down. He huffed in annoyance when he got to my boots, struggling to unlace them and pull them off, flinging each one across the stall with a jerk when it finally came loose.

Now, the only thing separating me from Kol's greedy gaze was my sexy little red lace panties.

He stared at me as if I were the most beautiful thing he'd ever seen, his eyes so dark with need that there was almost no trace of his usual chocolate-brown irises. He shoved off his pants, and then his hands were on me again, working their way up my legs. His lips followed, kissing and nibbling every inch of skin like it was sacred ground. When he nipped at the sensitive flesh of my inner thighs, I let out a moan, tangling my fingers in his hair. He took his time teasing me, making me squirm.

Finally, he moved to the apex of my thighs. He used his teeth to take hold of the edge of my panties, dragging them over my mound. But they were too difficult to remove this way, and Kol was too impatient. With a growl, he gripped them in his fingers and ripped them apart.

"Hey!" I pouted. "Those were brand new, and I really liked them."

He just grinned up at me. "I'll buy you plenty more. Now, spread your legs for me, Noelle."

His command sent a jolt of heat straight to my core. I did as he asked, needy and desperate for his touch. His fingers explored my wetness, his touch sending waves of pleasure crashing over me. His mouth followed, and he began to swirl his tongue around my clit in slow, torturous circles.

I was lost in a haze of pleasure, my body arching off the blankets as Kol worked his magic. His fingers slid inside me, curling in just the right way to hit that sweet spot. The pressure was now building, my orgasm hovering just out of reach.

"Stay still," he commanded, his hands holding my hips in place. I whimpered but did as he said while my fingers twisted in the blanket beneath me.

Kol's fingers pumped in and out, his tongue matching the rhythm. He feasted on me like a starving man, his mouth and fingers working in perfect harmony. Over and over, he sucked my clit into his mouth, his fingers thrusting in and out of me, making me see stars. My walls clenched around him, desperate for release.

I was lost in a sea of bliss. The sensation of his scruff against my inner thighs, the feel of his tongue on my clit, the way he expertly manipulated my body—it was all too much. I was teetering on the edge, so close to climax that I could taste it.

And then, just like that, he slowed down, his fingers and mouth retreating. I let out a groan of frustration. "Oh no, not this again," I whined, the words slipping out before I could stop them.

"Patience, sweetheart," he said with a chuckle, his breath hot against my folds. The vibration sent a shudder through me. Before I could protest further, he nipped at one of my swollen lips, grazing the sensitive flesh with his teeth. I yelped, more from surprise than pain.

He moved up my body, his lips trailing a wet path along my stomach, pausing to lavish my breasts with the kind of attention that had me arching off the blankets again. His mouth closed around a nipple, his tongue flicking over the pebbled peak while his hand kneaded my other breast. The bolt of pleasure shot straight to my core, reigniting the fire he'd so cruelly doused.

Kol kept moving but paused again, his eyes locked on the sparkling diamond necklace he'd given me, which hung between my breasts, catching the light. "You wear that well," he growled, his voice a low rumble that I felt deep in my belly.

He positioned himself over me, reaching back to take my legs, one at a time, and drape them over his shoulders. I gasped when he slammed his cock inside me. With my knees up like this, each thrust hit deeper, the angle pure perfection. I could feel every ridge, every vein of his cock as he filled me completely. My breath came in short, ragged gasps as he set a punishing rhythm, his hips snapping against mine with a desperation that matched my own.

The pulsing ache within me coiled tighter and tighter with each stroke, the pressure building to an almost unbearable level. His eyes never left mine, so focused it was like he was seeing straight into my soul.

I was so close, and from the look of sheer concentration on his face, I could tell he was fighting his own release, wanting to make sure I tumbled over the edge first.

His movements became faster, more erratic, as he chased his own climax.

"Kol," I breathed, my voice barely above a whisper. "I'm— I'm going to—"

I didn't get the chance to finish my sentence. With a final, powerful thrust, he sent me spiraling into oblivion. My vision whited out, every muscle in my body tensing as wave after wave of pleasure crashed over me. My walls clenched around his thick shaft, inciting him to shatter along with me. He groaned, his body trembling as he came.

Amid the aftershocks, while my heart was pounding in my chest and my breath was coming in short, sharp pants, he whispered, "I love you, Noelle." It was so soft I wasn't sure I had heard it.

Shock coursed through me, tears pricking at my eyes. When Kol finally came down from his high, he released my legs from his shoulders and collapsed on top of me, his body a possessive weight. We stayed like that, panting, our hearts beating in sync for a few blissful moments.

When I could speak, I asked, "Did you mean what you just said? Or was it the passion talking?"

He pushed up on his elbows, gazing down at me. That lopsided grin I loved so much spread across his face. "I think I've loved you since the moment I saw you—the sassiest blonde I've ever met, sitting alone, wiping tears from her eyes in the middle of an airport, wishing she'd never been born. You tore out my shriveled, icy heart and replaced it with one that beats only for you."

He brushed a stray curl from my forehead, his eyes searching mine. "I never believed in love at first sight, never thought I'd find the kind of love my parents or some of my buddies have found. But then, out of nowhere, fate intertwined our destinies. And here we are."

My heart swelled with a love so profound, it was almost painful. "It really is a wonderful life, isn't it?" I whispered.

His grin widened, his eyes crinkling at the corners. "Yes, sweetheart. It is."

"I love you, Kol." The words escaped my lips like a secret.

He held me close, and we lay there, enjoying this perfect moment. It was just us, lost in each other, in our own little world. A world where love conquered all, where the past didn't dictate the future, and where every day was a gift. It was a wonderful, wonderful life.

If *Christmas Cancellation* left you wanting more, step into Evie's Broken Heroes world, where the Thorin brothers await with their unforgettable stories.

The Thorin brothers share more than blood—they're all dedicated to saving lives in Tacoma, WA, working side-by-side in the medical field until their paths unexpectedly cross with the dark, dangerous world of the mafia. Having lost their parents young in traumatic events that shaped their lives, each brother believes that love is a fairytale that will never find them. Yet, one by one, they meet women who challenge their beliefs and open their hearts in ways they never expected.

Start with *Night Shift*, where brooding ER physician Atticus Thorin battles burnout until fiery redheaded nurse Samantha Sheridan turns his world upside down. Their sizzling age-gap romance takes a twist when her dark past catches up, igniting a heart-racing rescue that melts Atticus's carefully constructed walls.

Then dive into *Day Shift*, where Constantine "Conan to his buddies" Thorin, a tattoo-covered, golden-retriever ER nurse, finds himself unexpectedly captivated by a mafia princess with amnesia. As danger closes in, Conan must navigate deadly family rivalries and protect the woman who's stolen his heart, even if it means facing down the underworld itself.

Coming soon is *Swing Shift*, where Braxton Thorin, the bold paramedic, faces life-or-death stakes in war-torn Ukraine. With his courage and grit tested, Braxton's journey alongside a Russian mafia underboss and hacker, Nikolai Volkov, pulls him deep into a world of high-stakes danger, love, and a battle for survival.

The Broken Heroes series offers standalone romances, with each book featuring a brother who finds true love and a fulfilling happily ever after. While you can enjoy any of the books on their own, following the recommended reading order will give you the fullest experience of their intertwined journeys and bonds.

Grab your copies and immerse yourself in the thrilling lives of the Thorin brothers—each journey more intense and unforgettable than the last!

Enjoy the read?

Take a couple of minutes to leave a review!

Reviews are everything to an Indie Author, and I would greatly appreciate it if you would take the time to leave one or click on the star rating. All you need to do is leave a few words.

Thank you!

Acknowledgments

To my readers: Thank you for picking up *Christmas Cancellation* and giving your time to these pages. Your support, whether through reviews, messages, or simply your enjoyment, means the world. I am truly thankful.

Emily Cargile, your insight has elevated this book in ways I never could have done alone. Your edits are always precise, thoughtful, and exactly what the manuscript needs to be its best. It's been a joy working with someone who brings not only technical skill but also such empathy to the process; knowing this story brought tears to your eyes was one of the highest compliments I could receive. *Christmas Cancellation* is close to my heart, and as an "It's a Wonderful Life" retelling, it's all about the profound impact of one life on others. Thank you for helping bring that meaning to light and for understanding these characters as deeply as I do. Your dedication has made this book shine, and I'm endlessly grateful.

Jourdan Gandy, your guidance through this journey has been invaluable. From marketing insights to career direction, you've shared advice that is as clear as it is effective. Thank you for your constant support and your unwavering belief in my work.

Vanessa Medina, your creative talent makes connecting with readers a joy. Your ideas, humor, and sense of fun bring such vibrancy to every post and campaign. Thank you for everything you do to make this journey both smooth and enjoyable.

This story wouldn't be the same without each of you. Thank you for helping *Christmas Cancellation* come to life in such an unforgettable way.

About Evie

Evie James is a lifelong creative, book enthusiast, and romance author who crafts angsty, fast-paced contemporary novels filled with heartache, heat, and unexpected twists. She writes strong, sassy heroines who know how to push every button on a man and possessive alphas who would burn the world down for their woman. Evie guarantees a hard-won happily-ever-after in every book.

A true romantic and animal lover, she's a Cancer sign to a fault—deeply emotional, fiercely loyal, and guided by intuition. She channels these traits into her writing, creating characters and stories that resonate with passion and vulnerability.

When not writing, she can be found baking, spending time with her family, or doting on her four dogs in Nashville, TN.

Where to Find Me

Website: eviejames.com

Instagram: @evie.james.author

Facebook: @evie.james.author

TikTok: @evie_james_author

Made in the USA
Middletown, DE
05 December 2024

66230608R00177